Bad

Alex Walters has worked in the oil industry, broadcasting and banking and provided consultancy for the criminal justice sector. He is the author of thirteen previous novels including the DI Alec McKay series set around the Black Isle in the Scottish Highlands where Alex lives and runs the Solus Or Writing Retreat with his wife, occasional sons and frequent cats.

Also by Alex Walters

Detective Annie Delamere

Small Mercies
Lost Hours
Bad Terms

Alex
WALTERS
BAD TERMS

CANELOCRIME

First published in the United Kingdom in 2022 by

Canelo
Unit 9, 5th Floor
Cargo Works, 1–2 Hatfields
London, SE1 9PG
United Kingdom

A CIP catalogue record for this book is available from the British Library.

Print ISBN 978 1 80032 640 8
Ebook ISBN 978 1 80032 639 2

Look for more great books at www.canelo.co

Printed and bound in Great Britain by Clays Ltd, Elcograf S.p.A.

To Helen

Prologue

Summer, 1976

This was Jayne's favourite place.

The view always caught her by surprise, though she walked this way every day during term time. It was the way the grey stone houses clustered at the top of the hill, as if keeping their own secrets. In those narrow streets you could be in some northern mill or mining town.

She felt nervous as she made her way through the village. If there was going to be trouble, this was where it would happen. The clatter of footsteps behind her. The taunting, the chanting, the mocking laughter. All she could do was lower her head and keep walking, avoid catching their eyes. Avoid anything that might provoke them.

Sometimes they'd get bored and leave her be. More often, they'd cluster behind her, pushing her in the back, tapping her on the shoulder, trying to trip her onto the quaintly cobbled street. The blows were never hard enough to hurt but hard enough to be annoying and intimidating, underpinned by the ever-present sense that this time they might go further.

It didn't happen every day. She encountered them perhaps once every couple of weeks. She had no idea why that should be, and she'd never detected any pattern to their appearance. Something to do with their timetable, she assumed, or perhaps they just came up here when they were at a loose end. She couldn't envision what their world was like, other than as some *Malory Towers* fantasy, and she had no idea what motivated them to behave as they did.

She knew she should tell someone about them. But her mum and dad would think she was making a fuss about nothing, and in truth there wasn't much to tell. A bunch of posh girls made fun of her? That was all it amounted to. It wasn't as if she was easily bullied. She had no problems at her own school, and if any of this bunch tried anything more serious, she'd make them regret it. But she wasn't looking for trouble, so she just kept her head down.

In any case, before long they'd all be breaking up for the summer. Jayne herself had only a couple of exams left, and then she could forget about this journey until she started sixth form in the autumn. By then they'd all be older and maybe this nonsense would finally cease.

In the meantime, she'd developed her own small rituals and superstitions to help her through it. If the bus dropped her off early, she wouldn't encounter them. If it was raining, she wouldn't encounter them. Both of those were rational enough. But she'd also persuaded herself that if they hadn't appeared before she reached the end of the street, she'd make it home without trouble.

The point when she turned the corner had gained an additional significance for her. She'd always seen it as a magical moment, stepping out of the grey village street into open space. The view opened up, the land falling away to the valley below. She could see for miles across the Cheshire plain towards the far Welsh hills. An empty landscape of moorland, shapeless fields, lines of dry-stone walls, dotted with clusters of houses, the occasional church spire pointing to the heavens.

Some days, if she was sure there was no risk of being accosted, she would stop and simply stare out across the landscape. On the clearest days, she felt as if she could see forever, the whole world spread out before her. She would simply stare, trying to spot the distant landmarks across the miles of fields and moorland.

For weeks now it had been too hot to allow that clarity. The far reaches were lost in a haze of summer warmth, shimmering in the late afternoon sunshine. That simply made the experience even more magical, as if she were gazing into a mystical world, distinct from the reality of the grey stone surrounding her.

The heat was growing more intense with every passing day. She couldn't recall a summer like this. Waking every morning to clear skies and bright sunshine. Coming home every day, as today, through countryside baked in the heat, the warmth rising from the earth and the cobbles. Spending the day revising in an overheated classroom or taking her O-Level examinations in the spacious but still stifling assembly hall.

It wouldn't last, of course. They all joked about that. It was a cast-iron certainty that, as soon as the exams finished and the term was over, it would rain for the rest of the summer. For the moment, though, her mum and dad continued to complain about the heat in the same way they usually complained about grey skies and rain, and Jayne could at least enjoy this brief magical moment at the end of every school day.

She paused a moment longer, gazing at the panorama before her, and then began to walk slowly down the hill towards her home. Her route lay through a short stretch

3

of open moorland, then over a stile into the field where a footpath took her to the small housing estate where her parents lived. There was an alternative, longer route through the streets to the front of the estate. But as long as the weather was fine and the paths dry, she preferred this shortcut.

Oddly, although she was more isolated down here, she never felt any sense of threat once she'd turned the corner. There was no reason, as far as she knew, why the other girls couldn't follow her down here if they chose. But so far they hadn't, which was why she'd developed her private superstition.

Out on the moor the sun felt even hotter, the grass baked dry and brown by the weeks without rain. Jayne had heard her mum and dad talk about the risk of wildfires if the weather continued, and there had already been fires on the moors further north towards Buxton. The stream that normally ran alongside the path had dried up weeks ago.

She was halfway down the hill when she heard the sounds behind her. The footsteps, the giggling. The comments muttered too quietly for her to grasp the meaning, even if she had no doubt as to the intent.

She was tempted to look back, but the noises still sounded relatively distant. She imagined the girls had gathered at the top of the street, observing her descent down the path towards home. As long as she didn't look back, she told herself, they wouldn't follow. As long as she didn't look back, everything would be all right.

Perhaps, she told herself, the moorland was 'out of bounds' to the girls. Some arcane school rule might prevent them from leaving the village. Her knowledge was almost entirely derived from reading Enid Blyton and similar authors in her younger days, but she knew boarding schools applied laws and conventions that would have no place in her own newly established comprehensive. Her school had no shortage of rules about what the pupils could and couldn't do on school premises, but, given the school's large catchment area, almost no limits on where they could go or what they could do outside school.

Jayne was still determined not to look back. She kept her head down and walked steadily onward, trying not to be intimidated into increasing her pace. The last thing she wanted was to convey any impression she was feeling scared or anxious.

Every step took her closer to the edge of the field. Even if the girls followed her out on to the moors, they surely wouldn't be prepared to cross the stile. If she could just make it to that point, everything would be okay.

The noises were growing closer. The footsteps and the laughter were not far behind her now. She could hear the scuffling of shoes on dry earth, could almost feel the unwarranted malevolence directed at her own retreating back. She stared ahead, her eyes fixed upon the stile.

By now, the footsteps were only a few yards behind her. She could hear the hissed comments, even if she couldn't make out what was being said. Then, suddenly, with unexpected clarity, a voice said, 'You, girl!'

It was the voice of someone no older than Jayne herself, and Jayne guessed the speaker was impersonating one of the girls' schoolteachers. There was more giggling from behind her, presumably because the other girls had recognised the impression.

'You, girl! I say, stop!'

Jayne kept her head low, her eyes fixed on her destination, her steps steady as ever.

'I said stop! Are you being wilfully disobedient, girl?' More laughter. Jayne guessed this was some familiar catchphrase of the teacher in question.

Unexpectedly, she felt a hand on her shoulder. 'Are you listening, girl?' The voice was immediately behind her. 'Or have you gone stone deaf?' All said in a booming, exaggeratedly cut-glass accent, a mocking representation of an individual much older than the speaker.

This was the first time the girls had dared to touch Jayne in this way. Previously, there'd been sly pushes in the back, glancing blows to her arms, attempts to trip her. Always sufficiently light to be plausibly deniable. If she'd responded, Jayne could imagine the girls mockingly saying, 'Oh, we must have just brushed against you. Sorry if you're so *sensitive*.'

This was different. This was a hand firmly on her shoulder, trying to check her progress. Jayne wriggled free and continued walking, determined not to give the girls the satisfaction of stopping or looking back. The hand seized her shoulder again, even more firmly. 'Wilfully disobedient!'

Jayne decided she had no alternative. She stopped and turned, making every effort not to appear scared or intimidated.

The girl in front of her was probably a year or so younger than she was. She was Jayne's height but more heavily built. Three other girls were standing behind her, watching intently but looking as if they'd rather not be involved in what might be about to happen.

'What do you want?' Jayne hoped she sounded bored rather than as nervous as she felt.

'I want you to do as you're told.' The girl was chewing gum in a manner she presumably thought made her look tough.

'Why should I do anything you tell me?' Jayne started to turn away.

The hand grasped her shoulder again, pulling her round. 'Because you obey your superiors.'

Jayne was aware of the others giggling in the background. 'I don't see any superiors here.' She turned again, but the girl's hand was still gripping her shoulder.

Jayne could feel her irritation finally overcoming her fear of confrontation. She gripped the girl's hand firmly by the wrist and pulled it away from her shoulder, twisting the arm sharply. The girl gave a yelp of pain. 'Now leave me alone.' Jayne tuned away and continued walking.

She had expected the girl might try to grab her again, but for a moment nothing happened. Then she heard a noise behind her. Before she could turn, the weight of another body struck her squarely in the back, forcing her to the ground. She hit the bone-dry moorland with a thump, driving the breath from her body. For a moment she was held down, her face thrust into the hard earth.

She felt an agonising blow to the back of her head and someone kicked her hard in the ribcage. There were more blows and more kicks, but, after that first impact, Jayne was already beyond feeling them.

Chapter One

Spring, 2022

DCI Stuart Jennings turned up the collar of his overcoat and ducked his head against the icy March wind. 'My old dad always used to say there's no such thing as bad weather, only the wrong clothes.' He paused a beat. 'Mind you, my old dad was an arsehole.'

DI Annie Delamere suspected it was a line he'd used more than once, but she was happy to humour him with a smile. Given her own relationship with her mother, she was the last one to disapprove of acerbic jokes about parents. In any case, he was right about the weather. She was slightly better prepared for it than Jennings, in that she was wearing a heavy-duty waterproof rather than his undeniably stylish woollen overcoat. Even so, she could already feel the icy wind inveigling itself between the layers of her clothing. 'It is bloody cold. Brass monkey weather.'

'Going to get worse too,' Jennings said gloomily. 'According to the forecast. Rain, sleet, hail, snow. You name it. The usual glorious start to the year, and we have to spend it up here.'

In Annie's view, there were worse places to be, despite the weather. Even under a heavy iron-grey sky with the haze of impending rain hiding the horizon, the view was impressive. The moorland dropped away towards the village below them, before rising again to form the dark line of hills in the far distance. On a summer Sunday, the area would be thronged with day trippers. Today, apart from a few lights showing in the village, there was no obvious sign of human life.

The sense of desolation dissipated as soon as she turned to look behind her. Marked police vehicles filled the narrow lane, along with the CSIs' white vans and, further back, the pool car in which Annie and Jennings had travelled up here. On the far side of the road, there was a bustle of activity, as the team cordoned off the scene. Annie and Jennings had arrived just a few minutes before but had retreated to the far side of the road to allow the team to complete its preliminary work without interruption.

'Do we know who the house belongs to?'

'Couple from London, apparently,' Jennings said. 'Bought it a year or so back to use as a weekend retreat.'

'Not always popular around these parts.'

'Not popular in most rural communities, I'm guessing,' Jennings agreed. 'Pushing up the house prices and leaving the houses empty for half the time. On the other hand, if you've a property to sell, you're not going to say no.'

'Decent-looking place, though.' Annie imagined that the large stone building had once comprised several small labourers' cottages, but it had long ago been converted into a single and sizeable residence. There was an attractive randomness about its frontage. 'Must be worth a bob or two. What are the builders actually doing?'

'That's another part of the story. The owners have been battling the local authority to get planning permission for a major revamp. Not quite tearing it down and rebuilding it, but something along those lines.'

'Another opportunity to make themselves popular.'

'Exactly. There's been some local campaign to preserve the place. Try to get it listed status. But without success. Hence the start of the building work.' The wind had whipped up again, and there was a taste of rain in the mounting gusts. Jennings looked up at the sky, his expression suggesting that ideally he'd like to have a firm word with the elements. 'Let's see if Danny's ready to talk to us yet.'

Danny Eccles was one of the senior CSIs, an amiable, slightly rotund man who maintained his trademark cheerfulness in the face of even the most unpleasant crime scene. Annie occasionally wondered if Eccles ever paused to contemplate the evils he had to deal with. She suspected he'd long ago closed himself off from such thoughts, allowing it all just to wash over him. That was the way with CSIs. Some remained blithely impervious to their work. Others wallowed in the attendant gore and misery. The first group were generally easier to work with.

Eccles was standing at the front of the house, issuing instructions to both his own team and the uniformed officers preparing the scene. He broke off as Jennings and Annie approached. 'I see you've brought the weather with you.'

'Perfect day for exhuming a corpse, I'd have thought,' Jennings said.

'Not exactly exhuming. That's been rather done for us. Unfortunately.'

'What's the story exactly?' Jennings looked up at the house. 'Where's this building taking place?'

'At the back of the house. Condition of the planning permission. The front facade of the house has to remain untouched, other than some cleaning of the stonework.

But what sits behind it is being gutted and pretty well rebuilt.' He sniffed disapprovingly, and looked back at the imposing grey stone building behind him. 'Some people have more money than sense.'

'Seems to be the fashion, doesn't it?' Jennings said. 'When you buy a house, you don't just move in. You rebuild the whole bloody place first.'

'Where did they find the body?' Annie said.

'There was a one-storey extension at the rear that housed the kitchen and a couple of utility rooms. The plan's to replace that with a two-storey structure to create a bigger kitchen and more bedrooms upstairs. They've demolished the old structure and they're digging out the ground for the new foundations. They've got a bloody great digger pulling up the ground, and halfway down they find a human skeleton.'

'Do we know when the foundations for the extension were laid?' Annie asked.

'Builder reckons sometime in the 1970s. I don't know any more than that.'

'And we reckon the skeleton dates from then?' Jennings asked. 'The rest of the house must be a lot older.'

'We'll need forensics to give us a definitive view, but there are fragments of fabric round the bones that look like man-made fibres to me. That's why they've not decayed. My guess is that 1970s sounds about right.'

The first drops of rain were falling, driven almost horizontally by the pounding wind. 'Can we go and have a look?' Jennings asked.

'As long as you do what I tell you and don't touch anything.' Eccles smiled amiably.

'I think I can bring myself not to touch anything, Danny.' Jennings shook his head. 'Though if this weather keeps up, I might be tempted to climb in next to the body. Even the grave's got to be warmer than this bloody place.'

Eccles led them down a driveway past the house. At the rear, a sizeable and well-maintained garden backed on to the open moorland. The back of the house itself resembled a bomb site. Although the interior walls remained untouched, presumably to preserve the internal security of the house, a substantial area had been cleared. A digger stood at one side, and the ground immediately in front of the house was partly dug away. The police team was in the process of erecting a protective tent across the area, but for the moment the skeleton was visible in the middle of the area that had been excavated.

'The guy operating the digger lifted it fully out of the ground,' Eccles said. 'It suffered some damage in the process, but he was smart enough to put it down gently so the bones are pretty much where they would have been. We'll have to see whether the damage was caused only by the digger, or whether there might be other factors involved.'

'Such as whether any bones were broken before death?'

'Exactly. And whether there's anything there that will give us a cause of death.'

Jennings had moved to the edge of the excavated area, peering down into the hole. 'Male or female?'

'Looks female to me. Beyond that, I'd be wary of making any guesses. Something for the docs to tell you.'

'No doubt. I hope they'll be able to give us something useful. I'm not sure I fancy dealing with a forty-year-old corpse.'

'Are we assuming foul play?' Annie asked.

'I think we have to start from there,' Eccles said. 'Unless forensics or the pathologist give us a good reason to think otherwise. If our friend down there died of natural causes, why would someone dump her body in the foundations?'

'Isn't it supposed to be good luck?' Annie said. 'Putting a body in the foundations. "London Bridge is falling down, my fair lady." All that stuff.'

'Not very lucky for her.' Jennings gestured towards the skeleton.

'Maybe more so for whoever was responsible for her death. If it was murder, the killer's got away with it for more than forty years.' Annie paused. 'Or lived with it for forty years.'

The rain was coming down more heavily, and the uniformed officers in the excavated area below were struggling to complete their task in the face of the wind-whipped downpour. There was something almost hellish about the sight, Annie thought, as she watched the canvas sheets billowing in the wind, the officers struggling to stand upright on the churned, sodden earth. In the middle of that frantic action, the pale shape of the skeleton, the apparent sacrifice that provided the focus for their activity.

'I assume we've no clues as to identity?' Jennings was standing, head down, the rain dripping from his hair, his expression indicating he'd rather be anywhere else than here.

'I've only been able to have a cursory look down there so far, but there's nothing obvious that would help identify the body. Of course, there may be something that's been separated from the skeleton itself. We'll need to do a thorough search.'

'And some historical delving through missing persons in the area,' Annie added. 'If she's been missing for four decades, someone should have noticed her absence.'

Below them, the uniformed officers had finally succeeded in erecting the large protective tent. Someone had brought round a couple of large spotlights to illuminate the scene. It was still only late morning, but, as the weather had closed in, it felt almost like twilight.

Jennings shook his head in the manner of a wet dog, rain scattering from his hair. 'I think we'll happily let you get on with it,' he said to Eccles. 'I'm going to find somewhere warm and dry to sit, even if it's only back in the car.'

Eccles shrugged. 'You know what they say. There's no such thing as bad weather, just the wrong clothes.'

Jennings stared at him for a moment, as if suspecting some kind of telepathic collusion with Annie. 'Yeah. I'd heard that.'

Chapter Two

'Ms Pearson?'

Sheena Pearson looked up to see a tall, imposing-looking woman striding across the lobby towards her. She was exactly as Sheena had envisaged – well-spoken, her clothing expensive but unobtrusive, her manner one of effortless superiority. All of which was exactly what the parents would expect. Sheena rose to meet her. 'Ms Ellsworth?'

'Lavinia, please.'

'Sheena.' They shook hands with a slightly uncomfortable formality. 'Delighted to meet you.'

'And you. Welcome to the Lady Elizabeth Brennan School for Girls. We're very grateful to you for taking the time to visit us. What do you think of the place?' Ellsworth gestured vaguely in a way that took in the whole establishment around them.

One honest answer would have been that Sheena saw the place as a socially indefensible den of privilege. Another equally honest answer was that, for all her efforts, Sheena saw it as intimidating, oppressive and mildly terrifying. 'Very impressive.'

Ellsworth gazed at her for a moment, then smiled. 'I appreciate that you disapprove of us and would prefer to see us abolished. All I ask is you approach us with an open mind.'

'I hope I can do that. I'm genuinely interested to find out more about what you do.'

Ellsworth led them out of the lobby and along one of the adjoining corridors. Other than the receptionist who had greeted her on arrival and Ellsworth herself, Sheena had seen no signs of human life since entering the building. There was a calm and quiet about the place that was different from any other school Sheena had visited.

'This way.' Ellsworth ushered Sheena into an area accommodating the school management, with the head-mistress's office at the far end. 'Welcome to my humble abode.'

Sheena assumed the words were intended to be ironic. The main school was Victorian or perhaps early Edwardian, constructed in dimensions designed to intimidate pupils and visitors alike. The exterior of the building was a squat grey edifice sitting immovably against a picturesque backdrop of rolling green hills and verdant woodland. Ellsworth's office could have passed as the study in a country house of the period, with its high ceiling and vast windows looking out over the school playing fields.

Ellsworth gestured for Sheena to take a seat at a large meeting table which already held a tray of tea, coffee and seemingly home-made biscuits. 'It really is fascinating to meet you,' Ellsworth said. 'It's been a while since we were visited by someone of your – persuasion.'

It took Sheena a moment to realise Ellsworth was talking about Sheena's political affiliations rather than, say, her religion. 'I trust you'll also approach me with an open mind?'

'Absolutely. I may not share your opinions, but I respect your good intentions.' Ellsworth smiled in a way that suggested any condescension was entirely deliberate.

'You're not the first left-wing Labour MP to visit us. We had Mr Benn here to talk to the debating society a few years ago. A charming man.'

Sheena assumed Tony Benn had been the kind of socialist Ellsworth approved of. That is, one with an aristocratic background. She imagined that Ellsworth would be less impressed by Sheena's origins.

As if in confirmation of Sheena's thoughts, Ellsworth went on, 'I took the liberty of conducting a little background research on you. Just to prepare a brief biography to support your session today.'

'Of course.' Sheena held her smile while Ellsworth poured the coffees.

'I found it very interesting. You were at Cambridge?'

'King's.'

'I'm an Oxford woman myself. St Hilda's. It must have been quite an achievement for you. Gaining a place at Cambridge from a comprehensive.'

Sheena had no intention of rising to this or any other bait Ellsworth might offer. 'It was a good school.'

'Did you always aspire to be a politician?'

'I don't think I aspired to be anything. But I've always been interested in politics. And I've always been something of a political activist.'

'Most admirable.' Ellsworth's tone suggested she'd found Sheena's words entirely baffling. 'I'm sure your ideals will be an inspiration for our girls.'

Sheena still wasn't sure why she'd agreed to do this, or indeed what had prompted the invitation. She suspected that it had resulted from the 'building bridges' initiative currently being promoted by the leader's office. The idea was that the party should be improving its credibility and influence in sectors the membership had traditionally treated with suspicion – the City, business and, apparently, even private education. 'We don't win elections just by preaching to the choir,' the leader had said in a recent speech. 'We have to reach out across the divide to those who aren't our natural supporters. We have to show we have something to offer them.'

The invitation to today's event had come directly from Ellsworth herself, in the form of an old-fashioned letter. In recent years, the school had invited a number of local MPs, from each of the major political parties, to address pupils undertaking A-Level politics. The idea was to allow them to debate relevant political issues, as well as providing an introduction to the realities of life in the House of Commons.

Sheena's predecessor, an old-school right-winger in the party, had spoken here on a couple of occasions, but her own initial inclination had been to say no. She was no fan of private education, and the prospect of contributing to the schooling of these already privileged young women had felt like a compromise too far. At the same time, a more mischievous part of her was attracted by the idea of spreading her socialist doctrine in this environment. She had no expectation of actually converting anyone, but there was always the possibility of sowing the seed that might ultimately germinate into the future female Tony Benn.

'It'll be interesting to talk with them, anyway,' she said now to Ellsworth.

'They're a bright and opinionated bunch,' Ellsworth said. 'I'm sure you'll have a lively session.'

'I'm looking forward to it.'

Ellsworth looked at her watch. 'You're on at eleven. I thought it might be helpful if I gave you the grand tour of the place and provided you with some background.'

Sheena had already steeled herself for a prolonged lobbying session. 'I'd be delighted to look around the place. You seem to have some excellent facilities.'

'We do our best,' Ellsworth modestly. 'We're constantly investing back into the fabric of the school to improve the quality of our pupils' experience here.' Sheena could see that Ellsworth had already shifted into her sales pitch.

The tour of the school was undoubtedly impressive, especially if Sheena compared it to her own former school. There was a swimming pool, a dedicated theatre, numerous high-technology laboratories, and rooms full of serious-looking pupils. The school itself was set in acres of playing fields, with views over the surrounding hills. Ellsworth regaled Sheena with endless facts about the school, the numbers of boarders and day-girls, the structure and organisation of the establishment, famous alumnae, and much more. None of it was of much interest to Sheena, but she allowed it to wash over her.

'In fact,' Ellsworth said, at the conclusion of a litany of supposedly high-profile old girls which meant little to Sheena, 'we do boast one alumna who I imagine is well known to you.'

'Really?' Sheena was expecting to hear the name of one of her fellow MPs, most likely from the opposite side of the House.

'Margaret Delamere.'

'Margaret? Really?'

'I hope I'm not being indiscreet. It's just that I noticed from your biography that you're married to her daughter.'

'No, that's fine. It's not a secret. I just hadn't connected Margaret with the school.'

'Funnily enough I knew her quite well. I'm an old girl myself. Margaret was in the same year.'

Sheena wasn't entirely sure how to respond to this information. The truth was that Sheena herself had almost no relationship with Margaret Delamere. The little time they'd spent in each other's company had been enough to confirm that they had nothing in common other than mutual suspicion. That might have proved awkward in terms of Sheena's relationship with Annie, except that Annie largely shared Sheena's views of her mother. Margaret and Annie rubbed along together simply because they were mother and daughter, but their interactions were mostly characterised by jibes and disapproval. Margaret Delamere was not an easy woman to like.

'She was a lively character, Margaret,' Ellsworth went on. 'She eventually became head girl. Sadly she didn't get into Oxford, so we rather lost touch. I was initially surprised when she joined the police, but I suppose it made sense.'

'In what way?'

'She was always a forceful individual. Keen to stamp her authority on others. She was like that as a prefect. I imagine she'd have made an impressive police officer. She certainly did well for herself.'

'She certainly did,' Sheena agreed.

'I watched her career with some interest, though we haven't seen each other for years.'

Sheena nodded, trying to conceal her growing boredom. They had returned to the entrance lobby, and she surreptitiously glanced at the large clock above the reception. Nearly eleven. She'd be delighted to escape

Lavinia Ellsworth's company to talk to what she hoped would be a relatively enthusiastic group of teenagers.

'I must say,' Ellsworth continued, 'I rather assumed that Margaret would make Chief Constable. She was always something of a pioneer. I was surprised when she chose to take early retirement.'

'Still,' Sheena said, 'she's continued to do rather well for herself since.'

'She does seem to have reinvented herself rather cleverly, I must admit.' There was a sniff of disapproval in Ellsworth's tone.

Since her retirement from the force, Margaret Delamere had established a burgeoning career as a media pundit. She'd initially been invited to express her views on matters related to law and order, but had gradually expanded her repertoire of opinions to encompass almost all aspects of conservative politics. She was increasingly seen as a talking head willing to pontificate about almost any social issue from a predictable perspective. It was one of the many sources of tension between Margaret Delamere and her daughter.

Sheena looked pointedly at the clock. 'Should we be getting along?'

'Is there anything you need for the session? I've arranged for some coffee and biscuits in the room. We like to treat our sixth-form girls as adults.'

'How many will there be?'

'As I say, it's been primarily targeted at those doing politics A-Level in the lower and upper sixth, but we've also opened it to any other sixth-formers with an interest in the area. I think we can expect about a dozen or so. I hope that's all right?' Ellsworth sounded as if she didn't much care what Sheena thought.

'That sounds fine. Small enough to engage with them properly, but large enough to generate a lively discussion.'

She followed Ellsworth back along the corridor and into the meeting room. At Sheena's request, the room had been set up with a single large table around which a number of teenage girls were already sitting. There was a hubbub of chatter which died away as Ellsworth and Sheena entered.

Ellsworth gestured for Sheena to take a seat at the head of the table, then looked around the assembled group. 'Are we all here?'

The girls looked around at each other, each of them clearly hoping someone else would answer the head-mistress's question. Finally, one said, 'I think Red Mel's supposed to be coming.'

'Red Mel?' Ellsworth's tone indicated distaste, though it was unclear whether she disapproved of the nickname or what it implied.

'Sorry, Melanie Donnelly, miss.' Sheena fancied that there was an edge of insolence in the girl's tone, but Ellsworth ether didn't notice or preferred not to acknowledge it.

'I'm surprised she's not here.' Ellsworth turned to Sheena. 'She's one of our more enthusiastic and talented girls. As you might have guessed from the nickname, she has some strong, if slightly naive, political views. She was keen to meet you, and I know she had a number of topics she wanted to raise with you. Still, it's not quite eleven. She's probably been delayed in her previous lesson. We'll give her a couple of minutes before we kick off.'

There was a prolonged silence, punctuated only by occasional whispers and giggles from the girls. Finally, the door of the meeting room opened.

Sheena had assumed this would be Melanie Donnelly, but the newcomer was an older woman. 'Headmistress,' she said. 'Could I have a word outside?' She caught the full force of Ellsworth's glare and added, 'I'm afraid it is rather urgent.'

Ellsworth gave Sheena an apologetic smile. 'I am sorry. If you just bear with me for a minute…'

Sheena waited while Ellsworth left the room with the other woman, and then turned back to face the girls. She was inclined to get started despite the absence of the head and Melanie Donnelly. If Donnelly should arrive late, she could catch up.

She was about to speak when she became aware of the sound. It was sufficiently distant almost to blend in with the other ambient sounds in the building, but loud enough that, once you'd registered it, there was no mistaking what it was.

The sound of someone screaming.

Chapter Three

'No Zoe?' Stuart Jennings said.

'She's on leave. Today and tomorrow. You authorised it.' Annie Delamere had to go through this routine with Jennings whenever a member of the team was absent.

'Did I? Must have been feeling charitable.'

'I'm just glad she's taken some time off, finally. She needed it, and she never uses all her annual leave.'

'I know. I'm not being serious.'

No, Annie thought, but you're not being entirely unserious either. That was the thing about Jennings. She'd concluded he was probably decent enough, but you had to probe beneath the surface to be sure. Some of that was insecurity. He was still relatively new to the team, having transferred over a year or so before, and he was wary of those, like Annie and Zoe, who were longer established here. Annie also suspected he had some issues working with women. Not that he'd displayed any obvious sexist or misogynist tendencies – certainly not compared with some officers in the force. It was more that he tried too hard in the opposite direction, wary of saying or doing the wrong thing.

He and Annie had spent the first few months dancing uneasily round each other, each trying to work out what made the other tick. The fact that Annie's mother had been a former Assistant Chief and was, for good or ill, something of a legend in the force hadn't helped. Jennings seemed to believe Annie's family connections had helped her career, whereas in reality Annie had spent most of her working life trying to live them down.

In recent months, they'd begun to establish a more productive working relationship. Jennings had developed a growing respect, even if slightly grudging, for Annie's abilities, and Annie had recognised that, for all his foibles, Jennings was for the most part a fair and supportive manager. There was still some edge between them, but now it generally felt constructive rather than the opposite.

Jennings was sitting beside Annie's desk in the open-plan office that housed the Serious Crimes Team. Jennings had somehow managed to procure his own office, a relative rarity in the building, but he seemed to prefer being out here with the team. Which, depending on his mood, could either be a blessing or a pain in the backside for the rest of them.

Annie had just finished the kick-off meeting for the inquiry into the human remains found in the foundations of the moorland farmhouse. The Meresham Bones, as Jennings had taken to calling them, in honour of the neighbouring village. Jennings was fond of coming up with melodramatic terminology, which tended to be adopted ironically by the rest of the team. Jennings had been tied up in another meeting and had arrived only for the last few minutes.

'Decent bunch,' he said. 'We seem to have most of the team in place, anyway. Well done.'

'We're going to need a good team. I can't see this being an easy one. Not after four decades.' They'd been discussing this in the meeting. It was one thing to invest-igate a murder in its immediate aftermath, when the evidence and the witness memories were both fresh. It was another to investigate a case when the so-called 'golden hours' lay forty or more years in the past. Advances in DNA and forensics would no doubt help, but only if the evidence was there in the first place.

'We can only do what we can do,' Jennings said platitudinously. 'What have we got so far?'

'Not a great deal. Danny Eccles has given me what he can, but that's not a lot as yet. I'm hoping we'll get more from the pathologist's report, but who knows? For the moment, we're fairly sure that the skeleton is female and that she was fairly young at the time of death. There's some evidence of damage to the bones, notably the ribs, that might have occurred before death, but that's not yet certain. Again, we're hoping that the pathologist might shed some light. Obviously, we don't know what might have happened to the body after death – in particular, how it ended up there in the foundations. The bones certainly suffered some damage when the digger extracted them, though Danny thought the breakage in the ribs was probably separate from that.'

'Any ID?'

'Not yet. Nothing around the skeleton itself, but we're digging out the whole area in case there's something that's become separated from the body. As Danny said yesterday, there are traces of man-made fabric around the bones, so we can be fairly certain the remains are relatively modern. It's reasonable, at least for the moment, to assume they were dumped there when the rear extension was being built. It's possible they might predate that, but then they'd most likely have been discovered at that point.'

Jennings was clearly thinking through the implications of what Annie was saying. 'It's not possible that they post-date the extension?'

'It's not likely. I've been chatting to the builder leading the current project. The foundations for the extension were relatively shallow – which is why they're having to be redone – but they were topped with a hefty stone floor which has been broken up for reuse in the new construction. Digging down through that would have been a major undertaking.'

'So we can date that reasonably precisely?'

'Planning permission for the extension was granted in early 1976, and it looks like the building itself took place over the summer. We're trying to pin down more exact dates.'

'Do we know who owned the house then?'

'We've got a name from the Land Registry. Someone called Alan Harwood. We're trying to track him down, assuming he's still alive. He sold the place sometime in 1977. It's changed hands a few times since then.'

'Suspicious that he sold the house so soon after building the extension?'

'Maybe. Maybe not. He might have been doing the place up to sell it. He must be in the frame for this, although the current builder reckons the body could well have been concealed without the previous builder or the owner being aware. The body was just below the level of the existing foundations, so could conceivably have been buried shortly before the foundations were laid. It was only discovered now because they're digging substantially deeper this time.'

'Bit of a risk for a third party, though. What if the builder had noticed the ground had been disturbed?'

'We don't know if the original building work was continuous. If it paused for a period, that might have allowed someone to take advantage of the delay to conceal the body. There'd have been no reason for the builder to examine the ground closely before laying the foundations. It's all conjecture at the moment.'

'Any likely candidates from the time in question? Missing persons?'

'We're digging through all that now, but there's one obvious candidate.'

'Go on.'

Annie tapped on her keyboard, selecting an internet site she'd bookmarked earlier, and turned the screen towards Jennings. The site showed the front page of a copy of the *Daily Mirror* dated June 1976, the image of a teenage schoolgirl below the headline: 'FEARS GROW FOR MISSING JAYNE'.

'Jayne Arnold,' Annie said. 'Went missing on her way home from school. Last seen getting off the school bus in Meresham. Search went on for weeks, apparently, but she was never found. There've been suggestions she might have been one of the early victims of the serial killer Robert Black, but that's just supposition.'

Jennings peered more closely at the screen, trying to read the detail of the story. 'What do we know about her?'

'So far only what was in the papers at the time. I've asked for the archive files to be sent over. She was sixteen at the time of her disappearance, in the middle of completing her O-Levels—'

'O-Levels?'

She raised an eyebrow at him. 'You're older than I am, Stuart. You know what O-Levels were.'

28

'Like GCSEs in the olden days. I remember my granddad telling me about them.'

'She'd almost completed them, and had been due to finish school for the summer a few days later. She went to secondary school in Ashbourne, and got the school bus in from the village.'

'That was where she was last seen?'

'She was generally the only one who got off at that particular stop in Meresham. It was on the edge of the village, but the closest to her parents' house. Most of the other pupils from the village got off at the next stop in the centre. Jayne got off the bus as usual, and then somehow contrived to vanish between there and her parents' house just a few hundred metres away.'

'No other witnesses?'

'Doesn't look like it. Obviously, there may be stuff in the files that never made it into the papers. We'll have to see when the case notes arrive. I've skimmed through the news reports for the weeks after her disappearance, and there's no sense the police were making much progress. It's a small village and it was a hot day but there was no one around. According to the reports, she normally walked along the village street then across a field to the back of the housing estate where her parents lived.'

'What about the parents?'

'Nothing very remarkable about them. Dad was an engineer, worked in Derby. Mum was a housewife or stay-at-home mum or whatever they called them in those days. I've found a couple of reports of public appeals they did. There's nothing in the press reports to suggest they were serious suspects.'

'Doesn't mean they wouldn't have been. Child goes missing close to home, we'd always look at the parents first. And other close relatives.'

'The files will no doubt tell us all that. The press reports are mainly about the attempts to find her. 1976 was one of those long hot summers and all the local villagers turned out to scour the countryside. They found her schoolbag quite quickly in a dustbin behind one of the houses. That generated a bit of excitement in the press, but it turned out to be a dead end. After that, nothing.'

These kind of cases – missing children – always gave Annie a frisson of dread. This one was long before her time, of course, but she'd experienced a few similar cases during her time in the force. Most had ended happily, with the child being quickly found unharmed. A couple of the cases had had more tragic outcomes but had been quickly resolved. Even so, the cases had lingered long in Annie's mind. What had stayed with her, perhaps even more than the outcomes, had been the preceding uncertainty. The gap between the child being reported missing and the body being found. She wondered what that would feel like extended over decades.

As if reading her mind, Jennings said, 'What about the parents? Do we know if they're still alive?'

'We're trying to find out. There doesn't seem to be anyone of that name in the village, but it's likely they'd have moved. If they were in their thirties or older at the time, they'd be getting on now.'

'As will almost anyone connected with the case,' Jennings agreed. 'Even her contemporaries would be in their late fifties or sixties. It's going to be a challenge.'

'Well, as you say, we'll do what we can.'

'If her parents are still alive, this might at least allow them a bit of closure,' Jennings said.

Annie had never been convinced by the concept of 'closure', which she sometimes felt offered more comfort to others than to those directly affected by this kind of incident. 'Maybe you're right. Or perhaps it'll just open old wounds and still not give them the answers they need.' She paused. 'Assuming, of course, that neither of them was responsible for putting her down there in the first place.'

Chapter Four

'I think we'd better stay put for the moment.' Sheena Pearson looked round at the girls seated in front of her.

'Someone might be in trouble,' one of the girls pointed out. Not unreasonably, Sheena thought, because the distant sound of screaming was increasingly difficult to ignore. It sounded like someone in acute distress, although Sheena was still young enough to recall that a teenager's notion of acute distress wasn't necessarily the same as an adult's.

'I'm sure the staff have it all in hand. I don't think our presence is likely to add very much. Perhaps we should just get on with our session...'

She was already losing the girls' attention. She was conscious she had no authority over the group and, after a moment, one of the girls rose and, with no word of explanation or apology, walked past her and out of the door. A minute later, another of the girls followed.

So much for the politeness of the privately educated, Sheena thought. The remaining girls did at least have the grace to look mildly embarrassed. 'I think we'd better go and see,' one of them said.

Sheena shrugged. 'I'd much rather you stayed. But I've no power to prevent you leaving.'

That was all the permission the girls needed. They filed out of the room, leaving her sitting at the head of the table, feeling unaccountably as if she'd failed some test. It was partly just the intimidating atmosphere of the place. The whole school felt as if it wasn't intended for the likes of her. She remembered having similar feelings when she'd first arrived in Cambridge, overwhelmed by the grandeur of the frontage of King's College and the chapel, feeling that everyone around her was more sophisticated, more socially adept than she would ever be. Luckily, it had taken her only a few weeks to realise that most of her fellow students were as intimidated as she was, and only a little longer to find a group of like-minded friends who'd sustained her through her three undergraduate years.

Those initial feelings had come flooding back as she'd walked through the doors here. This wasn't her world, and it never would be. It wasn't even that the girls here were particularly posh. Some of them would be here on scholarships, and many of the paying pupils were simply the daughters of those who'd managed to acquire wealth through one means or another. But whatever the girls' backgrounds, this school was designed to prepare them for roles in the upper echelons of society, either in their own right or – because this was a place still steeped in traditional values – as the wives of famous men.

The screaming still hadn't ceased, although it seemed to have taken on a more desolate tone, as if now expressing misery rather than the initial horror. Sheena's first instinct had been to remain where she was. There was probably little she could contribute to whatever was happening out there, and she didn't want to add to the staff's burdens by not being where they expected her to be.

On the other hand, if there was some major issue, perhaps she ought to see if there was anything she could do to help. After a moment, she rose and made her way back out into the corridor. The corridor itself was deserted, but she could hear the hubbub of voices coming from the direction of the main entrance.

As she rounded the corner into the entrance lobby, she was startled to find it crowded with pupils. Ahead of her, in the entrance, she could see a group of staff urging the girls back, encouraging them to return to their classrooms. None of the girls showed much sign of obeying, although they'd drawn back from the entrance itself.

Sheena eased her way slowly through the crowd, making her way towards the staff group. It took her a few minutes to ease herself through to the front. One of the teachers turned and regarded her with a mix of suspicion and disapproval.

'I'm here as a visitor,' Sheena explained. 'A guest of the headmistress. Sheena Pearson MP.'

The suffix had its familiar semi-magical effect. As soon as they realised you were a Member of Parliament, people tended to take you more seriously, regardless of their own politics or even their attitude to politicians. It was as if the post itself conferred some kind of authority or respectability. Sheena tried hard not to abuse this phenomenon, but it did occasionally come in useful. The teacher stepped back to allow Sheena to pass.

'What's going on?' Sheena asked.

'Some sort of accident. We're not sure of the circumstances but Ms Ellsworth is dealing with it. We're just trying to prevent the girls from getting too close.'

The school's main entrance led into a courtyard, with an archway leading out to the front of the building. Beyond the archway, another cluster of staff was gathered, blocking Sheena's view of what they might be observing.

She walked down the steps and through the archway, then made her way around the gathering until she could see what they were looking at. There was an odd silence, with none of the curious chatter she might have expected. A moment later, she realised why.

A human body was lying on the tarmac, face down, its limbs spread at disturbing angles. Lavinia Ellsworth and a male teacher were crouched beside the body, though neither appeared to have much idea what they ought to be doing.

Involuntarily, Sheena looked up and behind her. Her assumption, from the position and state of the body, was that the girl had somehow fallen from the upper floors of the school, although Sheena could see no open windows.

'I take it someone's called an ambulance?' she asked one of the teachers on the edge of the group.

The teacher gazed at her for a second as if trying to decide whether Sheena could be safely ignored. 'I believe so.'

'What about the police?'

The teacher looked as if she'd prefer to give Sheena a detention for impertinence. 'The police?'

Sheena didn't bother to answer, because she'd already heard the ambulance siren and she could see the blue light passing in the road outside the school. Moments later, the ambulance pulled to a halt in front of the school, metres from the body. Two paramedics emerged and immediately took charge. The crowd fell back, and Lavinia Ellsworth walked over to join Sheena. 'Dreadful business. I'm so sorry that this should have occurred while you were here.'

'Do you know what happened?'

'She must have fallen from one of the upper floors, but goodness knows how. The windows should be limited so they can't be fully opened. I can only assume she must have been playing the fool in some way.'

'Have you called the police?'

'Why would I do that?'

'Because it's an unexplained death,' Sheena said. 'The paramedics will be referring this to the police in any case.'

'Unexplained?'

'In the sense that you don't know what caused her to do what she did.'

'You're surely not suggesting—'

'I'm really not suggesting anything, other than that at present the circumstances are unknown. The police will treat it as a potential crime until they're confident it isn't.'

Ellsworth looked as if she was going to argue, but then she nodded. 'I suppose you have inside knowledge of those kinds of matters.'

'I'm aware of how the police work,' Sheena said blandly.

Ellsworth nodded, and walked back over to where the two paramedics were still leaning over the body. As she approached, one of the paramedics shook his head. He rose and spoke at some length to the headmistress. At the conclusion of the discussion, Ellsworth walked over to the group of staff. There seemed to be some debate, at the end of which most of the group dispersed back towards the school. A handful remained, positioning themselves at points on the paths leading to the front entrance, presumably to prevent anyone from approaching the scene. It seemed as if the headmistress was finally imposing some discipline on the situation.

Ellsworth walked back over to join Sheena. 'You were right.' Her tone suggested she was congratulating a bright pupil on giving a smart answer. 'They've already called the police. Unfortunately, the poor girl is beyond help. They don't want to move the body until the police arrive. I can't believe this has happened. We've had the occasional serious accident before, but nothing like this.'

'Is there anything I can do?'

'I don't think so. We're going to cancel lessons for the rest of day, and we'll be contacting the parents of the day-girls so they can be collected early if possible. We'll have to deal with boarders as best we can, but it doesn't seem right just to continue as normal. I'm very sorry you've had a wasted journey.'

'That really doesn't matter at all. I'll be happy to rearrange for a more suitable time.' She paused. 'Do you know who the poor girl is yet?'

Ellsworth hesitated for a moment. 'It's really very odd. I recognised her straightaway, but that was partly because she was already in my thoughts.'

'I'm not sure I understand.'

'She was the girl who was due to attend your session. The girl who was missing. Melanie Donnelly.'

Chapter Five

'Small world,' Stuart Jennings said, as they turned off the main road.

'Isn't it?' Annie agreed. 'In more ways than one.'

'That partner of yours seems to have a nose for trouble. She quite frequently ends up in the wrong place at the wrong time.'

Annie was driving, and was more concerned with finding their destination than in engaging in a verbal joust with Jennings. 'She just happened to be there. Supposed to be giving a talk to their politics students.'

'Surprised they let a red-hot radical like Sheena through these gates.'

Annie had just turned off the road through the ornate gates in question. The squat Victorian facade of the Lady Elizabeth Brennan School for Girls was in front of them, its brooding stone offering a stark contrast to the pale rolling hills behind. Ahead of them, in front of the school, there was an ambulance, a cluster of squad cars, and the CSIs' white van. The area had already been sealed off and the crime scene tent erected. A uniformed officer stepped into the road in front of them, signalling for them to stop. Annie lowered her window and proffered her ID. The officer nodded and waved them through.

The previous day's rain had passed, and it was a fine cold spring day, the sky a clear blue, the low sun casting long shadows across the school grounds. Annie and Jennings climbed out of the car and walked over to join the uniformed officer directing proceedings. He nodded to them. 'Stuart. Annie.'

'Morning, Paul. Sad business,' Jennings said.

Paul Burbage was well known to Annie. She'd had several dealings with him on recent cases, and found him a bright and reliable officer. He'd had a couple of conversations with her recently about applying for a transfer to CID, and she thought he'd fit in well. 'What's the story, Paul? Accident, or something else?'

'Most likely an accident, I'd have thought,' Burbage said. 'But you'll need to talk to Danny. There seem to be some questions.'

Annie looked past him at the crime scene tent. The CSIs would be inside, taking their photographs and measurements, capturing any evidence that might inform the investigation. 'What's happening in the school?'

'Head teacher's cancelled lessons for the day. They've a mix of boarding and day pupils. The boarders have been allowed to return to the dormitories. They've got various communal rooms and leisure facilities over there. Day pupils have been allowed to go home, as long as they can be collected by a parent. Otherwise, they've joined the boarders.'

'Where's the headmistress?'

'In her office. She said she'd be available whenever you wanted to talk to her.'

'Wouldn't like to be in her shoes this morning,' Jennings said. 'Hell of a thing to happen on your watch.'

Burbage hesitated. 'Ms Pearson's still in there, too. She thought it was better to wait until you arrived in case there was anything she could do.'

Annie nodded. 'Okay. We'll have a chat with Danny and then go and talk to the head.'

'Good luck with it. This sort of thing is always tragic, but when it's someone so young...'

Annie nodded. Burbage had mentioned previously that he had a young daughter, still just a toddler, so she could imagine what he might be thinking. 'Too right.'

Jennings had already wandered across to the tent, and was chatting to one of the white-suited CSIs. Annie walked across to join him, just as Danny Eccles emerged.

'Wasn't expecting to run into you again so soon,' he said.

'Not in the same place, anyway,' Jennings said. 'Or as near as damn it.'

'Aye, funny that, isn't it?' Eccles gestured towards the far end of the playing field. 'That's Meresham over there. Nearest village. Five or ten minute walk, I'd guess.'

'So what have we got here?'

'Not sure. The obvious answer's a tragic accident. The victim is Melanie Donnelly. Seventeen years old. One of the boarders. What we know for sure is that she fell from one of the upper storeys. The initial assumption was that she'd somehow contrived to fall from a window, but the upper windows are all supposed to be limited so it shouldn't be possible, however much someone was messing about.'

'Window limiters can be broken,' Jennings pointed out.

'Well, quite. I've had all the relevant rooms sealed off, so we can examine those once we've finished down here. There is one other possibility.'

'Which is?'

'That she came off the roof. It is theoretically possible to get up there, apparently. There's a walkway between the wall and the pitched roof that's used for maintenance purposes. Strictly out of the bounds to the pupils and supposedly securely locked, but I guess you never know. Again, we've had it protected until we can have a look at it.'

'What would she be doing on the roof?' Jennings asked.

'Not a clue.' Eccles looked at Annie. 'Funnily enough, she was supposed to be in the session with your partner, apparently. So no one knows what she was doing upstairs anyway.'

Jennings shook his head. 'I should have known.'

Annie ignored him. 'Anything else, Danny?'

'If you want a personal view, I'd say she probably came off the roof. And with a bit of force. We'll have to get someone to have a closer look at it, but for me the position of the body doesn't look right for having fallen from one of the windows. I think she'd be closer to the building. Don't treat that as definitive, but it's the way it looks to me.'

'With some force?' Annie said. 'Suggesting…?'

'That she didn't fall,' Jennings said. 'That she jumped or was pushed.'

'Christ.'

Eccles nodded. 'Quite. But, as I say, treat that with caution for the moment.'

'It's where we'll need to start, though,' Jennings said. 'Until we've reason to believe otherwise. Any evidence she was involved in a struggle?'

'Difficult to tell,' Eccles she said. 'Given that she subsequently had an argument with a hefty great piece of tarmac. Something for the pathologist to advise on.

Speaking of which, I'd better get on so we can have the body removed.' Eccles's tone was matter-of-fact, almost jovial.

'Okay, Danny. Thanks for the input. We'll see what the headmistress has to say.'

They made their way round the tent to find the archway that led into the main entrance to the school. Jennings stopped in front of the archway and gazed up at the building. 'Impressive place.'

'I'd better tell you before someone else does,' Annie said. 'My mother went here.'

'Now why doesn't that surprise me? Had a bob or two, did they, your grandparents?'

'Comfortably off, let's say. My granddad was MD of a manufacturing business in Derby. Not massively wealthy, but did all right. This sort of place was more affordable in those days.' She felt as if she was almost apologising for her grandparents' educational choices.

'Did you go to a place like this as well?'

'Not me. I wouldn't have wanted to.'

'Always the idealist.'

'It wasn't about that. I just wanted to stay with my friends.'

'There's something about places like this,' Jennings said. 'There's no wonder the pupils come out believing they can do anything.'

'It's not exactly Eton,' Annie said. 'But I know what you mean.'

Inside, the atmosphere seemed to be one of quiet and calm, very different from most of the local schools that Annie had visited in the course of her duties. But then this was hardly a typical day.

The receptionist bade them take a seat while she called the headmistress's office. Moments later, Lavinia Ellsworth came hurrying along the corridor to greet them. 'Please come this way. We really do want to do everything in our power to help you. Such a tragic accident.'

They followed Ellsworth back to her office where Sheena Pearson was sitting waiting for them. She smiled as Annie followed Jennings into the room. 'Afternoon, Stuart,' she said to Jennings. 'I thought I'd better stay around in case you wanted to talk to me.'

Jennings nodded to her, and then glanced back uncomfortably at Annie. 'Thanks, Sheena. I take it you didn't witness the incident itself.'

'I arrived at the scene just after it had happened.'

Jennings nodded. 'That's fine. We can get a statement from you later if we need to.'

'In that case, I'll leave you to it. I'll see you later, Annie. I'm guessing much later.'

'I imagine so.'

Ellsworth turned back to Annie and Jennings. 'Now,' she said, 'please let me know what I can do to help. This has been such an awful business. I'm really not thinking very clearly. I'm sorry we have to meet in these circumstances. I was telling Ms Pearson that I knew your mother. We were at school here together.'

Annie glanced at Jennings, her expression challenging him to say nothing. 'I knew she was a pupil here. She talks about it sometimes.' In fact, her mother very rarely said anything about her schooldays. Annie had always had a vague idea that her mother hadn't enjoyed her time here, though that had never prevented her from extolling the virtues of private education in general. 'It must have been strange for you to come back as headmistress.'

'It was, a little. I'd taught at various independent schools around the region and still knew the school quite well. When I saw the job being advertised, I was reluctant to apply, for precisely that reason. But there's no question that it's one of the most prestigious schools in the area, so I thought I'd be foolish not to give it a go. And here I am, five years later.'

'Can you tell us what happened this morning?'

'I'll do my best. As you know, Ms Pearson was due to speak to a group of our sixth-formers this morning, including poor Melanie. I'd arranged for Ms Pearson to arrive at about ten thirty so she could get herself settled before the session at eleven. I'd been showing her round the school before we arrived at the meeting room just before eleven. Some of the girls were already there waiting for us.'

'But not Melanie Donnelly?'

'I was a little surprised, to be honest. Melanie was one of our most able pupils, and she had a particular enthusiasm for politics.' Ellsworth was silent for a moment, as if contemplating the short life of the young woman she was describing. 'She was particularly keen to meet Ms Pearson, not least because she shared some of her political views. As you might guess, that's not common in an environment like this. Some of the other girls in her year called her Red Mel. Affectionately, I mean.'

Annie let that go for the moment. 'What happened after that?'

'It wasn't quite eleven, so I was prepared to wait a few minutes before we started. Though the girls know I'm a stickler for punctuality. Then we were interrupted by Mrs Bennett—'

'Mrs Bennett?'

44

'My secretary. I went back with her to the entrance and – well, saw what had happened.'

'So this would have been about eleven?'

'Almost exactly eleven, I'd have said.'

'I assume you weren't the first on the scene?'

'It was the team in the admin office who'd spotted her first. One of them had just happened to look out of the window and saw her lying there. A couple of them went out to see if they could do anything, but it was clear she was beyond that. Someone had called an ambulance. By the time I arrived there, word had spread to the neighbouring classrooms, and the teachers were trying to exert some control. To be honest, it was all a bit panicked and chaotic.' She looked slightly embarrassed. 'We have procedures in place to deal with serious accidents, but those are designed for sports injuries and the like. This just knocked everyone back.'

'Do you have any idea when she might have fallen?' Jennings asked. 'How long before you arrived, I mean?'

'They'd spotted her just a few minutes before. At first, they thought she'd collapsed or fainted. It was only when they went out there that they realised what had happened.'

'No one saw her fall? No one in the admin office, I mean,' Annie asked.

'I don't think so.'

'Presumably none of the girls has said anything about witnessing what happened?'

'Not that I'm aware of, but I've been mainly tied up trying to organise the rest of the day, so I've not had much time to talk to anyone in detail. Some of the staff may have heard something.'

'That's something we can follow up,' Annie said. 'Let's talk about Melanie herself. You said the other girls called her Red Mel. Was she a popular girl?'

'I'd have said so, mostly. The nickname was affectionate rather than mocking. My impression was that the other girls saw her as slightly eccentric, but in a likeable way. She wasn't particularly outgoing compared with some, but she seemed to get on well enough with the others.'

'Did she have any particular close friends?' Jennings asked.

'You'd have to ask her form teacher or her tutor. They knew her better than I did.'

'Thank you. I'm afraid we will need to talk to a number of staff members, and also to some of the pupils. We'll ensure any dealings with the pupils are handled with appropriate sensitivity.'

'I expected that would be the case.'

'What about Melanie's parents?' Jennings said. 'Would you like us to contact them to break the news?'

Ellsworth gazed at him for a moment. 'I think it would be better coming from me. I'm effectively *in loco parentis* here, and I should take that responsibility.'

'I understand.'

'We're already in the processing of contacting them,' Ellsworth went on. 'Although Melanie was a boarder, they live relatively close by.' She mentioned the name of another Peak District village, further north in the county. 'I understand they travel overseas very frequently in connection with the father's business, which was why they placed Melanie as a boarder. I called the contact numbers we have, but they went to voicemail. The ringtone on the mobiles suggested they were outside the UK.

I didn't want to leave a message on a matter like this, so I thought I'd try again once we're finished.'

Jennings, who had been examining one of Ellsworth's bookshelves, leaned forward. 'Can we go back to the – incident itself? I know it's speculation at this stage, but do you have any idea how it could have happened?'

'Something like this really shouldn't be possible. We know girls of that age can be prone to acting foolishly, but we thought we'd taken every precaution to prevent consequences like this.'

'Is that what you think's behind this?' Jennings said. 'Foolish behaviour?'

'That seems the most likely cause,' Ellsworth said. 'Girls can act irresponsibly. Even our girls, who for the most part are a sensible bunch. They can get carried away or overexcited, and then they don't think about what they're doing. It's partly the old cliché about feeling you're immortal at that age. You take risks or accept dares without really believing in the consequences.'

'You think that's what happened in this case?'

'How else to explain it? My concern is about how it could have happened. It shouldn't have been possible for her to fall from any of those windows.'

'We'll get that looked at,' Annie said. 'To see if any of the window limiters have malfunctioned. I'm afraid our CSIs have sealed off all the relevant classrooms until we can ascertain where she was prior to the fall.'

'What about the roof?' Jennings said.

'The roof? I'm not sure I understand.'

'We understand there's some kind of walkway up there. Between the top of the wall and the bottom of the pitched roof.'

'You're suggesting Melanie might have fallen from there?'

'At the moment, we're just considering all the possibilities. Is there any way Melanie could have gained access to the roof?'

'I don't see how. It's closely secured and there are very few keyholders. Me and the deputy head, the head of the maintenance team. I think that's all, though my secretary can give you a definitive list. In any case what would Melanie be doing up there?'

'We have to look at all options until we know more.'

It was clear that Ellsworth wasn't fooled by the blandness of Jennings's tone. 'I have the impression you think this might be something other than a tragic accident. What exactly are you implying?'

'I'm implying nothing, Ms Ellsworth. You'll appreciate that with any unexplained death we have to consider every possibility.'

'Such as?'

It was Annie's turn to intervene. 'Unpleasant as the prospect might be, we can't ignore the possibility that either Melanie took her own life, or that she was the victim of some kind of foul play.'

'I can't believe you're seriously suggesting—'

'I appreciate it's a distressing prospect,' Annie went on. 'But we have to consider it. I'm sorry.'

Ellsworth took a breath. 'Yes, of course you're right. Though I think both are highly unlikely.'

'What was Melanie's state of mind recently?' Annie asked.

'Again, you'd have to ask her form teacher or her personal tutor, but from my contact with her, I'd say she seemed happy enough. There were no issues with her work or her application, and as far as I'm aware she was up to date with all her assignments. She was on target for an extremely strong set of A-Level results.'

It was perhaps revealing, Annie thought, that having been asked about Melanie's state of mind, Ellsworth's instinctive reaction was to discuss the girl's academic performance. But that no doubt went with the territory. 'You'd not seen or heard anything to give you cause for concern?'

'Nothing that I'm aware of. I'm sure that if other members of staff had any concerns they'd have raised them with me.'

'You said you thought Melanie was generally fairly popular. Was there anyone who might have had reason to harm her? Anyone she really didn't get on with.'

'I really can't envisage it. As I say, she wasn't the most extroverted individual, but I'm not aware that there was any enmity or bad blood between her and anyone else. Again, other teachers might have a better idea than I do about her relationships with the other girls. I hope any issues would have been brought to my attention.'

Annie remembered from her own schooldays that the pupils had been very adept at keeping their relationships – positive or negative – well away from the prying eyes of the teachers. That might be a little different in the more claustrophobic environment of a boarding school, but she guessed the girls here had plenty of secrets the staff knew nothing about.

What she didn't know was whether any of those secrets were relevant to Melanie Donnelly's death.

Chapter Six

'A girl could get used to this,' Margaret Delamere said.

'Don't tell me you're not already used to it.' Alastair Winters smiled in a manner that remained just the right side of unctuous. 'A woman like you must always be in demand.'

'If you say so, Alastair.' She wasn't remotely fooled by his flattery, no matter how thickly he laid it on. She'd initially encountered the slick local television presenter a few months earlier when he'd chaired an event at which she and various other opinionated pundits had debated policing and public order issues. He'd been an effective chair, but she'd already seen enough of him to recognise that his only real interest lay in furthering his own career. That was fair enough. If their interests happened to coincide, as Winters seemed to think they might, she'd be happy to stick with him.

The other chap, this Trevor Railstone, was supposed to be the potential executive producer – or whatever the appropriate term was – for the proposed TV show, but so far had contributed little to the conversation. That might mean this was really Winters's show, or it might mean that Railstone wasn't a man to show his hand until he needed to. Margaret had enough experience to know that those with the loudest voices weren't always the most influential. In any case, she was keeping her own powder dry until she was clear what exactly was being proposed. She'd been round this particular loop more than once already in recent years.

If nothing else, she'd get a decent lunch out of it. Winters had suggested they meet at one of the county's more upmarket restaurants, set in an elegant country house on the edge of the national park. The dining room was furnished in a style she might have characterised as chintzy and old-fashioned, but which was clearly designed to meet the expectations of a clientele which seemed mainly to comprise well-off retired couples or foursomes, with the odd smattering of neatly suited business types. The restaurant drew its produce from the adjacent fields and its own well-tended gardens, and its windows offered imposing views of the nearby hills and woodland. The food was determinedly unostentatious but so far had tasted glorious.

Even so, it was perhaps time she brought them back to business. 'I'm still not entirely sure what it is you have in mind.'

This time it was Railstone who responded, perhaps because he wanted to pre-empt whatever Winters might have to say. 'What we have in mind, Margaret, is a rein-vention of political television.' His emphasis on the word made it sound as if he were talking about some concept in quantum physics.

'That sounds very interesting,' she said.

'More than just interesting,' Railstone went on. 'I want to get back to the days when political programming could really spark debate. When it set the agenda. When it was what people talked about at work the next day.'

Margaret wasn't sure she could actually remember any days like that, but it didn't seem the moment to challenge him. 'I suppose the audience is more diverse these days.'

'Exactly.' Railstone waved his knife excitedly at her, then clearly realised his gesture looked potentially threatening. 'That's the point. Most people out there don't really know about or care about politics. It passes over their heads, even though it affects every last detail of their lives.'

'What I think Trevor means,' Winters interjected smoothly, 'is that television hasn't yet found a language to communicate contemporary politics in a way that really engages the widest potential audience.'

If that was so, Margaret thought, Alastair Winters didn't necessarily sound like the man to remedy the situation. 'I'm still not clear what you actually have in mind.'

They paused while the waiter served the next course in the tasting menu – a vibrant-looking concoction of cod cheeks, mussels and samphire. Railstone said, 'There are various issues, we think. The fact is that people have lost faith not just in politicians but also in political commentators. They see them all as part of the same political elite, talking among themselves. We need not just to find a new language and new topics, but new *people*.' He sampled his food before continuing. 'If you think of the politicians who've engaged the public in recent years, it's the ones who convey a sense of authenticity.'

'If you can fake that, you've got it made,' Winters offered.

Railstone ignored him. 'So that's what we're looking for. Someone who can engage with the audience. Someone who talks their language. Someone who can introduce them to a politics that isn't just about the House of Commons and Early Day Motions and Private

Members' Bills and all that nonsense, but about the realities of their lives.'

Some of this speech sounded suspiciously well-rehearsed, and it occurred to Margaret to wonder whether she was the first recipient of it. 'I'm still not sure where I fit into this.'

'We've been watching you, Margaret,' Railstone said. It sounded vaguely threatening. 'We've been watching you for a while now.'

'That's very flattering.'

'We like what we've seen. We think you have that authenticity.'

Margaret looked at him in surprise. She'd never had a low opinion of her own abilities, but she'd never seen herself as an authentic voice of the people. Certainly the idea would come as a surprise to her daughter. 'Really? Aren't I a little – well, old?'

'I think you're being harsh on yourself,' Winters said. 'Mature, yes, but by no means old.'

'But it's also the point,' Railstone said. 'Of course, you don't speak for the whole country. But you speak for the silent majority mostly ignored by the political classes – the respectable middle- and working-class folk whose voices are never listened to. You speak for them clearly and straightforwardly, with no nonsense. You know what you're talking about, particularly with regard to law and order. Even those who don't share your perspective can understand and recognise that. They may not agree with you, but they respect you.'

'It's good of you to say so. I just draw on my experience and say what I think.'

'That's the point. You're not trying to kowtow to some interest group or say what people want to hear. You tell the truth as you see it. People recognise that.' Railstone took the last mouthful of his food and clattered his fork down onto the plate. 'I've watched you in your recent television appearances, Margaret. You're a breath of fresh air. You must be getting more and more invitations to appear.'

'A few,' she acknowledged. 'I'm happy to accept as long as I feel I can make a useful contribution.' Margaret decided that, gratifying as all this might be, it was probably time to cut to the chase. 'It's good of you to say all this, Trevor, and I can't pretend I'm not flattered. But I'm still not sure what you have in mind.'

There was another pause while their empty plates were removed. 'What we have in mind, Margaret, is a new kind of political show. Something which looks at the areas of politics other shows don't reach. Day-to-day social issues. We want to talk to ordinary people about the realities of their daily lives and what that means in political terms. We want to talk to those operating in political spaces outside Westminster.'

None of this sounded particularly original to Margaret, but she'd already learned enough about the world of television to know that the pitch often bore very little similarity to reality. 'What kind of spaces?'

'It seems to me,' Railstone said, 'that we're reaching a point in this country where traditional party politics — and certainly the politics of the two major parties — are fragmenting. It's not about left and right any more. Some of the biggest issues transcend that divide. It's about values. Personal identity. The kind of country Britain should be.' He took a breath. 'We want presenters who can lead people through those issues. Help them understand what this might mean for them.'

'Presenters?'

'That's perhaps not the right word. Guides, mentors. People who can offer a vision.'

'But who can also present a television programme, of course,' Winters added. 'Or, at least, co-present.'

'With you?'

'With an experienced TV hand. We're envisaging a panel of equals, but, as Trevor said, people from outside the traditional world of both politics and television. People who can bring a new voice, a new perspective.'

'You see me as one of those?'

'We think you'd be perfect.'

Margaret waited while the waiter delivered the next course, some kind of foie gras dish of which her daughter would wholly disapprove. 'Who else do you have in mind?'

'We really only want a couple of main presenters, alongside Alastair, of course,' Railstone said. 'We were thinking perhaps Gareth Thomas.'

Thomas had been another participant on the panel with Winter, Margaret recalled. A young, fairly bumptious left-wing journalist. Undoubtedly articulate and persuasive, even if Margaret had disagreed with almost every word he'd said.

'There's a definite chemistry between you,' Winters commented.

Like potassium and water, Margaret thought. 'Interesting choice. I don't agree with Gareth on much, but he's passionate and well-intentioned, I'm sure. And he's knowledgeable in his own field.'

'You speak to very different constituencies,' Winters conceded. 'But you both speak to groups who've disengaged from the political mainstream. That's what's exciting about this.'

'I take it this would be a local programme?' Margaret had only ever seen Winters as a presenter on the regional TV news, though she guessed he had aspirations to do more.

'That's the exciting part,' Railstone said. 'We've got some interest in it being networked nationally. The idea would be to run a pilot series as part of the regional news and current affairs budget, but if it goes well there's every chance of it being taken nationally.'

Margaret had had previous discussions about the possibility of a regular television slot which, for various reasons, had come to nothing, so she'd remain sceptical about this until it actually happened. But there was no reason not to go along with it. If the show did happen, even at a local or regional level, it could lift her post-retirement career to a different level. 'It all sounds very exciting.'

'So we can count you in, Margaret?' Railstone said enthusiastically.

'In principle, certainly. I assume there are lots of details to be ironed out.'

'We're still at a relatively early stage. We haven't spoken in detail to Gareth yet, but he's also keen. Obviously we'll need to develop the format.'

'You're seeing Alastair as presenter?'

'I see my role more as a moderator,' Winters said. 'As Trevor said, we haven't worked through the details yet, but we're envisaging a live, audience-participation element. That's where I'd come in.'

'As long as it's not too much of a bear-pit,' Margaret said. 'I can't abide those programmes where everyone just shouts over each other.'

'Absolutely,' Railstone said. 'We want to avoid that at all costs. We want discussions that generate more light than heat. We won't be afraid to bring in genuine experts in specific fields who can aid the audience's understanding. But we'd want them subject to proper, meaningful scrutiny. Too often on TV, we rely on the appeal to authority. "Trust me, I'm an expert." That's what we want to avoid.'

'I suppose it's a question of balance.'

'We need balance,' Railstone conceded. 'But we also need strong, fearless opinions. That'll be the magic formula.'

To Margaret's untutored ears, none of this sounded hugely original, but she supposed that wasn't the point. 'I'd be delighted to be involved. If you really believe I've something to offer.'

'Don't underestimate yourself, Margaret,' Winters said. 'You offer something genuinely rare and fresh – honesty in your views, and the wit and eloquence to communicate them to the man and woman in the street. I see you and Gareth as a formidable pair.' He raised his glass of sparkling water. 'It's splendid that we all seem to be on the same page. If we weren't all driving, I'd order a bottle of champagne to celebrate. Especially as Trevor's picking up the tab. As it is, I'll just have to toast you with this stuff.' He waved the glass in her direction. 'To you, Margaret, and to the success of this exhilarating new project!'

Margaret clinked her own glass against his. 'To the project. Let's hope it's the start of something big.'

'To the project,' Railstone echoed. 'We're on our way!'

Chapter Seven

Alice Cartwright was a small woman, who seemed to have been shrunk even further by the morning's events. She stared fearfully at Annie, as if expecting some kind of physical attack. 'Tell me about Melanie,' Annie said, as gently as she could.

Cartwright blinked and Annie could see the tears swelling in her eyes. She'd clearly been in a highly emotional state when she'd first arrived for the interview, and Annie had offered to postpone it until Cartwright felt more able to proceed. Cartwright had shaken her head – the most active gesture Annie had so far seen from her – insisting that she wanted to get all this 'over with'.

That had seemed to be the general attitude across the school. Annie and Stuart Jennings had decided to begin some initial interviews immediately so they could decide how best to handle the case. They'd hoped that interviews with some of the key individuals, along with the findings of the CSI team, might give them a clearer sense of where to focus their resources. Jennings himself had returned to HQ to set the administrative wheels in motion, leaving her to conduct the first interviews. She suspected he'd been only too keen to escape this predominantly female environment.

'You were her personal tutor, I understand? What does that mean exactly?'

'Each girl's allocated a personal tutor when they first join the school. The idea's that, as far as possible, the personal tutor remains consistent as the girls progress through the school, so we're able to form a closer relationship with them than their form and subject teachers. We provide pastoral care, so we should be the first point of contact for dealing with any personal or emotional problems. I've been Melanie's tutor since she joined the school, so you can imagine what a shock this has been.'

Cartwright's emotion was understandable. Annie wondered to what extent the teacher might be blaming herself for Melanie's death, whatever its causes. 'Tell me about Melanie.'

'I don't really know what to say. She was a lovely girl. Very bright, too.' She hesitated. 'I probably shouldn't say it, but she was much brighter than most of our girls.'

Annie raised an eyebrow at the unexpected bluntness. 'The school gets very good academic results, I understand.'

'We do, because we're good at what we do. But we're a sausage machine. We churn out girls who are good at passing exams. They'll do well in life. But we don't encourage them to think for themselves. We don't encourage real creativity.'

It was clear that Cartwright's apparently timid exterior concealed a much steelier personality. 'And Melanie was different?'

'In her quiet way, she was a genuine rebel. Not the sort to cause trouble, but more than capable of thinking for herself. And she could be surprisingly stubborn if she really cared about something.'

'What sort of things did she care about?'

'Well, the most obvious example was her politics. I didn't share her political views, and to be honest I'm not even sure she fully believed in them herself. But she felt it was important to go against the grain, to challenge what other people thought or how they behaved. Most of the girls here never even think to question their own values. Melanie spent her time questioning herself and challenging others.'

'Did that make her popular?'

'I'm not sure it made her popular, exactly, but I don't think she was disliked. When she challenged people, she did it very subtly. I don't think I ever saw her have an argument with anyone. At worst, people thought she was a bit eccentric, and some of them made fun of her a little. All that Red Mel stuff. There was no malice in it, and she seemed to take it in good part.'

Annie wondered about that. Her own memories were that her teenage years were a mass of swirling hormones and mood swings. Any small perceived slight could quickly turn into a huge trauma. Friends were best friends forever and enemies were always mortal. Nothing was ever in proportion. Maybe that was different for the girls here, but Annie doubted it. It was possible that Melanie had been able to accept the mockery, but it was equally possible she'd been a seething bundle of anger and resentment. They might never know for sure unless she'd confided in one of the other girls.

'Did she have any particular close friends?'

'One or two. A girl called Kate Holloway, and another called Nadine Vance. They were probably the closest to Melanie. They shared a lot of her interests. Not so much the political stuff, but books and music and suchlike. They're devastated by what's happened.'

'We'll need to talk to them at some point, but that can wait till they feel up to it. This must be a dreadful shock. Especially to girls of that age.'

'It's a shock for all of us. I can't imagine what it must be like for them. I don't think you even consider death when you're young.'

'Were there any tensions between Melanie and any other girls?'

'Tensions?'

'You said that some of the other girls thought her a little eccentric. I was wondering whether that ever turned into anything stronger.'

'Bullying, you mean?'

'That sort of thing.'

'We have a very strong line on bullying. It's one thing that we absolutely won't tolerate. You can imagine that in an environment like this, any instances of bullying could be very toxic.'

It sounded to Annie as if Cartwright was trotting out a well-rehearsed line. The line they'd no doubt take with any current or prospective parent who raised the subject. The question was whether the reality matched the rhetoric. 'Perhaps bullying is a little too strong a term. I just wondered if there was anyone that Melanie didn't get on with.'

'I'm not aware of anyone. There were plenty of people she didn't particularly mix with, I think. There are always different circles here. The girls who are keen on sports. The ones who are into all the usual teenage stuff. The more intellectual types. There's some overlap between them, but a lot of the girls stick to those with similar interests.'

'Do you think she was happy here?'

Cartwright was silent for a moment before responding. 'I'd have said so, on the whole. Some of the girls throw themselves wholeheartedly into this kind of environment, and Melanie was never one of those. I sometimes wondered if she'd have been happier in a different kind of school. But like most of the girls here, she found a circle of friends and a set of interests that suited her, and she made it work well enough.'

To Annie's ears, it sounded an odd conclusion. That Melanie Donnelly had had no choice but to make the best of a lifestyle for which her parents were presumably paying a very substantial amount of money. But Annie knew she could easily have ended up in a similar position if she hadn't resisted her own mother's aspirations. She wondered whether the headmistress had yet managed to contact Melanie's parents, and if so how they'd reacted to their daughter's death. 'I'm sorry if this sounds an insensitive question in the circumstances,' Annie said, 'but have you had girls who haven't, as you put it, made it work here?'

'Sometimes. For a variety of reasons. And with a variety of outcomes. We usually spot quite quickly if a pupil isn't fitting in. Sometimes it's because they're shy. Sometimes they come with a chip on their shoulder because they didn't want to be here in the first place. Sometimes it's the ones who seem the most brash and self-assured who turn out to have the biggest problems. We try to intervene as sensitively as we can, helping them to build friendships and relationships, making sure they don't become isolated. In most cases, that's enough.'

'You didn't seen any signs of those problems with Melanie?'

'I'm not aware of any issues. She was generally a very well-balanced girl. It's such a tragedy. She was a girl with tremendous promise.'

'Did she have any particular ambitions?'

'She had a real interest in politics. She was concerned about fairness and justice. A lot of it was teenage idealism, but she took it seriously. Whatever she ended up doing, she'd have made the world a better place.'

There were worse epitaphs, Annie reflected. She was wondering how to phrase her final question to Cartwright, but knew it had to be asked. 'I'm sorry to have to ask this, but you clearly knew Melanie well. Do you think it's possible that her death was anything other than a tragic accident?'

'I don't know, to be honest. We try to be conscientious about safety issues, though I suppose accidents can always happen. I just didn't see Melanie as the sort to take silly risks. There are daft girls here who'd hang out of windows for a dare, but Melanie was never one of those. On the other hand, I can't really see her as a victim of bullying, either.'

'The victim doesn't usually get to choose,' Annie pointed out.

'I'm not saying it's impossible. But Melanie was strong-willed. She did what she wanted and didn't really care what others thought.'

'That might antagonise some people.'

'It might. But my impression was that most of the girls – certainly most of the girls in the sixth form – broadly liked and respected her.' She stopped again. 'There is the third possibility. That she took her own life. I'm trying to be objective about this. I know there's nothing predict-able about self-harm, and that sometimes it's the most unexpected people… But it doesn't feel like something she would do. I'm sorry – I don't think I'm being very helpful to you.'

'I just wanted an honest opinion, which is what you've given me.'

'What I would say,' Cartwright added, 'is that I suspect you won't find it easy to get to the bottom of this.'

'Why do you say that?'

'It was what you just said. About giving an honest opinion. I've tried to do that, but I don't know how many others will. I don't mean they'll actively lie to you. But they'll all have an agenda. Ms Ellsworth will be understandably desperate to protect the reputation of the school, not to mention her own reputation. The other teachers will be keen to ensure no blame attaches to them. The girls – well, they'll have countless agendas. Some will be keen to protect Melanie. Some will want to hog the limelight. Some will want to criticise the school or the teachers, or a particular teacher. I don't envy you trying to disentangle the truth from all that.'

'It's what we do,' Annie said. 'And we encounter the issues you've just described in more or less every case we deal with.'

Cartwright looked sceptical. 'Everything takes on a greater intensity in a place like this, though. The rumour mill's going all the time, and most of what it generates is nonsense. It's just worth bearing in mind.'

'I'll do that.' As she spoke, Annie was wondering exactly what sort of rumours Cartwright really had in mind.

Chapter Eight

Annie had decided to see Kate Holloway and Nadine Vance together. Her first instinct had been to talk to the two girls, supposedly Melanie Donnelly's closest friends, separately, but Alice Cartwright had advised her that, like Melanie herself, both girls were quiet individuals. 'If you talk to them separately, you might find they both clam up. They always seem more relaxed when they're together.'

The interview had been delayed to allow the girls time to recover from the immediate shock of their friend's death. In the meantime, their parents had been advised that the interview was taking place, and had been happy for it to be conducted in their absence. Alice Cartwright had agreed to attend to provide reassurance to the parents, although the girls were being interviewed only as possible witnesses.

At first glance, the two girls could almost have been mistaken for twins. They were a similar height and build, and both had dark hair, Kate's short and straight while Nadine's was a longer mass of apparently natural curls. As Cartwright ushered them into the small classroom being used for the interviews, both looked as nervous as if they'd been summoned to the headmistress's study for a dressing-down.

Annie did her best to offer a welcoming smile. 'Good morning to you both. I'm DI Annie Delamere, but you can call me Annie. I hope this doesn't need saying, but I'd like to stress that you aren't in any kind of trouble. I know it must be intimidating to talk to a police officer, but all I'm trying to do is learn more about Melanie. I understand you were both friends with her?'

The two girls looked back at her with earnest expressions. Finally Kate nodded. 'We were probably her best friends.' There was a slight catch in her voice, although her face showed no emotion.

'This must have been a great shock,' Annie said. 'I'm very sorry.'

The two girls exchanged a glance, which Annie felt was intended to convey some sort of meaning between them. Kate said, 'It's been awful. I just couldn't believe it. Then when the police came...'

'I'm sure there are rumours about why the police are involved,' Annie said. 'But I do want to reassure you that our presence here is entirely routine. We're obliged to investigate any death where the circumstances aren't completely clear.'

Kate nodded, though her expression remained sceptical.

'Tell me about Melanie. Have you been friends throughout your time at the school?'

'Not really.' This time it was Nadine who responded. 'I mean, we always got on okay with her, but we weren't really best friends until the last couple of years.' This time Nadine looked across at Cartwright, as if seeking some direction as to how much she was allowed to say. 'We always thought of Mel as a bit of a loner, to be honest. Very nice, but she preferred to keep to herself. She used to go off to the library to read by herself at lunchtime, that sort of thing. Kate and I do a bit of that, but we mainly spend time chatting together.'

Annie nodded. 'But you'd got to know her better in the last couple of years?'

'It was when we started doing GCSEs,' Kate said. 'We were doing a similar range of subjects so we got to know her better in class. We liked a lot of the same things.'

'What kinds of things?' Annie asked.

Kate shrugged. 'Books, mainly, I suppose. All three of us are—' She stopped, checking herself. 'Well, were, I suppose, doing English.' She looked suddenly downcast, as if the reality of Melanie's death had only just struck her. 'We liked the same sort of books.'

'I understand Melanie was very interested in politics. Is that something that interests the two of you too?'

Nadine looked mildly embarrassed. 'We're both doing politics A-Level so, yes, in that sense. Though not quite in the same way as Mel was. Mel was very passionate. She was always campaigning about something.'

'You didn't share her political views?'

'It wasn't really that. It wasn't that we disagreed with her. I mean, she was very well-intentioned. But her views were a bit more extreme than ours. It was one reason we liked her, to be honest. Because she'd say and do things we generally wouldn't.'

'What sort of things?'

Again, Nadine glanced over at Cartwright, whose face remained expressionless. 'She'd started a school newsletter online, and she ran various campaigns in the school, for example. Topical issues she was interested in. Climate change. Black Lives Matter. Things in the news.'

Cartwright gave a cough that might have been intended as a warning to the girls, Annie thought. It

67

was interesting that Cartwright hadn't mentioned this campaigning during their previous discussion. 'We try to encourage the girls to develop an interest in the news and topical matters,' Cartwright said. 'Particularly the sixth-formers, and obviously this tied in with Melanie's politics studies. So we never had any issue with her campaigns. Obviously, we have to be careful as a school that we're not seen to be taking a political stance or endorsing the senti-ments being expressed, and we have to ensure other pupils don't feel offended. But we're always keen to encourage our girls to express their right to free speech.' As in her previous conversation with Cartwright, Annie had the sense of a well-rehearsed official line.

'Were any of Melanie's campaigns controversial?'

This time it was Kate who responded. 'Most people liked Mel, even if they thought she was a bit batty—' She stopped, as if concerned that she'd overstepped a mark. 'Well, you know what I mean. I don't think most people really cared about her politics, and if they did they just laughed at her.'

'Did she mind that?'

'I don't think so. She thought she was right and they were wrong. Her view was that most of the girls here had already been indoctrinated to grow up like their parents. She didn't think they were capable of thinking any other way. Mel liked winding them up, but it was all friendly.'

Annie was beginning to wonder about that. The picture of Melanie Donnelly emerging from this discus-sion felt subtly different from that provided by the head-mistress or Alice Cartwright.

'Was there anyone who particularly disliked Melanie?' she asked.

68

There was a silence before Kate said, 'I don't think so, not really. If she had arguments with people, it was mainly about politics. I don't think anyone but Mel took those seriously. The thing is, you had to know Melanie to understand what she was like. She was one of those people you couldn't really dislike.' Tears filled her eyes now, and she looked across at Nadine as if embarrassed that she'd revealed her feelings.

'I understand,' Annie said. 'I'm so sorry about all this.' She suspected she'd taken the discussion as far as it was likely to go for the moment. Both girls had been holding themselves together well, but their grief wasn't far below the surface. Annie was still young enough to recall how intense those emotions could feel for teenagers. 'I can appreciate what a shock this has been for you both. I don't think we need to take it any further today.' She looked over at Cartwright. 'I may want to talk to Nadine and Kate again before we're finished. I assume that won't be a problem?'

'We'll do everything we can to help.'

Kate and Nadine were still exchanging glances, as if there was something more they wanted to say.

'Is there anything else you want to tell me about Melanie before we finish?'

Kate hesitated for a moment. 'We don't think it was an accident. What happened to Mel.'

Annie could see Cartwright preparing to intervene. 'Why do you say that?'

'She wasn't stupid. She didn't mess around. I just can't imagine her falling accidentally.'

'It's not just that,' Nadine added. 'She didn't like heights. She was really nervous about any risk of falling. We had a school trip in London, and she was only one

69

who wouldn't go on the London Eye because she couldn't face being that far off the ground.'

'I don't recall that—' Cartwright began.

'It's true, miss,' Kate said. 'Mrs Dores had to stay with her while the rest of us went up. Mel was a bit embarrassed by it, but there was nothing she could do. She wasn't even keen on looking out of the windows on the upper floors here.'

Annie had little doubt the girls were telling the truth, or at least the truth as they understood it. 'Of course, accidents can happen in numerous ways,' she said vaguely, 'but that's a very helpful piece of information. Thank you, and thank you for your time this morning.'

'We just want you to find out what happened to Mel,' Kate said.

'That's why we're here. We'll do our very best.'

Annie thanked the girls again, and maintained her bland smile while Cartwright ushered them out of the room. Moments later, Cartwright reappeared. 'I hope that was helpful. They were more forthcoming than I'd feared.'

'They obviously cared about Melanie. I was interested to hear about the newsletter and the campaigns.'

'I'm sorry. I should have mentioned that. It just slipped my mind completely. It's been a fraught time.'

'Yes, of course.' Annie decided to press a little harder. 'It sounds as if Melanie might have been a more controversial figure than I'd realised.'

Cartwright sat herself down beside Annie. 'I wouldn't really have said controversial. We were keen to support Melanie with the newsletter idea. We'd never really had anything like that before – produced by the pupils, I mean. The first few were largely produced by Melanie herself, just to get it going, but the idea was that she'd play an editorial role and we'd open it up to other girls to contribute. The head's only condition was that she or I should have an opportunity to vet each edition before it went out. Not that we didn't trust Melanie, but we were conscious there might be sensitivities she might not be aware of.'

'Did you have to remove anything?'

'Melanie was a very sensible girl, and she was keen not to abuse the opportunity she'd been given. She talked about some political issues, as Kate and Nadine said, and obviously had her own take on those, but there was nothing inappropriate or provocative.'

'Would it be possible for me to see some copies?'

'Of course. I'll email them to you this afternoon.'

'Thank you.' Annie flicked briefly through her interview notes. 'The other interesting part was about Melanie's fear of heights.'

'I must confess that was news to me. I'll check the file to see if there's any mention of it. I don't recall the London incident.'

'It would be an odd thing for the girls to make up.'

'Oh, certainly. It may be they've misunderstood or exaggerated what Melanie told them.'

'It would be useful to know,' Annie said blandly. 'Just to ensure we've got a full picture.'

'Of course,' Cartwright said. 'I appreciate you have a job to do.'

There was a pointed edge to her words, and Annie was more than happy to take the hint. 'We'll be continuing our interviews with the other relevant teachers this afternoon, but I'll leave you to get on with things. My next task is to talk to Melanie's parents.'

'I don't envy you that,' Cartwright said. 'The head saw them this morning. They're devastated, as you can imagine.'

'I feel for them,' Annie said. 'It's an awful thing to happen to any parents.'

Cartwright nodded, sympathetically. 'The worst thing imaginable.'

Chapter Nine

Annie hadn't realised there were places like this in the Peak District, and she couldn't really imagine why they were needed. She assumed the set-up made the householders feel more secure, but she couldn't envisage what sort of threat they feared to justify this lifestyle.

She drew up to the imposing gates and lowered the car window. There was a list of house names with a bell beside each. She pressed the bell for the address she been given and waited while the gates swung smoothly open. As she passed through into the estate, the gates immediately closed behind her.

She followed the road round slowly, checking the house names until she spotted the Donnellys' residence. It was at the far end of the estate, in a premium location. The house overlooked the suspiciously artificial-looking lake beside the estate, and commanded excellent views of the glorious landscape beyond. Annie couldn't imagine how much these houses were worth. She also couldn't imagine why anyone who could afford to buy one would choose to live here. It had the air of an upmarket suburban estate transplanted into the middle of the moorland.

She supposed that was the point. The people who bought these places wanted to feel the security of suburbia while enjoying the benefits of country living. In the Donnellys' case, their judgement was no doubt further influenced by the time they spent outside the UK. When the school had finally succeeded in contacting them, they had turned out to be on a business trip to Dubai. They'd flown back over the weekend and had visited the school that morning. Annie had arranged to talk to them at their home afterwards. It wasn't an interview she was looking forward to.

She'd looked up Tony Donnelly on the Companies House website and discovered that he was a director of a number of building and construction businesses in the UK and overseas, with particular interests in the Middle East. Most of the businesses had registered offices in London, but there was a substantial network of foreign subsidiaries. Further investigation had revealed that this imposing building was only one of several houses owned by the Donnellys, including a couple abroad. This seemed little more than a country bolthole, standing empty for much of the year.

None of this had been exactly what Annie had expected. She'd assumed the Donnellys would be well-off because they could afford the fees required to send Melanie to an upmarket boarding school. But her brief investigation into Tony Donnelly's background suggested wealth she couldn't easily imagine. Some months before, while working on a case, Annie had had some dealings with Michelle Wentworth, a prosperous local businesswoman. That experience had been eye-opening, but Donnelly was in a different league again.

She climbed out of the car and stood for a moment looking at the house. It was set back from the road behind a substantial and well-maintained garden. Nothing looked quite natural. The plants and flowers were obviously real enough, but the garden as a whole was clearly the product of meticulous planning and frequent care. Everything looked mildly incongruous against the backdrop of the wild grey moors and distant hills.

The rain had held off for the moment, though the sky remained heavy and a cold, blustery wind was blowing in from the moorland. Annie pulled her coat more tightly around herself and made her way up the gravelled driveway towards the house.

As she approached, the large oak front door opened and a man stepped out to greet her. He was tall – well over six feet, she estimated – and heavily built, with the air of someone who had once been athletic but was now slightly out of condition. He was casually dressed, in a black polo shirt and jeans, but to Annie's inexpert eye the clothing looked expensive.

'DI Annie Delamere.'

The man held out his hand. 'Tony Donnelly. Pleased to meet you.'

The strength of his handshake matched his build. This was a man accustomed to dominating proceedings.

'I'm sorry it has to be in these circumstances. I can only offer my deep condolences. I'm very sorry.'

'It's an awful business.' His tone suggested that he might have been describing some failed business deal rather than his daughter's death. 'Come inside.'

The interior of the house was largely as she'd expected – spacious, impressively designed, slightly anonymous. She wondered to what extent the Donnellys had bothered to impose their own personalities on the place after they'd bought it.

Donnelly led her into the living room. Again, the room looked immaculate, the furniture expensive and well-chosen, the pictures on the walls tasteful and appropriate.

It felt like a show house or, perhaps more accurately, an architect's impression of a show house. The picture included in the brochure to attract potential buyers.

The only incongruous element was the woman hunched on the sofa. She was a relatively slight woman, her skinny body wrapped round itself as if seeking protection from the outside world. Annie could see that she had recently been crying.

'Barbara, this is DI Delamere.'

Barbara Donnelly rose unsteadily and held out her hand. Annie felt almost as if she was physically supporting the other woman, preventing her from falling back onto the sofa behind her. 'I'm so sorry for your loss, Mrs Donnelly. I appreciate it must have been a dreadful shock for you. If you feel up to answering some questions, that would be very helpful. But if you're not yet ready, I'm very happy to return at some other time.'

'It's better for us to get it all over with.'

Tony Donnelly had answered before his wife could offer a response. She nodded. 'Tony's right. Better to get it over with.'

'Please do take a seat.' Donnelly gestured towards the armchair beside the sofa. 'I'll fetch us some coffee. I'm sure we could all benefit from a cup.' He shook his head. 'We normally have some staff when we're here, but our return was a little unexpected this time, so I'm having to work out where everything is.'

Annie's instinct had been to refuse the coffee, but she felt it might be useful to have Barbara Donnelly to herself for at least a few minutes. Her husband was likely to dominate any subsequent discussion, whether deliberately or simply through the force of his personality.

'I don't know how this can have happened.' Barbara Donnelly's tone suggested she might be talking about her life in general, rather than simply the death of her daughter.

'That's what we need to find out, Mrs Donnelly.'

'Melanie was such a careful girl. I just can't believe it. How could the school have allowed this to happen?'

'Again, that's the purpose of our investigation. We need to understand the circumstances of your daughter's sad death.' Annie paused. 'Perhaps it would be best if you just tell me about Melanie. What sort of girl she was. If that isn't too painful for you.'

'It feels good to talk about her. I feel guilty now I didn't do more for her.' She looked over at the door, as if fearful her husband might overhear what she was saying. 'We were always too busy, you know? Tony always had another business deal more important than spending time with Melanie.' There was a bitterness in Barbara Donnelly's tone that took Annie by surprise.

'When did you last see her?'

'At Christmas. We came back for the Christmas holiday to be with her. I've always insisted on being here during her school holidays, even if Tony has to jet off all over the world as usual. That's why we bought this place, to give Melanie a home not too far from the school. This place had all the facilities a child might want. We've an indoor pool, a games room, a gym. You name it.' She sounded like someone reading from a brochure. 'I suppose Melanie enjoyed that.'

Annie wondered how this lifestyle had squared with Melanie's espoused socialism, but she guessed the answer was provided by Barbara Donnelly's tone. 'So you had a family Christmas here?'

'We even had Tony here for Christmas itself, which is almost unprecedented. We spent a fortune, as we always did – presents, decorations, over-the-top Christmas dinner. Had various friends – by which I mean Tony's business associates, for the most part – round for meals and drinks.' She paused. 'I think Melanie hated every second of it.'

'What was Melanie's general state of mind?'

'If you're asking whether she might have taken her own life,' Barbara Donnelly said bluntly, 'I'd say no. I might be wrong, but I don't think so. That wouldn't have been Melanie. She didn't get depressed. She got angry.'

'How was she at Christmas?'

'To be honest, I'd say she was pissed off. Pissed off with Tony, mainly. But also pissed off with me. And pissed off with the rest of the world, probably.'

'Was there any particular reason for that?'

'No more than usual. She was at that age. The age when you're too old to spend time just with your parents, but not quite old enough to do much else. Melanie always resented that she wasn't able to live what she thought of as a normal teenage life. Have the same circle of friends at school and at home, for example. At the end of every term, her friends would disappear off to whichever part of the country or world they came from, and Melanie would be stuck back here with mainly just me for company. I did my best for her. We'd invite some of her friends up here to stay, and once or twice that worked. But mostly they were just too far away.' She gestured vaguely to the house at large. 'Whatever facilities we might have here, it's not much of a life for a teenage girl.'

It was difficult to have too much sympathy for a girl who had been born into this level of privilege. But Annie

78

could imagine how miserable it might be for a girl having to live, essentially on her own, in this bizarrely cloistered community. 'You said your daughter was angry with your husband. Again, was there any particular reason for that?'

'It was mainly the usual blanket resentment, but the particular focus was on whether Melanie should learn to drive. She was soon to turn seventeen and wanted to start taking lessons. We'd talked about buying her lessons as one of her Christmas presents. But Tony said he wasn't sure it was a good idea.'

'Why not?'

'I think it was a genuine concern for her well-being. He might not always have had the best way of showing it, but he loved Melanie. He's more distraught at what's happened than I am, though you'd never know.' She looked over at the closed living-room door. 'That's why he's absented himself. Not just to make coffee. But because it's hard for him to talk about any of this. He was concerned about her driving by herself. He was worried about her safety, but he also didn't want to accept she was growing up.'

She broke off as her husband returned, bearing a tray of with coffee and mugs. He made a show of pouring drinks for the two women, as if delaying the moment when he had to engage with the discussion. Finally, he sat down on one of the other armchairs, a mug of coffee cradled to his stomach.

'DI Delamere was just asking about Melanie's state of mind when we last saw her.'

'At Christmas?' Donnelly was silent for a moment. 'Her usual teenage self, I suppose. Not easy to get on with. We did what we could for her. Spent a fortune on presents. Had people over so she wouldn't be bored.' He looked across at his wife, as if challenging her to gainsay what he was saying. 'I don't think there was anything out of the ordinary.'

'She didn't seem in a particularly low mood?'

'I wouldn't have said so. A bit morose, but that was usually the case when she was here. Like I say, teenagers.' For the first time Annie detected a trace of emotion in his expression. 'I'm sorry. I keep having to remind myself that she's – no longer with us. It just doesn't feel real.'

'That's understandable,' Annie said. 'Tell me about Melanie.'

It was Barbara Donnelly who responded first. 'She was a very bright girl.' She looked across at her husband and gave an unconvincing laugh. 'I don't know where she got that from. Tony and I aren't academic. Melanie came top in everything. She was planning to apply for Cambridge. That would have been a first in the family.'

'She was clever all right.' Tony Donnelly sounded almost resentful of the fact. 'Maybe not quite as clever as she thought sometimes, but she could run rings about me on most subjects. Especially politics.'

'I understand she had strong political views,' Annie said.

'You can say that again.' Donnelly said. 'I blamed the school for encouraging her, but I suppose it's right to allow kids to go through those phases.'

'You believe that's all it was? A phase?' This was Barbara Donnelly, her tone unexpectedly sharp.

Her husband shrugged. 'It's the old thing, isn't it? If you're not a socialist at twenty you don't have a heart, but if you're still a socialist at forty you don't have a brain. Mind you, I never went through a socialist phase, so that tells you something.' He gave a hollow laugh.

'What did Melanie think of your lifestyle?' Annie gestured at the house around them. 'With respect, you're clearly not short of money.'

'It's all relative, though, isn't it?' There was a touch of defensiveness in Tony Donnelly's tone. Annie wondered he'd had variants of this debate with his daughter. 'Compared to some of the people I deal with in the Middle East, we're on our uppers.'

'She disapproved of our lifestyle,' Barbara Donnelly added.

'Though not to the extent of rejecting its benefits,' Tony Donnelly said.

'Like she had a choice.' Barbara Donnelly was glaring at her husband now, as if daring him to argue back. Her tone had changed, and Annie could feel old family tensions rising to the surface. 'She didn't want to go to that school, but you made it very clear she had no option.'

'It was the only practical—'

'She didn't want to come back to this place. She didn't care about the pool and the games room and all the other stuff you had installed supposedly for her benefit. She didn't want your presents at Christmas, and the only thing she did want you refused her.'

'I said—'

'You wanted to preserve her forever as your little girl. You didn't just want to protect her. You wanted to control her.'

'Barbara, I *loved* her—'

'I've no doubt you did, in your own way. And I've no doubt that you're devastated – much more than you're prepared to reveal – that you've lost her. But for you it's like losing one of your fancy cars. It's the loss of a highly prized and valuable possession.'

They were glaring at each other now, each daring the other to say more, to raise the stakes even higher. It was as if they had forgotten Annie's presence. For her part, Annie had been content to allow the argument to proceed in the hope it might reveal more about the couple's relationship. Well, it had done that, she supposed. 'You were telling me about Melanie.'

Tony Donnelly was still staring at his wife. 'I'm sorry. We're both a bit overwrought at the moment. This has all been a real shock.'

'As I say, she was clever,' Barbara Donnelly said. 'And she had real principles. Her concern about our lifestyle wasn't so much that we were well-off. It was how we'd acquired our money.'

Her husband snorted. 'We acquired our money through hard work and graft. I never started out with any privileges. My family—'

'Tony!' Barbara Donnelly's tone was that of an owner to its disobedient dog. 'No one wants to hear your "poorer than thou" sob stories. We're talking about Melanie. She never questioned that you'd worked hard for your money. That wasn't the point.'

'What was the point?' Annie prompted.

'She had a problem with some of the places I do business now,' Tony Donnelly said. 'I've built a genuinely international business. We've partnered on construction projects with countries across the world. North America. Australia. Asia. As well as across Europe. We're a British success story.' He sounded as if he was delivering the commentary on a corporate video. 'But we're a business, not a moral crusade.'

'I'm not sure I follow,' Annie said.

'Melanie would have had us limit our business to the countries and regimes she approved of. She didn't like the fact that we have partners in Russia and China, and she certainly didn't like some of the Middle Eastern counties we've worked with. She just didn't live in the real world.'

'That's not fair, Tony,' Barbara Donnelly said. 'She didn't disapprove of your work in itself. She just wanted you to apply some moral standards.'

'That's not how it works. She seemed to think that you can just turn business off and on like a tap. She asked me how much money I really needed, as if it was possible just to stop. But it's a treadmill. There's a business to maintain, staff to pay, loans to service. Sure, we're well-off. Wealthy, even. But it's not like I'm sitting there with billions in the bank. Maybe one day, I hope. But until then, we have to take the work where it comes. Beggars can't be choosers.' Donnelly stopped, as if even he was aware of the inappropriateness of his phrasing.

Annie decided it was time to move the conversation on. 'You said Melanie was expecting to apply to Cambridge. What ambitions did she have in life? What did she want to do?'

'I don't think she entirely knew,' Barbara Donnelly said. 'But her interest in politics had led her to think about various options. Politics itself, of course. But she'd also talked about a career in journalism.'

'I imagine it's a challenge to break into that sort of work.'

'That's what I told her,' Tony Donnelly said. 'I told her she needed to be realistic.'

'She was,' Barbara Donnelly countered. 'That was why she was trying to gain some experience at school with the newsletter. She'd approached the local newspapers and radio to see if she could do any intern work there during her holidays. She thought if she did something like that and then got involved in student journalism, it might give her the foundation she needed.'

Tony Donnelly sniffed. 'And of course she'd have been able to do unpaid internships because I'd have been subsidising her through real work. But she didn't see any contradiction there.'

'What did Melanie tell you about her newsletter at school?' Annie asked Barbara Donnelly.

'Not a great deal. The teachers were supportive. A lot of it was harmless stuff about the school. Sports reports, reviews of books the girls had read or the films they had at their film society. The usual sort of school stuff. Melanie contributed some of the more serious pieces about national or international politics.'

'One of her teachers mentioned campaigns,' Annie prompted.

'Again, that was Melanie all over. I'm not sure the school entirely approved of those, but Melanie was careful to include a spread of opinions rather than just pushing her own views, so it was presented as a debate.' She finally gave a faint smile. 'Like I say, Melanie was clever. Though there was one topic that caused a bit of a kerfuffle.'

'What was that?' Annie couldn't recall any of the teachers mentioning any contentious issues.

'Melanie was keen to do something on all this stuff about supposedly rewriting history. It was after that fuss with the slaveowner statue in Bristol. The one that was thrown into the river. It was a topical subject, and Melanie thought it would make a good debate in the newsletter. She'd lined up a couple of other girls to write more conservative pieces, and Melanie was writing something about how we needed to recognise the injustices under-pinning so many British institutions.'

'So why did it cause a fuss?'

'Because this time Melanie was a bit too smart for her own good,' Tony Donnelly said. 'She thought she could make it even more topical by discussing the school itself.'

Annie was beginning to see where this was leading. 'She found some skeletons in the school's closet?'

Donnelly shrugged. 'If you think they're skeletons. I didn't think the school had anything to be embarrassed about. But they were worried about bad publicity. We had a grumpy call from the head, expressing concern and saying the school wouldn't allow it to proceed. I'm not sure what she expected us to do about it. I just told them they should take whatever action they thought appropriate. They were the ones who'd allowed her to get caught up in this nonsense in the first place.'

'What kind of information did Melanie uncover?'

'I don't know the detail,' Barbara Donnelly said. 'Melanie was very frustrated, because she felt it was the first time she'd had an opportunity to carry out some original investigative journalism of her own. She tried to get me to intervene, but I told her the head had the reputation of the school to consider. Which just meant that Melanie painted me as the villain of the week.'

'Good to see you getting a taste of it for once,' Tony Donnelly said.

His wife ignored him. 'She sent me some extracts to show me what she was doing. Some of it was quite inter-esting. Apparently, the school's founder, Lady Elizabeth Brennan, was the wife of a slave trader. The initial funding for the school had roots in the trade and in the early days many of the pupils were the daughters of traders. Melanie's point was that this account of the school's origins is absent from the school's current prospectus. But she'd dug out one from twenty years ago which did include those details. She said the school wasn't being honest about its history. That they didn't used to be embarrassed and it was only because attitudes had changed that they were now brushing it under the carpet.'

'That wasn't the real problem, though, was it?' Tony Donnelly said. 'I mean, the slave link was far enough back in the past that no one was really going to care much about it. It was the more recent stuff that really gave old Ellsworth the jitters.'

Barbara Donnelly nodded. 'I suppose so. Melanie, in her wisdom, had decided to do an analysis of all the benefactions and grants given to the school over the years. She told the school librarian that she was doing some research into the school's history as the basis for an article for the newsletter. The librarian showed her masses of archive material that had been gathering dust for decades. Melanie just locked herself away and worked through everything.'

'What did she find?'

'I only know what Melanie told me at Christmas. In the early days, the school received money from the empire, from the slave trade, from dubious overseas sources. Interesting, but nothing too explosive. But then Melanie started to look at donations made to the school over the last few years.'

'And that was what seemed to ruffle Ellsworth's feathers,' Tony Donnelly said. 'She called a halt to Melanie's research, and told her in no uncertain terms to move on to some other topic.'

'Do you know why?'

Tony Donnelly shrugged. 'I'm guessing it was just too sensitive. I can't say I blamed Ellsworth. Look, this is all very fascinating, but we're dancing round the real question.'

'What's that, Mr Donnelly?'

'How Mel died. That's all I want to know. Unless I'm missing something, there are only three possibilities. Either she fell, she jumped or someone pushed her. I'm right, aren't I?'

'In broad terms, yes. Of course, there could be countless—'

'So which is it?'

'That's the purpose of this inquiry, Mr Donnelly. To ascertain, as clearly as we can, the circumstances of your daughter's tragic death.'

'You like to talk around the houses, don't you? Let me put it my way. If this was any other girl, I'd think it was most likely just a stupid accident. Some teenager messing about and losing their footing. That stuff happens. We've had experienced workmen do it on site, however many health and safety procedures we put in place. But it's not Melanie. It's not what she'd do.'

'Some of her friends said she was scared of heights. Is that true?'

Barbara Donnelly nodded. 'It was a real thing for her. One reason we didn't take her overseas with us. She wouldn't fly. She didn't like being anywhere where she thought there was a risk of falling. So, yes, Tony's right that Melanie would never climb up to the roof through choice.'

'If it wasn't an accident, that only leaves two alternatives,' Tony Donnelly said. 'To be blunt, suicide or murder.'

'Well—'

'I'm not an idiot,' Donnelly said. 'Please don't treat me like one.'

Annie took a breath. 'As I say, in broad terms you're right, Mr Donnelly. Those are the three potential causes of your daughter's death, with some possible overlap between them. I understand what you're saying about Melanie's fear of heights, but I've been doing this job long enough to know accidents can happen in the most unexpected ways. It's also possible someone else was involved, but had no intention of it ending in the tragic way it did. In short, we have to look at any possibility, including those that may seem unlikely.'

'Including suicide or murder?'

'Including those.' She decided, given Donnelly's own bluntness, to be direct. 'Let me ask you, Mr Donnelly. Do you think your daughter took her own life?'

Donnelly was clearly taken aback by the question. 'My gut feeling is no. I don't think she was that sort of person. But I also know that there isn't a "that sort of person", and that these things aren't predictable. She didn't strike me as depressed, even given her mood over Christmas – more like angry. Angry with us, angry with the school for the whole newsletter thing. Angry with the world, but I thought that was mainly just being a teenager.' He shrugged. 'So I don't know. I don't think it's likely. But it's possible.'

'What do you think, Mrs Donnelly?' Annie asked.

'The same, I suppose. If she was feeling anything like that, I hope she'd have talked to me about it. Maybe I'm fooling myself. But I've found nothing that would indicate – well, anything like that.'

Annie nodded. Melanie's room at the school – as a sixth-former, she had a room to herself – had been checked with similar results. The police had examined her laptop and phone with her parents' agreement, and had found nothing to indicate that Melanie had had any intention of taking her own life. But as Annie knew, that might prove very little. 'What about murder, then? Can you think of anyone who might have wanted to harm your daughter?'

Donnelly was silent for a moment. 'No. I can't. I've been trying to think of anything like that, anyone who might have had a reason to wish her ill, but it makes no sense.'

'You don't think she was being bullied at school?'

'Again, you can never be entirely sure of these things, can you?' Barbara Donnelly said. 'But I'd never seen any sign of any problems. She was a strong character, not easily cowed. She was never the most sociable type, but she had her own small circle of close friends.'

'I've met a couple of them,' Annie said. 'They were clearly very fond of Melanie and spoke very positively about her, if that's any consolation to you.' She turned to Tony Donnelly. 'And again you're right, Mr Donnelly, those are essentially the possible causes of your daughter's tragic death. The problem we have, as you can see, is that none of them seems very likely.'

Chapter Ten

For the moment, the rain was holding off, but the heavy clouds suggested the weather would soon be closing in. The wind was rising too, bitterly cold from the moorlands to the east.

Zoe Everett ducked her head against the cold, her eyes already watering. She wasn't even sure what she was expecting to achieve with this visit, other than an opportunity to get away from the office and kickstart her brain. She was sleeping badly, and she'd spent the morning feeling as if her head had been stuffed with cotton wool, struggling to concentrate on even the most mundane tasks. By mid-afternoon, after yet another mug of coffee had failed to have the desired effect, she'd decided that what she needed was a breath of air and a different perspective on the work.

She felt mildly resentful that she'd returned from leave to find she'd been landed with this cold case, though she knew Annie's intentions had been positive. For some months now, Annie had been trying to identify assignments to help Zoe develop her skills and experience, ideally cases where Zoe could act with a high degree of autonomy. Annie had no doubt expected the Meresham inquiry to provide another such opportunity. Not the most high-profile job, but one that would require solid organisational and management skills.

'Stuart wants me to focus on Melanie Donnelly,' she'd said. 'So I thought you might want to take over the Meresham case for the moment. I know I can trust you just to get on with things. We can review it again in a day or two when we see what progress we're making on the Donnelly investigation.'

The truth was that the wheels on the Meresham case were grinding slowly. Over the preceding days they'd interviewed the occupants of the houses nearest to where the body had been found, but with no conspicuous success. Most of the householders in the village were incomers, and few had been there longer than a decade. That was the nature of many Peak District villages. House prices had risen, and many long-term inhabitants, or their descendants, had sold up, making a few quid in the process. The houses had been bought either by relatively well-off commuters to Sheffield, Derby or Nottingham, or by even more prosperous types looking for a weekend bolthole or a holiday cottage investment.

In parallel with that, the team had been trying to track down any living relatives of Jayne Arnold, the girl who'd gone missing back in 1976. The case was notionally still open, an unresolved cold case from decades before. The files would repay a thorough examination, but Zoe's initial skim through the papers had added little to what she already knew. Jayne had been an only child. Her parents had lived on what had then been a new housing estate on the edge of the village. Jayne had had only a short walk, perhaps ten or fifteen minutes, from the school bus stop to her home. Somehow, in the course of that short walk, she'd disappeared.

It had been a baking hot day – one of many in that famously long hot summer. Despite that – or perhaps because of it – the village streets had apparently been deserted, and no one had witnessed Jayne's movements that afternoon. The school bus had a reputation for unreliability, and Jayne's mother hadn't initially been worried at her daughter's non-appearance. She'd eventually contacted the bus company to be told the bus had run to its normal schedule, but it had only been when Jayne's father had returned from work that they'd finally contacted the police.

In practice, those few hours' delay had probably made little difference. With no witnesses to Jayne's movements, the police had had little to work with. Despite Annie's comments to Jennings, the father had never seriously been in the frame. At the likely time of the disappearance, he'd been at work in Derby, fifteen or more miles away, and there'd been plenty of workmates to vouch for his presence there long after his daughter had stepped off the school bus. In the absence of other contenders, the mother had briefly been considered as a possible suspect – although Annie had the impression that the police at the time had found it difficult to conceive of a woman as a potential killer – but there was no evidence to support the idea.

There were no other close relatives, except for an uncle on the mother's side living in Leicester who'd had no contact with his sister, other than a ritual exchange of Christmas and birthday cards, for several years. The police had conducted interviews throughout the village, but had found no witnesses or credible suspects. Zoe might have found that suspicious in itself, but there was no suggestion that the police at the time had concerns. It was a small village, and people were either still at work or indoors sheltering from the heat. To add to the police's frustration, it had been early closing day, so even the village's one small general store, which might have attracted a few potential witnesses, had been closed.

The case had gained some national notoriety at the time, dominating the front pages of the newspapers for several days, the ghostly image of young Jayne in her school uniform gazing out at readers as if seeking their help. But days and then weeks had passed with no news and no progress, and it had eventually vanished from the nation's collective mind, just one more unsolved mystery.

The first challenge now was to determine whether the human remains really were those of Jayne Arnold. It seemed likely – the pathologist's initial view was that the skeleton was that of a female of approximately Jayne's age at the time of her disappearance – but they couldn't proceed without confirmation. Ideally, they needed to track down either Jayne's dental records, which would be a challenge after forty years, or an appropriate relative for DNA comparisons. Their best hope was that one or both of Jayne's parents was still alive and could be traced.

They had already confirmed from Land Registry records that the Arnolds had sold their house in Meresham a few years after Jayne's disappearance, but had not succeeded in tracking their movements any further. The one-man solicitor in Ashbourne who had handled the sale and presumably any subsequent house purchase was long gone, and so far they hadn't tracked down any records he might have held. They'd found no other record of the parents that post-dated their move from Meresham. For the moment the trail remained cold.

Even so, Zoe was relatively confident that, if the parents were still alive, they'd eventually be tracked down. They might well make themselves known now that the finding of the human remains had been released to the media.

The question was how long that would take. In the meantime, they would receive the pathologist's report on the body, familiarise themselves with the original case, and continue trying to identify anyone who might be able to shed light on how the body had been placed in the foundations. The key task was to track down Alan Harwood, the owner of the house at the time the foundations were laid, again assuming he hadn't died in the intervening years. They had no information on Harwood, other than that he'd owned the house for a couple of years in the mid-1970s.

If they were to make progress on the case – and it was a big if, given the circumstances – it would almost certainly be the result of steady and painstaking work, possibly over a period of weeks or months. There had been a flurry of media interest in the story following the discovery of the bones, but Zoe guessed that would die away if there were no immediate developments. In the meantime, Zoe had no option but to press on with the investigation.

Fair enough, Zoe thought. She was all too conscious that, at least in recent weeks, she hadn't done much to justify Annie's continued faith in her. She'd struggled to concentrate. She'd made mistakes. She'd missed appointments and been late for deadlines. Not in any major way, and some of her colleagues were less reliable even at their best. But Zoe had fallen below the standards she expected of herself, and she knew she'd fallen below the standards Annie normally expected of her too.

Part of Zoe's motivation in coming here was to try to bring the case back to life, at least in her own head. Because she'd been on leave when the remains had first been discovered, she hadn't participated in the initial examination of the site. Since her return, she'd been working on the basis of the extensive photographs and evidence gathered by the CSI team. In practical terms, that didn't matter too much. If there was anything to be gleaned from the site, that would emerge from the detailed examination and forensic work. Her focus had been on investigating why and how the body had come to be here in the first place, which for the moment was inevitably a largely paper exercise.

Even so, she wanted to get a feel for the location. See where the bones had been found, and gain a sense of what it would have taken to conceal them. Explore the layout of the village where Jayne Arnold went missing. Walk the route that Jayne would normally have followed between alighting from the school bus and arriving home. None of this would directly progress the investigation, but it would make it all much more immediate in Zoe's mind.

She left her car on the roadside, opposite the cottage where the remains had been found. Her intention was to walk from there into the village, following the route that Jayne would have taken. She'd then make her way back there and examine the excavated area at the rear of the cottage. She took another look at the sky, wondering how long she had before the heavens opened.

She tramped her way slowly up the hill towards the centre of the village. In physical terms, little would have altered here in the years since Jayne Arnold had disappeared. People would have died, moved on, moved in. But the grey stone cottages that comprised the heart of the village wouldn't have changed substantially in the intervening years. A lick of paint, replacement windows or doors, a redesigned garden – those were likely to be the only external differences to these buildings. The interiors would have been redecorated, perhaps even rebuilt, but none of that was visible to Zoe as she made her way to the top of the hill.

The school bus, and the few other buses that now passed this way, still stopped at what Zoe assumed was the same spot where Jayne Arnold had alighted. There was a bus shelter there now which looked relatively new. Zoe imagined the teenage girl emerging from the bus, looking both ways before crossing the road into the village.

Jayne's route would have taken her down the street to Zoe's left, almost opposite the bus stop. Zoe turned into the street and paused again, taking in the view that would have greeted Jayne. A narrow street lined with stone cottages. The street was dark and gloomy on this overcast spring day, but even during the summer of 1976 it would have lain in shadow for much of the day.

As Zoe walked down the street, there was almost no sense of the expanse of countryside beyond. The buildings closed in on themselves, resentful of outsiders, keeping whatever secrets they might hold.

Other than a few lights showing in the houses, there was no sign of human life. In Jayne Arnold's day there'd been a village shop, but that was long gone and Zoe could no longer identify where it might have been.

As she reached the junction where Jayne would have turned right, the sense of open space returned. Jayne's usual route led steeply downhill, the moors ahead. There were a few houses at the summit of the hill, then the short road ended in open moorland. To the left, there was a hedgerow with a field beyond.

Zoe hesitated for a moment, then descended the hill-side and walked along the hedge until she found the stile giving access to the field. She climbed over it and made her way along the edge of the field until she reached a further stile on the far side, at the rear of the small housing estate.

The estate itself looked well-maintained but a little old-fashioned. These would have once been desirable residences, as the estate agents might put it. They were all bungalows, each individually designed and set into its own neat plot of land. It had a similar feel to the modern estate where Zoe herself lived on the outskirts of Derby, but there the houses and the gardens were all essentially identical.

She wondered how much of this route Jayne had traced on that final day. What seemed certain was that she'd never entered the front door of her parents' house, just a hundred or so metres away from where Zoe was now standing. This was another house that looked unchanged from the pictures that Zoe had seen in the case file. Today, no lights were showing and there was no car outside, the occupants presumably at work or otherwise absent.

Zoe climbed down from the stile, glancing back over her shoulder as she did so. There was a figure standing on the far side of the first stile across the field. From this distance, in the gloom of the overcast day, it was difficult to make out the figure clearly, but Zoe had the impression it was someone staring across the field in her direction. As Zoe looked back, the figure stepped away, disappearing behind the shelter of the hedge.

Zoe continued through the estate until she reached the main road. Most of the houses looked unoccupied at this time of the day, and she guessed most of the householders here now commuted for work into the surrounding towns and cities. If a latter-day Jayne were to vanish today, her disappearance would be as unnoticed as Jayne's had been forty-six years earlier.

Zoe turned left to walk back uphill into the village, completing her circular route. As far as she could see, there had been no further building in the village since the completion of the estate some fifty years before. It felt as if, with Jayne's disappearance, the whole place had become frozen in time, awaiting the moment when her bones would finally be disinterred as in some dark fairy tale.

She made her way back down towards her car and the cottage. The CSIs had completed their work, and Zoe understood the builders weren't planning to return till the following week, so she'd be able examine the site at her leisure.

There were still remnants of police tape on the front gate and fencing. Zoe opened the gate and made her way around the side of the house into the rear garden. The garden was an attractive space, sheltered by trees but with a westerly aspect that would be a suntrap on summer afternoons. Today its air was one of gloom, a combination of the heavy sky, the dark overhang of the trees, and the blackness of the yawning gap excavated immediately beside the house. Zoe felt the first drop of rain hit her face.

She made her way to the far end of the pit and peered into its depths. The earth had been dug away for another half metre below the level where the bones had been found, but nothing further had been discovered. She stared into the pit for another few seconds, identifying the spot where the remains had been found, then she looked up.

The figure was standing in the shadow of the trees on the far side of the garden. Zoe thought at first that it was her imagination, some trick of the fading light. It stood motionless, well back in the gloom of the trees, a hundred or so metres from her. It was wearing a hat of some kind and a dark overcoat, hands thrust deep into the pockets.

She felt a chill finger run down her spine. She felt sure, without quite knowing why, that this was the same figure she had glimpsed earlier.

'Hello,' she called. 'Can I help you?'

The figure made no response, but continued to stare at her, unmoving. There was something unnerving about its stillness, particularly given the increasing force of the rain. Zoe took another few steps forward. 'Is there something I can do for you?'

The figure still hadn't moved. Zoe began to walk along the edge of the excavated area, conscious of the slipperiness of the grass beneath her feet. At that moment, the figure finally moved, taking several steps towards her. Involuntarily, she recoiled, although there was nothing obviously threatening about the figure's movements. Suddenly, Zoe's own weight was dragging her backwards. She could feel the ground at the edge of the excavation crumbling beneath her. Then she was falling backwards, the breath knocked from her body. More earth showered down on her, the icy rain pounding on her skin, and she realised she was screaming.

Chapter Eleven

'I'm sorry. It just didn't occur to me that it was important.' Alice Cartwright shifted awkward in her seat.

It occurred to Annie that she'd interviewed murder suspects who looked more relaxed, but she suspected this was simply Cartwright's natural demeanour. It was one reason why Annie had decided to raise this first with her rather than with the head. 'The problem is that we don't yet know what might be important, which is why we need as full a picture as possible.'

'Yes, I appreciate that. I just wasn't thinking very clearly.'

In truth, Annie imagined that Melanie's research into the school's benefactors was unlikely to be pertinent to their investigation. She just felt mildly irked and intrigued that neither Cartwright or the headmistress had thought to mention the controversy during their previous discussions. It left Annie wondering what other details the two women might have withheld. 'You told me nothing inappropriate appeared in Melanie's newsletter.'

'Nothing did,' Cartwright insisted. 'This was really just a fuss about nothing.'

'Tell me what happened.'

'It started with Melanie researching aspects of the school's history. She was actually doing that as part of her A-Level history project initially, looking at historical attitudes to slavery and abolition. She'd thought the school's origins and funding might provide an interesting case study. We were only too happy to encourage her in that.'

'Even if it uncovered some uncomfortable truths about the school's past?'

Cartwright stiffened. 'We've never been secretive about the school's history. There's nothing we can do about it, after all. In fact, when Melanie first raised the topic, Lavinia was quite enthusiastic. She felt it would give the school a way of addressing a potentially contentious issue without being seen to take sides, and encouraging the girls to consider and debate the issues.'

'So what went wrong?'

'I'm afraid Melanie pushed it just a little too far. She was keen to write something about how attitudes are influenced by historical context, and she'd identified some interesting changes in the language and content of the school's prospectuses over the years. One of her questions was whether anything has really changed.'

'I'm not sure I follow.'

'I suppose her point was that we're prepared to condemn the slave trade because it's safely in the past, but that we may well be turning a blind eye to equivalent injustices in our own time.'

Annie had seen enough in her police career to convince her that Melanie had been correct. She wondered, for example, how often Tony Donnelly had been prepared to ignore exploitative or unsafe working practices in the delivery of his international construction contracts. 'I'm not sure that's even a particularly controversial opinion.'

'I fear you may be right,' Cartwright said. 'But Melanie wanted to illustrate it by highlighting examples from the school's own current and recent benefactors. As you can imagine, that had the potential to cause the school very considerable embarrassment.'

Annie nodded. 'I can see that. Did Melanie have any particular benefactors in mind?'

She could see Cartwright hesitate before responding. 'I don't know if she'd really got as far as looking at individual cases—'

'We've no wish to cause you or the school any unnecessary embarrassment,' Annie said. 'But, as I said, it's important that we have a full picture of Melanie's life in the weeks before her death. Especially if she was researching something potentially controversial.'

Cartwright was silent for a moment. 'You'd have to speak to Lavinia for the details. But as I understand it Melanie had been looking at a number of our recent and current benefactors. The one that cause Lavinia most concern was Mr Challis.'

'Challis?' Annie looked up from her note-taking, her head suddenly filled with memories. triggered by a name she hadn't heard for a long time.

'Ryan Challis,' Cartwight said. 'He's been very generous to the school in recent years, and he's a very active supporter of our work. You've probably come across him. He's very well known in the area.'

Annie's own recollections of Challis were more personal than she could acknowledge to Cartwright, but that was an issue for another time. 'I know the name. He runs a building company, doesn't he?'

'I believe so. He seems to have a number of business interests.'

Annie wasn't about to offer Cartwright any opinion of Challis. Apart from her own personal associations, she'd come across his name a few times, usually on the periphery of some investigation or other. He had a police record from years before, though mostly minor stuff and as far as she knew he'd kept his nose clean in recent years. Or, more accurately, she thought, he'd managed not to do anything that had attracted the attention of the police.

There were a number of characters like Challis around the county, just as there no doubt were in every other part of the UK. Moderately successful business types who, for the most part, operated on the right side of legitimacy, but had reputations that were far from squeaky clean. Challis had had a few run-ins with the local authority on planning permission issues, and she could recall some dealings with trading standards. From what she recalled, he'd gone bust once or twice, usually as a way of wriggling out of his obligations to creditors, but he'd always come bouncing back, because that kind always did.

The surprise was that he should have any connections with an upmarket boarding school. She couldn't recall much about Challis's domestic circumstances, but she wouldn't have been surprised to discover he'd sent his children to that kind of independent school. It was what people like Challis did in a bid to acquire social respectability. Although Donnelly was clearly in a different league from Challis, she imagined that would have been at least part of his motivation in sending Melanie to the school. An attempt to step away from his own working-class background into a new social world.

'What was Melanie's concern about him?'

Cartwright still looked uncomfortable. 'I think you'd have to ask Lavinia about that. To be honest, I did wonder whether Melanie's interest wasn't more personal. Challis's youngest daughter, Samantha, is our current head girl. I wondered if Melanie assumed Challis had effectively bought the appointment for her.'

Melanie might have been right, Annie thought, although Challis was hardly the first parent to have tried to buy influence in that way. The school would claim that any such donations, however welcome, would have no impact on the school's educational and pastoral independence. Perhaps that was true too, though Annie suspected that it was an unusual head teacher or board of governors that would be able to disregard such considerations entirely.

'So was Melanie planning to write something about these donations in the newsletter?'

'I believe she was toying with the idea, although I honestly don't know what she'd really have been able to say. But when she raised the subject with Lavinia, she was simply told not to proceed. As I say, it was really all a fuss about nothing.'

'How did Melanie feel about being told not to continue?'

'She was a little disgruntled at first. But she was a sensible girl, and I'm sure she understood the reasons.'

Annie wondered about that, and about Melanie's state of mind in those final weeks. If nothing else, a picture was emerging of Melanie Donnelly as a more complex and perhaps more provocative figure than her teachers had initially suggested. Annie recalled that at their first meeting Cartwright had warned her that everyone in the school would have an agenda, though she'd insisted that didn't apply to her own testimony. It was now clear that, whether by accident or design, Cartwright herself had failed to share potentially significant information about Melanie's final weeks.

She wondered again whether there was anything else they weren't being told.

Chapter Twelve

Annie was turning out of the school gates on to the road when her mobile rang. She glanced across at the display to check the name of the caller and sighed audibly. The last thing she needed right now was a conversation with her mother.

Annie had endured a long but largely unproductive afternoon at the school following her meeting with Alice Cartwright, including a further session with Lavinia Ellsworth. The CSIs had completed their examinations of the relevant classrooms over the weekend. The most significant finding had been that none of the window limiters appeared to be faulty. 'There are only half a dozen or so rooms she could conceivably have fallen from,' Danny Eccles had told her. 'The windows were sound in all of them. They opened no more than three or four inches. Melanie Donnelly was a slim girl, but even she couldn't have fitted through that space.'

It wasn't really what Annie had wanted to hear. If Melanie hadn't fallen from one of those windows, the only other option was that she'd fallen from the roof. If so, that reduced the likelihood that her death had been straightforwardly accidental. If nothing else, it raised the question of why she'd been up on the roof in the first place. Neither Alice Cartwright nor the head had been able to offer any suggestions. 'It's strictly out of the bounds to the girls,' Ellsworth had said, 'and it's normally kept securely locked. Melanie knew her own mind, but she wasn't the sort to break the rules without good reason. There are plenty of girls here who might try to go up there just to say they'd done it, but not Melanie.'

With these thoughts still churning in her head, Annie contemplated letting the call ring out to voicemail, but she knew that would only be delaying the inevitable. She reached out and took the call.

'Mum?'

'I hope you're using the hands-free. People expect police officers to set an example.'

'Yes, I'm using the hands-free.'

'Out and about yet again.' Margaret sniffed disapprovingly, as if she'd caught her daughter on some unauthorised jolly.

Annie bit back her instinctive response, which was to point out that, for all her former seniority, Margaret had never gained any significant experience of detective work. 'I'm working on an investigation.'

'Of course you are, dear.' Margaret's tone was that of an indulgent parent congratulating their child on a successful dolls' tea party. 'Another one of your murders, is it?'

'An unexplained death, anyway.' Melanie Donnelly's death had been reported on the local news, so Annie had little doubt her mother would be aware of it. 'I'm just leaving your old school, as it happens.'

There was a welcome silence for several seconds. 'Oh, yes, that poor girl. A dreadful accident, I assume. I'm not sure why you're wasting your time on that.'

'Because I don't have any choice. At least until we've clarified the circumstances of the death.'

'It's not likely to be anything else, though, is it? Schoolgirls don't get murdered. Not in a boarding school, anyway.'

'What can I do for you, Mum?'

'It's nearly a week since you called.'

'I'm sorry. It's been a bit of a frantic week, what with this and the body found up in Meresham—'

'You're not going to get anywhere with that, though, are you?' Margaret said bluntly. 'Not after forty-odd years.'

'Who knows?' Annie was trying, as ever, not to allow Margaret to provoke her. 'It's surprising what forensics can do now.'

'I know you have it relatively easy these days. I sometimes wonder what we'd have achieved in my day if we'd had a similar level of technology available to us.'

Annie could think of several possible responses to that, but decided that Margaret wouldn't react well to any of them. 'Did you call for anything in particular, Mum?'

'I thought you might want to congratulate me.'

Annie could already feel her heart sinking. Anything that Margaret felt worthy of congratulations was likely to be a source of either trouble or embarrassment to her daughter. 'Congratulate you?'

'I might be getting another shot at a proper TV career.'

Annie suppressed a sigh. They had been through all this a year or so before, when Margaret had been in initial discussions about some sort of television show. That had come to nothing, not least because one of the 'personalities' involved had ended up serving a life sentence for murder. Annie had hoped the experience might serve as a warning to Margaret, but that wasn't the way Margaret's mind worked. 'Well, that's good,' she offered after a lengthy pause.

'Don't bother to sound too enthusiastic. I thought you'd be pleased for me.'

'I am. But you know how it ended last time.'

'That was hardly anything that could have been predicted.'

'So what's the programme?'

'It's just a pilot at this stage. But there's a strong possibility it might be networked nationally if it goes well. A different kind of political discussion show.'

'Is that right?'

'The idea is to reach the kind of people that conventional politicians have lost touch with, the people outside the Westminster bubble.'

Annie assumed that this was a not-very-veiled jibe at Sheena. 'The people Sheena deals with every week in her surgeries, you mean?'

'Real people,' Margaret said. 'That's what I mean. The people that politics forgot.'

'Is this the strapline for the show?'

'It's one of the ideas we're toying with. The plan is to involve me and that journalist, Gareth Thomas. Two very different perspectives on the issues.'

'The two of you certainly offer that,' Annie conceded. 'I've met Gareth a couple of times through Sheena. He seems decent enough, though he's very effective at winding people up. The two of you will probably get on famously.'

'I'm sure he means well,' Margaret sniffed. 'Even if he's a bit wet behind the ears.'

'I wouldn't underestimate him. From what I've seen, he's a sharp operator.'

'Are you suggesting I'm not?'

Annie wasn't sure how to answer that. Margaret was bright enough, and her forty years in the force had provided her with the political nous needed in the senior ranks. But there were moments – and this had been particularly true in Margaret's post-retirement career – when she could be unexpectedly naive. 'I'm just saying that this is a new environment for you. Don't take anything for granted.'

'I should have known you'd find it impossible just to congratulate me.'

'Of course I congratulate you. I'm sure you'll do brilliantly.'

'As long as I've your endorsement, that's obviously all that matters,' Margaret said, tartly.

That was her mother's great skill, Annie thought. Whatever you said, she'd put you in the wrong. There was never any point in arguing with her. 'When does all this happen?'

'The producer's very keen to get started. So we're planning to kick off some initial filming this week.'

'I hope it goes well then.'

'Whatever you might think, I am more than capable of stringing a sentence together, you know.'

Annie had criticised Margaret for many things over the years, but lack of articulacy had never been one of them. 'Look, I need to go. I've a couple more calls to make.' It wasn't entirely a lie. She'd promised Stuart Jennings an update after she left the school, and she wanted to touch base with Zoe on the Meresham case.

'I can appreciate you've got more important things to do that waste time talking to me. That's fine.'

'I'm at work, Mum.'

'And no doubt very busy. I'll leave you to it.'

Margaret had already ended the call. Annie had tried to build a more constructive relationship with her mother but it had never worked. She wasn't even sure why. Granted, Margaret clearly took some perverse pleasure in provoking her daughter, and Annie found it difficult to resist the provocation. But they were both adults. They ought to be capable of getting past that. By now the mutual antagonism just seemed too deeply ingrained.

Or perhaps, Annie added to herself, they were just too similar.

Now that really would be a scary thought.

Chapter Thirteen

The screaming seemed to be coming from all around her, the noise shrill and piercing, the sound of a woman in absolute terror. Zoe wanted to block her ears, shut out the sound, pretend everything was all right and there was nothing to fear.

It took her another moment to realise she was the one screaming, and another few moments to force herself to stop. She lay gulping for air.

It had felt as if she was somehow outside her own body, observing what was happening but able to do nothing to prevent it. It had been the strangest feeling, a mix of detachment and absolute terror. Now, it was as if she was coming back together, the sense of dread receding like an outgoing tide.

She opened her eyes. She was lying on her back at the bottom of the pit. She had half-fallen, half-slid down here, bringing a heap of earth down with her, and she was partly covered by the sodden soil. Her legs were angled above her, and all she could see was the dull metallic grey of the sky. The rain was falling heavily, and her face and hair were soaked.

She finally regained sufficient energy and breath to begin to extricate herself. She pulled her body free of the fallen earth, scrambling round until she was on her knees, looking up towards the edge of the pit above.

It was beginning to occur to Zoe that escaping this predicament might be more difficult than she'd originally assumed. The edge of the pit was three or four metres above her, the slope steep and slippery. She might scramble her way up there, but it wasn't going to be easy.

She felt in the pocket of her coat for her mobile phone and realised it was missing. It must have slipped out during her fall. She peered around the spot where she'd fallen, but could see no sign of it. She'd been assuming that, if all else failed, she could at least call for help. She'd feel an idiot, and the story would be shared force-wide within hours, but she could live with that if it meant she could get warm and dry.

As far as she could see, she had only one other option. She looked down at herself, scowling at her mud-smeared coat and trousers. She'd already ruined her work suit, so there was no point in worrying too much more about that.

She tried walking upright up the slope, but the muddy ground slipped from beneath her feet and she found herself falling forward onto her hands and knees. Her second attempt, crawling up the slope, was more successful. She dragged herself to within a half-metre of the top of the slope before the earth gave way beneath her weight and she again slid downwards.

Cursing, she hauled herself to her feet and looked around, trying to work out where the sides might afford her the best chance of reaching the edge. The far side of the pit looked less steep and was dotted with protruding roots. That would probably provide her with the easiest route.

She stumbled over and, foregoing any concerns about her own dignity, dropped to her knees and dragged herself painstakingly up the slope. She had one setback, when she felt the ground slipping away beneath her as before, but she grabbed one of the protruding roots and hung on. The root took her weight, and she managed to scramble another foothold in the earth below.

She pushed herself up again, grabbing hold of another root, and pulled herself, centimetre by centimetre, towards the edge of the pit. She was relieved now that she'd decided to swap her office shoes for a pair of sturdy walking books before embarking on her trek round the village. At that point, her primary concern had been the risk of ruining her shoes in the impending rain. Now, as she dug the toes of the boots into the sodden earth, the decision might have literally helped save her life.

Finally, her fingertips reached the edge of the pit, and with another shove of her feet in the earth, she forced herself further up until her arms were resting on the ground above. It took her another few moments, her feet thrusting against the side of the pit, her cold hands grasping at the grass above, before she was finally able to drag herself free. She rolled away from the edge, fearful of another landslip, and then lay, gasping for breath, on the rain-soaked lawn.

It was several minutes before she was able to pull herself to her feet and look around. The garden was deserted, and there was no sign of the figure she'd seen earlier. Zoe was cursing her own stupidity. She could scarcely even comprehend the emotions that had gripped her only a short while before. It struck her now that the terror had grown stronger after she'd fallen. It had been in that moment, when the earth had been falling around her and she'd momentarily thought she might be buried alive, that she'd begun screaming.

There was something there. Something tantalisingly close to emerging into her conscious thought. Even as she tried to grasp it, it slipped from her, dissolving like the rain between her fingers.

What was wrong with her? She was becoming increasingly sure something was. Annie, and no doubt Stuart Jennings, would assume it was something to do with her work, that she was still traumatised by the dramatic events she'd experienced over the past year, two cases which had placed her life directly at risk.

But it felt as if those traumas had triggered something else, something deeper within Zoe herself. She felt sure this was about more than just what had happened to her in the past year, even though she had no idea what that something else might be.

Zoe took another look around the garden. At least now, this felt real. She could imagine that moment, forty-six years before, when someone had brought that body into this garden and had buried it in the pit that now yawned in front of Zoe. Probably in the small hours of a stiflingly hot summer's night. How much effort must it have taken to dig even a shallow grave in the hardened earth? Who would have been capable of something like that?

She emerged from the garden on to the road where her car was parked. As she crossed the road, she took one more look at the house, then unlocked the car and slid herself back behind the wheel, relieved she'd finally escaped the incessant freezing rain. Minutes later, she was heading back towards the shelter of home.

Chapter Fourteen

'So what do you think?' Jennings said. 'What are we going to say to the coroner's office?'

Annie sighed. She'd already started to talk to Jennings about this during her drive back from the school, but the signal quality had been poor and, after the call had been interrupted for the third time, they'd agreed to continue when she was back at HQ. That had given her more time to consider the answer to Jennings's question, but she still hadn't reached any firm conclusion. 'I'm not sure what to think. There's enough to justify a forensic post-mortem. But I'm not sure what that's really going to tell us.'

'Is there enough to justify further investigation?'

'If you're asking for an honest answer, I'd say yes. There's enough doubt in my mind. I feel as if we'd risk betraying Melanie Donnelly if we didn't.' She offered Jennings a smile. 'Well, you asked.'

'I did, didn't I?' Jennings rubbed his eyes. 'It's not like we don't have enough on already. Okay, talk me through it again. Tell me your doubts. Why do you think that Donnelly's death might not have been an accident?'

'Let's start with the practicalities. The CSIs have examined all the classrooms from which Melanie might have conceivably fallen. The relevant windows all have limiters to prevent the window opening more than a few centimetres. It wouldn't be possible even for the smallest girl in the school to have squeezed through that gap, let alone anyone of Melanie's stature. They've been thoroughly checked and they're all perfectly sound.'

'It's not possible that one could have been removed and subsequently replaced?'

'In theory it might be, but that would imply foul play, so it just takes us full circle. But I'm told it wouldn't be a simple task. It might have been possible for one to be removed in advance, but it would have been tricky to replace it without being noticed. I think we can fairly safely conclude that Melanie didn't fall from any of those windows.'

'So where did she fall from? The roof?'

'There's nowhere else.'

'But that's not readily accessible to the pupils?'

'Strictly out of bounds, according to the rules. But some of the girls have told us that it's not unknown for pupils to get up there. It's the kind of thing they do for dares. Walk around the roof without being caught.'

'I assume the roof's well secured? So how do the girls get up there?'

'There's only a single point of access which is kept locked, and the keys are supposedly held only by a limited number of designated individuals. But the doors weren't alarmed, so if an unauthorised person did get hold of a key, they could get up there without anyone being aware. That's something the school's looking at.'

'I bet they are. But how would an unauthorised person get hold of a key if they're strictly controlled?'

'Kids are surprisingly ingenious about that sort of stuff, aren't they? My guess is the key-holding wasn't as strictly controlled as it should have been. There are no keys obviously missing now, but I wouldn't be surprised if they'd gone missing in the past. We've asked the question, and nobody seems entirely sure.'

'Okay, so we think she came off the roof. Do we have any other evidence to support that?'

'Not really. CSIs checked for prints on the entrance to the roof, but there were so many it's not likely to be possible to identify Melanie's from among them. There's no DNA evidence, and no obvious sign of anyone having been up there at the time of Melanie's death.'

'No CCTV?'

'No CCTV up there. We've checked the CCTV cameras around the school, but there's nothing of significance.'

'So no hard evidence that she was up there, but realistically it's the only option. Still doesn't mean it wasn't an accident.'

'It's not hard to imagine someone messing around on the parapet, losing their footing and – well, ending up as Melanie did.'

'So why don't you think that's likely?'

'Melanie's personality. By all accounts, she was a sensible girl, the last person who'd have been playing silly buggers on the rooftop.'

'People can surprise you. I bet you've taken the odd dare in your life, haven't you?'

'Does that include working with you?'

'I knew you must be here for a reason. Seriously, people aren't always consistent. Maybe she was talked into doing something daft.'

'Of course it's possible. But it doesn't square with the fact that she supposedly had a real fear of heights.'

'Maybe it squares perfectly, if that was why someone challenged her to go up there. Perhaps she felt obliged to accept the dare, so as not to lose face. Then she panicked when confronted with actually doing it.'

'From what her friends and her parents said, her fear was pretty severe. They didn't think she'd have been able to put herself in that position, even with someone egging her on. And from everything I've heard about her, she doesn't sound like someone who'd have succumbed easily to peer pressure in any case.'

'And the other options are suicide, murder or possibly manslaughter.'

'Personally, I'm inclined to discount the idea that she took her own life, though we can't ignore it. There's nothing in her recent past to suggest that she was depressed or unhappy, other than the usual teenage angst with her parents. We've checked with her GP and with the school, and there've never been any reported mental health issues. And we come back to the fear of heights. Even if she had wanted to take her own life, is that the method she'd have chosen?'

'So what about the other options? Murder or manslaughter?'

'There's no evidence she was being bullied at school, She wasn't the gregarious type, but she doesn't seem to have had any real enemies. It's possible she was the unfortunate victim of some ill-conceived joke. Someone trying to wind her up by forcing her on the roof. If someone did that for a laugh, and Melanie panicked...'

'What about all the newsletter stuff? Any possible motive there?'

'It's not exactly Watergate, is it? But it's one of the areas that does intrigue me. Not least because the school were cagey about it. Neither the head nor Alice Cartwright mentioned it when I first spoke to them. It was something that clearly meant a lot to Melanie, so I'm surprised. Then they both told me that they'd never had reason to censor anything. But it does look as if Ellsworth put a stop to Melanie's research into school donations.'

'The school's not going to publish anything that might risk offending its wealthy benefactors, is it?' Jennings said. 'I imagine the head would have seen that as common sense, not censorship.'

'No doubt. I'm just surprised they didn't mention it, given it happened only just before Christmas.'

'It's not much, though, is it? Hardly a motive for murder. Local builder exposed as wanting to buy a bit of influence for his daughter.'

'Exactly. It might be nothing more than Ellsworth being cautious. This whole incident's embarrassing enough as it is, so the last thing she wants is to air any other dirty linen in public, however trivial. None of this is really answering your question, is it?'

'Not so's you'd notice. What else have you got?'

'Not much. We've spoken to most of the staff, particularly those who'd had recent contact with Melanie, but that's not added much to what we got from Ellsworth and Cartwright and from Melanie's friends. Bright girl, studious, destined for great things, all that stuff. No particular signs that she was unhappy. No evidence of any conflict with any of the other girls. Everything consistent with the picture that had already been painted. We've interviewed all the sixth-form pupils, but again, nothing new there. The ones who knew her well confirmed what her friends had told us. The rest didn't have a strong opinion of her, other than maybe that she was a bit of a swot. Nobody had anything negative to say about her.'

'What about this head girl?'

Annie hesitated. She'd known they'd get round to this eventually, and she'd been wondering how much to say. None of it was likely to be relevant to this case, but she didn't know how much Jennings knew already. She didn't want to hold something back and find herself being caught out later. Avoiding Jennings's eye, she fumbled through her file in search of the relevant set of interview notes.

'We've spoken to her, as part of the overall sixth-form interviews. Samantha Challis. The officer who interviewed her didn't exactly warm to her. Found her supercilious and snooty, as if she was doing us a favour by sparing time for the interview.'

'She'll go far.'

'No doubt. She didn't have much to tell us. She knew who Melanie Donnelly was, but she made it very clear they weren't friends.'

'Did it go any further than that? Any sense Challis was antagonistic towards Donnelly?'

'I wouldn't have said so. More that she just had no real interest in her.'

Jennings nodded slowly, and Annie could see he was thinking. 'I've been wondering why the name Ryan Challis rings a bell.'

Annie had been waiting for this. Jennings would have read through the file notes in advance of the meeting. The only question, given his relatively recent transfer into the force, was how much he'd already known. 'Challis has been on our radar a few times.'

'That's what I thought. Does he have a record?'

'Only in the dim and distant, and all trivial stuff. Possession, low-level dealing, petty theft. Spent a few months inside, and that put him on the straight and narrow, or so he'd like you to think. Ryan Challis's straight and narrow is a lot twistier than most people's.'

'He's a builder?'

'Among other things. He has fingers in a lot of pies. One of those wheeler-dealer types who turn a dollar wherever they can. He's been bankrupt more than once, but he always lands on his feet. Various run-ins with the authorities over the years – planning permission, tax, trading standards. But he knows how far to push things. If he gets found out, he pleads wide-eyed innocence and pays up. Most of the time he doesn't get caught.'

'That sort usually get caught eventually.'

'He's come close once or twice.' Annie took a breath. 'Look, Stuart, I don't know if you know this already, but you'll spot it soon enough if you look up Challis's files.'

'Go on.'

'One of the things Challis is good at is networking. Surprisingly so, maybe, given the character he is. He devotes a lot of time to hobnobbing with the local great and good. Councillors, local authority officers, lawyers, accountants, anyone who might be in a position to support Challis's business. There've been rumours for years that Challis was paying backhanders to oil the wheels.'

Jennings was watching her with apparent curiosity. He liked to keep one step ahead, and she wouldn't have been remotely surprised if he'd already examined the records to satisfy his curiosity about Ryan Challis. She felt as if she was being tested.

'A few years back,' she went on, 'we had a whistle-blowing complaint from within the local authority. The informant claimed Challis had been paying bribes to council officers and officials to help secure planning permission for various developments he was involved in. We kicked off a full-scale investigation into the allegations – which, as far as I'm aware, was the first time we'd ever had a serious look at Challis's operations.'

'But he wasn't prosecuted?'

'I was just a newbie PC at the time. My understanding is two factors kiboshed the inquiry. The official reason was that that we couldn't find substantive evidence of wrongdoing. There was no question Challis had glad-handed some of the officials in question – decent lunches, a slap-up day at some sporting event, that kind of stuff. One or two were disciplined because they'd failed to make appropriate declarations. But we weren't able to prove anything more substantial, or at least anything the CPS thought would stick.'

'And the unofficial reason?'

Annie gazed back at Jennings but it was clear that, if he did know anything, he wasn't going to say. 'The rumours at the time were that they'd opened up a much bigger can of worms than they'd expected. That Challis's network was more extensive than anyone had realised. And that among those involved were several senior police officers. I don't know how much truth there was in it. But there were some very awkward questions being asked inside the force.'

'And a few high-profile early retirements, if I recall correctly.' Jennings's face was a picture of innocence, but Annie didn't have much doubt now that he knew.

'Including my mother.'

'The blessed Margaret. I wondered if she was part of this. I recall her retirement was – unexpected.'

'You might say that. Not that she's ever shared the details with me. You probably know as much as I do, if not more. I only really know what I gleaned from the gossip at the time – and people weren't inclined to share much of it with me – and the few hints she's dropped subsequently.'

'So do you think there was anything in the story? The backhanders, I mean.'

'I don't honestly know. I don't see her as someone who'd just accept a bribe for services rendered. But I can imagine her being seduced by a few upmarket dinners in the right company. She'd see it as part of her own networking and tell herself she wasn't doing anything wrong. All I know if that she suddenly decided to take early retirement.'

'You think she was leaned on?'

'I don't think she'd have gone voluntarily. She'd never talked about early retirement, and she still had ambitions for the top job. So I think someone had a quiet word with her. She left with her reputation, not to mention her pension, intact. The alternative would have been an inquiry and, whatever its outcome, that would have left a much bigger cloud over her career. As it was, there was a bit of gossip, but she went out with all the usual ceremony.'

'Must have been awkward for you.'

'It's always been awkward. If I'd realised how awkward, I might have chosen another career, or at least another force. Mum and I have never exactly been close, but everyone assumed I was getting some sort of special treatment. If only they'd known. I'm not sure Mum's ever done much for me except make my life more difficult. Which she continues to do. You know she's still talking about doing some political show on TV?'

'Lord save us,' Jennings said. 'Just what we need.'

'Exactly. But the blessed Margaret, as you call her, will always do what she wants.' She smiled. 'I'm not sure this is getting us very far with Melanie Donnelly, though.'

'Not really. As you say, there's probably enough there at least to justify a forensic post-mortem. It's worth having another chat with the head and the personal tutor about the newsletter stuff, and what sort of discussions went on about the donations story. Beyond that, is there much more we can do?'

'Not that I can see, unless the post-mortem findings give us something more to work with. All we really have is a few possible reasons for questioning whether it was an accident, but no strong reasons for believing it was anything else.'

'It may just be one of those where we end up presenting the coroner with the evidence, such as it is, and let them take it from there. What about the Meresham Bones? Where are we up to with that?'

'I've left Zoe with it for the moment. It's another one that doesn't look too promising. My biggest hope is that the media coverage might bring people out of the wood-work. It would save time if any of the relevant parties made themselves known to us.'

'Fingers crossed we get some response then. How is Zoe, anyway?'

'She seems okay. I'd like to persuade her to take some proper leave. But you know Zoe. If she feels she's being nagged, it just makes her more stubborn.'

He nodded vaguely. 'Whatever you think best.'

She could tell from his distracted manner that his mind had already moved on to other matters. That was the way with Jennings. He gave you the attention he'd allotted to your particular issue, then detached himself from the discussion in a way that indicated, more clearly than words, that the meeting was over. She'd found it disconcerting at first, but now found it almost endearing. At least it ensured meetings didn't drag on unproductively.

She began gathering up her papers. 'Okay, Stuart. I'll see what I can do.'

Chapter Fifteen

Lavinia Ellsworth couldn't recall the last time she'd had a decent night's sleep. She'd never assumed the job of head teacher would be an easy one. She'd witnessed enough in her previous deputy head role to appreciate the challenges of leadership in this environment. Even so, she hadn't fully appreciated the step-change involved in moving into the top job. It wasn't just that there was more work and more responsibility. It was the knowledge that every buck stopped with her.

That was onerous enough at the best of times, and this was far from the best of times. The death of Melanie Donnelly had been a shock. It had been a shock at a human level because, despite herself, she'd rather liked the girl. So her death had been a personal blow as well as a managerial nightmare. But it was the managerial nightmare that was dogging Ellsworth now. Whatever the cause of Melanie's death might turn out to be, it had happened on Ellsworth's watch. If there was a can to be carried, it was Ellsworth's duty to pick it up.

From that perspective, despite the police investigation, it almost didn't matter how Melanie had died. If it had been a tragic accident, questions would be asked about pupil safety in the school. If Melanie had taken her own life, questions would be asked about the school's handling of mental health issues. If – heaven forbid – Melanie had been murdered, then there could be questions about almost anything. Even now, as she'd realised when talking to the police inspector, Ellsworth was nervous about where those questions might lead.

Her key task over the coming weeks would be to protect and rebuild the school's reputation – with parents, prospective parents, staff and the pupils. Not to mention, most importantly, the school's board of governors. They had faith in her abilities, particularly the new chairman, but that wasn't the point. In the end, if there was enough pressure for the school to be seen to be doing something, she would become the scapegoat. It would be unfair and counterproductive, but it was what she was paid for.

Her worries were made worse by consideration of Melanie's parents. They were far from the most difficult of parents, from Ellsworth's perspective, and they would deal with Melanie's death rationally and fairly. But the Donnellys were even wealthier and more influential than most of the girls' parents. If they decided action needed to be taken, they wouldn't hesitate to stir up trouble.

Tonight, Ellsworth had gone to bed at ten thirty and fallen asleep relatively quickly. She'd been woken around three by the ringing of the landline. She'd picked up the bedside extension still half asleep, certain that the call would herald some further crisis in the school. Instead, there was only silence. Some transnational automated cold call, she assumed, heedless of the time of day.

With the certain knowledge that she wouldn't sleep again that night, she pulled on her dressing gown, came downstairs, made herself a milky coffee, and tried to find something productive to occupy her mind.

She wondered now if she'd have been better off not taking advantage of the school's on-site accommodation.

There were undoubted benefits in being close at hand in an establishment like this. On the few occasions when they'd had medical or similar emergencies in the night, she'd been glad she could deal with them personally and immediately. But she never really switched off from the job. Her first thought on coming downstairs was to get on with some of the endless administration that swamped her desk.

She'd just sat down at the desk, a coffee by her side, when she heard the ring of the doorbell. She looked at her watch. Three thirty a.m. No one would be disturbing her at this time of night without good cause. Perhaps the phone call had been an attempt to contact her after all. All she knew was that, whatever the reason for the visit, it was unlikely to be positive news.

She sighed, pulled her dressing gown more tightly around her, and hurried to the front door.

Chapter Sixteen

Zoe was standing in the kitchenette, a steaming mug of coffee in her hand, staring blankly into space.

'Something on your mind, Zo?' Annie had come in search of a restorative coffee herself before kicking off the morning briefing. She began delving in the cupboard for a mug.

Zoe blinked as if returning to consciousness. 'Miles away.'

'Sorry I didn't get chance to chat yesterday afternoon. Bit hectic.'

Zoe hesitated. 'I went up to Meresham, actually. Took a bit longer than I'd expected. I thought it was worth getting a bit of a feel for the area.'

Annie had a sense there was something Zoe wasn't saying. 'Probably a good idea. It's hard to get a clear grasp of the location from the files. I take it there's nothing new in terms of confirming the identity of the remains?'

'Not yet. We know the body's female and of approximately the right age to match Arnold. There are some broken ribs and other damage to the bones which the pathologist thinks predate death. There's no sign of any healing, so it looks like the body suffered some serious physical assault which directly or indirectly resulted in the death. There's no evidence of any previous fractures, and nothing on the record to suggest Arnold had suffered any broken bones prior to her disappearance, so that doesn't help us.'

'No progress with dental records?'

'We're checking with all the local dental practices, but I'm not hopeful after forty-six years. There's nothing in the records to tell us who Jayne Arnold's dentist was at the time.'

'So our best hope is still to find a living relative, I guess. Anything coming in from the media reports?'

'We're getting quite a few calls, which they're working through at the moment.'

'What was your impression of Meresham?'

'Gave me the creeps, to be honest. I know I wasn't seeing it at its best, but it struck me as a bleak place.'

'Just another stone-built Pennine village. But I know what you mean. It's as if they're designed to keep out the weather and strangers alike.'

'I followed the route Jayne Arnold would have taken. Hardly saw a soul all the way, except…' She stopped.

Annie had been busying herself with making her coffee as they were talking. Now she turned. 'What is it, Zo?'

'I told you I went to the cottage. While I was there at the back of the house, there was someone watching.'

'A man?'

'They were in the shadows at the far side of the garden, so I wasn't sure. I had the impression it was a woman. Just watching me.'

'Maybe you'd triggered the local neighbourhood watch. You know what those villages can be like. Or some rubber-necker,' Annie said. 'We've not published any information in the media about exactly where the body was found, other than that it was in Meresham. But

131

I'm guessing the locals know all the details by now. Came for a gawp and was surprised to see you there.'

'Seems likely. I was just a bit spooked by the whole place.'

Annie still had the uneasy sense that Zoe was keeping something back. 'Sure you're okay?'

'I'm sure.'

Annie considered probing Zoe further but saw Stuart Jennings waving through the glass partition between the kitchenette and the main office. 'Stuart's looking agitated. I'd better see what he wants.'

'I'll go and check what responses we've got to the media reports. I'm still living in hope of tracking down one or both of Jayne Arnold's parents.'

Jennings was pacing up and down in front of Annie's desk, with the air of an anxious parent awaiting the return of their child from a late night out. 'I've been looking for you.'

Annie held up her coffee. 'I was on the other side of the corridor getting myself a drink before the briefing. I'm assuming that's still allowed?'

'I think you'd better postpone the briefing,' Jennings said.

'What is it?'

'The headmistress—'

'Lavinia Ellsworth. What about her?'

'This morning.' Jennings stopped, as if searching for the right words. 'She was found dead.'

Chapter Seventeen

As Annie turned into the school gates, the heavy rain turned briefly to hail, the stones drumming heavily on the car windscreen and roof. Her view was momentarily obscured, and then the return sweep of the wipers cleared the screen once more. It felt almost like an omen.

She followed the road round the side of the school and then down a track between two of the sports pitches. Ahead of her, she could see the pulse of blue lights, the cluster of official vehicles in front of what looked like an oddly suburban Edwardian villa.

She pulled to a halt behind one of the marked cars and climbed out into the rain. Uniformed officers were scurrying ahead of her, sealing off the scene. As she drew closer, one of the officers stepped forward to intercept her path. She flashed him her ID and he nodded her past with a smile of greeting.

Tim Sturgeon, the duty crime scene manager, was standing in front of the house under a large golf umbrella. Sturgeon had a reputation for micromanagement which could be wearing for his colleagues, but which at least guaranteed a well-managed scene.

'Morning, Tim.'

'Annie.' He lifted up the umbrella as if to gain a better look at her. 'Perfect day for it.'

'Isn't it always? What's the story? I only got the gist before I set off.'

'Nasty one.' He lifted the umbrella to offer her some shelter and gestured towards the house behind him. 'Body found in the living room. CSIs are just setting up in there.' One of Sturgeon's skills was the ability to provide all the relevant information in a few terse sentences.

'Cause of death?'

'You'll have to ask the experts for a definitive view, but it looks like strangulation to me. Except...'

'Except what?'

'There's some nasty bruising to the face and head, as if – well, as if someone's given her a damn good kicking.'

Annie looked around at the apparently genteel location – the neat villa, the surrounding thickets of oak and ash, the rolling hills disappearing into the morning's rain. 'A kicking?'

'If we'd found her in the back streets of Derby on a Saturday night, I'd have been less surprised. But that's the way it looks. I've only seen the face, but I'd wager the rest of the body's in the same condition.'

'When was she found?'

'Just after nine thirty this morning. She's normally over at the school early, but it wasn't till after nine that anyone really started to wonder where she was. Her secretary had been ringing around to find out if anyone had seen her, but drew a blank. She contacted the head of maintenance who held a spare key to the house, and they came over here and found her. It was the secretary who called the emergency services.' He gave a bleak smile. 'She sounds the efficient type.'

'Any idea of the time of death?'

'Not yet. She'd had apparently been in the school yesterday evening, so presumably some time overnight.'

'You said she'd been strangled. Any murder weapon?'

'No sign of any ligature. From the bruising, I'd say the murder weapon was probably someone's bare hands.'

'Bare hands? Jesus.'

'You can see why I said it looked like a nasty one.'

'I'm beginning to. Thanks, Tim. I'll leave you to it. Where are the two who found the body?'

'I asked them to wait back at the school in one of the rooms you've been using for interviews. Seemed best to keep them out of the way. The deputy head was also over here. Woman called Diane Astor?'

Annie had met Astor on one of her previous visits. At the time, Annie had formed the impression that Astor had very much been in Ellsworth's shadow, with none of Ellsworth's presence or gravitas. 'How was she?'

'Flustered would be a generous description, I'd say.'

'I wouldn't want to be in her shoes this morning, to be fair. Hell of a thing to deal with.'

'I won't argue with you there.'

The school had allocated a number of rooms for the temporary use of the police team, and the secretary and head of maintenance were waiting for Annie in one of the smaller rooms normally used for teaching the senior pupils. The secretary, a severe-looking woman called Andrea Bennett, leapt to her feet, a look of anxiety on her face. The head of maintenance, a relatively elderly man, rose more slowly. He looked as if it might take a lot to faze him.

'Is there any news?' Bennett said.

'The scene's being sealed off and the Crime Scene Investigators are now on site. We may know more when they've finished their work.' She gestured for them both to sit. 'We've met before, Mrs Bennett. I don't think we've met, Mr…?'

'Garner. Frank Garner.' He half rose again and held out his hand for Annie to shake.

'Pleased to meet you, Mr Garner. I appreciate you've both had a terrible shock this morning. Do you feel able to answer a few questions?'

Bennett nodded. 'Of course. It's such an awful business.'

'You entered the house together?'

'Frank holds the key, so I needed him to gain entry. I was a bit worried about what we might find so I was looking for some moral support, to be honest.'

'Did you have a reason to be concerned about Ms Ellsworth?'

'Only that it wasn't like her to be so late into school, and it certainly wasn't like her not to answer her phone. I was afraid she might have had some sort of accident or been taken ill.'

'I wish I'd gone in on my own,' Garner said. 'But I felt uncomfortable doing that. I keep a key to the house in case of emergencies when Ms Ellsworth's away for any reason. Burst pipes, that sort of thing.'

'Talk me through what happened when you arrived at the house.'

'We rang the bell a few times,' Bennett said. 'I brought my mobile over with me, so we tried the phone again, just in case. I'd wondered whether she'd gone out to some appointment she'd forgotten to mention, though she was normally punctilious about keeping me informed. Even if something had arisen overnight, she'd have left me a message or sent a text. We could see her car parked at the back of the house, so it didn't look like she'd gone very far.' She coughed, as if realising she was talking too much.

Garner took up the thread. 'There didn't seem to be any alternative but to go in. I remember being surprised that the deadlock was already unlocked, so I only had to use the latchkey. Made me wondered whether Ms Ellsworth had popped out somewhere after all.'

'Do you know if she usually kept it deadlocked?' Annie asked.

It was Andrea Bennett who responded. 'I don't know for sure. But this place is rather remote, so I'd imagine she locked up securely overnight. We've had a couple of burglaries at the school over the years, but they seemed mainly to be after laptops and IT equipment.'

'You unlocked the door. Then what?'

'I called out Ms Ellsworth's name,' Garner said. 'Just so she'd know it was us. At that stage, I was envisaging she might have had some sort of fall or be lying in bed unwell. There was no response, so we went into the hall and then the living room...'

'That was when we saw her.' Bennett's expression suggested she was reliving that moment. 'I thought she must have collapsed or fainted...'

'I think I realised straightaway,' Garner said, 'though I've no idea why. Just something about the way she was lying. It didn't look natural. I told Andrea to back away while I checked her pulse. Then I saw the bruising on her face...'

'Who'd do something like that?' Bennett said.

'I couldn't find any trace of a pulse,' Garner went on, 'and I didn't have much doubt she was dead. I told Andrea I thought it was best we got out of the room, so we came out and called for an ambulance and the police.'

'Did anything else strike you? Did anything look out of place, for example?'

'I'd only been in there a few times before. Ms Ellsworth sometimes has—' Bennett corrected herself. 'She sometimes had what she called "at home" sessions for different groups of the staff, as well as for some of the senior girls. Just an informal tea. Her way of getting to know people, I suppose. She liked to have me there to help with the organisation.' She paused. 'There'd definitely been a struggle. A couple of the ornaments on the coffee table had been knocked to the floor. I didn't notice anything else out of place.'

'What time did Ms Ellsworth leave work yesterday evening?'

'Relatively late, I think. I'd finished at five as usual, but she still had some meetings set up with a few of the teachers.'

'In the evening?'

'A number of the teachers live on site so there's twenty-four-hour support for the girls. It's sometimes easier to arrange one-to-one meetings with them out of hours. These were half-yearly performance appraisals, which she conducted in her office.'

'What time would they have finished?'

'She started them after the girls had finished eating and headed back to their dormitories and rooms. I think she had three to get through, so I don't imagine it would have gone on beyond eight.'

'Then she'd have headed back to the house?'

'I assume so.'

'Can you give me the names of the staff members she saw last night?'

'Yes, of course. It's all in the diary. I'll check when we've finished here.'

'Thank you. I'm sorry if any of these questions sound intrusive, but I'm keen to get a sense of Ms Ellsworth's lifestyle—'

'I've no real idea about her private life.' Andrea Bennett gave an almost imperceptible sniff, as if such considerations were below her interest. 'As far as I'm aware, she didn't have any close family. As for friends, I really couldn't say.'

'What about among the school staff? Did she have any particular close friends there?'

'Not especially. She was probably closest to the senior team – the deputy head, the heads of year and so forth. But apart from the "at home" sessions, I'm not aware she ever invited them back to the house.'

Annie felt she'd learned as much as she was likely to from Bennett and Garner. If there was gossip to be discovered about Lavinia Ellsworth, it would emerge quickly enough once they began talking to the rest of the staff. Ellsworth's house had been discreetly located, but it was still on the school grounds. If there was anything significant to be discovered about her private life, the grapevine would no doubt reveal it.

She closed her notebook. 'Thank you to you both. I appreciate this must have been a tremendous shock, and I'm very grateful you were able to talk to me now. We'll need to take a formal statement in due course, but I always find it helpful to speak when events are still very fresh, difficult as that might be. We'll need to establish a full murder inquiry. I'm afraid that will inevitably be disruptive to the school's normal operations, though we'll do our best to minimise the impact. I assume the deputy head's now taken temporary charge?'

'I haven't had chance to speak to her properly yet, but that would normally be the case when the head's – unavailable, yes.'

'I'll need to speak to her as soon as she has a moment, though I appreciate she'll have a lot on her plate this morning.'

'I'll let her know. Is there anything else I can do for you in the meantime?'

Annie rubbed her temples, thinking ahead to the effort that would be involved in this inquiry. If nothing else, her earlier conversation with Stuart Jennings had been rendered largely superfluous. Whether or not there was any connection between the deaths of Lavinia Ellsworth and Melanie Donnelly, their proximity in location and time would mean that Donnelly would be a continuing focus until the police could be confident the two weren't linked.

Now they had a reason to scale up the inquiry, with all the associated resources. Annie thought about the hours of interviews ahead, the painstaking work needed to invest-igate Ellsworth's life and background, the endless adminis-tration and co-ordination. As always at the start of a major investigation, she felt a mix of excitement and mild dread. Once they got started, the excitement would dominate, interspersed with bouts of frustration and even boredom, but for the moment the dread, fuelled by a sense of fatigue, still held the upper hand. She thought back to the mug of coffee she'd abandoned to head over here.

'There is one small thing,' she said in response to Andrea Bennett's question, 'if it doesn't sound too self-indulgent in the circumstances. I don't suppose you could organise me a coffee?'

Chapter Eighteen

'Bingo!' DC Andy Metcalfe called from across the room.

Zoe Everett looked up from her computer. 'Bingo?'

'That's what you say, isn't it? When you get a result?'

'It is if you're playing bingo.' She smiled to show she was only teasing him. Metcalfe was the newest member of the team, and he displayed a mixture of enthusiasm and occasional naivety which she couldn't help finding endearing. He reminded her of herself when she was a newbie.

She imagined he was going through some of the same tensions and uncertainties she'd been through. In her case, the usual issues of inexperience had been compounded by the fact that she was a young woman in what had still been a largely male environment. For Andy, the complicating factor would be that he was black in what, at least among the officers, was still a predominantly white workforce. She imagined, or at least hoped, that he hadn't encountered much explicit racism, just as she hadn't faced too much overt sexism or misogyny, except from one or two of the real old-school types. It would be more what remained unspoken or said behind his back. Zoe had overheard more than one colleague imply that her own appointment and promotion were nothing more than tokenism, and she imagined similar comments being made about Andy.

Despite his lack of experience, Andy had already proved himself to be a bright, enthusiastic and conscientious officer. She'd worked with him on a couple of enquiries since his arrival, and found him easy to deal with. He appreciated the limits of his experience, but was keen to learn.

'What have you got?'

Andy had been working his way through the telephone and online responses to the media reports about the Meresham discovery. The response team had filtered out any obvious non-starters – mainly the inevitable attention-seekers who were usually first on the line after any media appeal or report – but that had still left a sizeable number of potentially useful calls.

In practice, most had proved insubstantial – either more time-wasters or well-intentioned but irrelevant or unhelpful reports. There were a number who claimed to have seen Jayne Arnold after her disappearance forty-six years earlier. Although the case was largely forgotten now, at the time it had received major and continuing media coverage. Zoe had devoted several hours to looking through the newspapers of the time. Jayne's absence had haunted that long hot summer, her pale face staring blankly from the front pages. For many months, and ultimately for several years, the police had received calls reporting a supposed sighting of the girl in locations ranging from the south coast to the Highlands of Scotland. None of these had ever come to anything, and the vast majority had been dismissed as nothing more than wishful thinking.

The current batch of similar reports was even more worthless. Some referenced sightings dating back many years, often rehashes of earlier reports. A few claimed recent sightings, though generally with no explanation as to how the witness had recognised Arnold four decades after her disappearance.

Zoe's main objective was to identify the remains. She was also conscious that the unexpected news of Lavinia Ellsworth's death was likely to change the whole picture. If Ellsworth's death was the result of foul play, the resulting investigation would swallow up any available resource. The case of the Meresham Bones, already the coldest of cold cases, would be accorded even less priority.

For the moment, all she could do was press on. She waited while Andy Metcalfe brought over the printouts he'd been working through. She cleared a space on the corner of her desk while he took a seat beside her.

He was clearly keen to milk his big moment, and Zoe was happy to let him. 'Right. I've pulled out a few of the responses, plus there's another pile on my desk of ones I've discarded for various reasons. It might be worth getting someone else to skim through those with a fresh eye in case I've missed anything.'

'I can have a look through them. So what about these ones?' She gestured towards the small pile of printouts Andy had placed on desk.

'These are the ones that seem worth following up. They're a mixed bunch. There are a couple from people who were living in Meresham around the relevant time.'

'Sounds useful. Well done.'

Andy shrugged. 'All I've been doing is reading. But that's only the appetiser.'

'Go on.'

'We've also been contacted about a man who claims to be Peter Arnold.'

'Peter Arnold? You mean...?'

'Jayne's father.'

Zoe grinned at him. 'I don't care if you were just reading, you've done a brilliant job, Andy. That's our first breakthrough.'

'I was a bit taken aback when I saw it.' He paused. 'The slightly less good news is that we weren't contacted by Arnold directly, but by the head of the care home where he's now living. He's pushing eighty now and, according to the transcript, he's suffering from some sort of dementia. I don't know how much use he's going to be as a witness.'

'It may not matter all that much. From what I've seen in the files, we pretty much wrung everything we could out of him at the time, so he's unlikely to have much new to tell us. His main value's as a source of DNA. Where is he?'

'Not far. Care home's just outside Somercotes.'

'Fancy a drive over there?' She was conscious that, before very long, both she and Andy Metcalfe might find themselves shifted on to the Ellsworth inquiry, and was keen make as much progress on this one as she could before that happened. 'Should only take us fifteen minutes or so.'

Andy nodded enthusiastically. 'Fine by me.'

'And once more for the record, Andy – well done.'

Chapter Nineteen

The coffee had taken a while, presumably because, Annie reflected, everyone here had more important things to worry about than pandering to her culinary whims. That was fair enough. Only Annie herself understood how much the hit of caffeine was likely to improve her temper and efficiency.

Eventually the door opened to admit Andrea Bennett brandishing a well-stocked tray. She placed the tray deftly down on the table while also managing to hold open the door behind her with her foot. She was followed by Diane Astor, the deputy head, a short, slender woman with her pale blonde hair tied back. She had the air of one of the pupils who'd been summoned to her own study, Annie thought.

'I'm sorry I've been so long,' Bennett said. 'You can imagine what things are like out there.' She gestured to the woman behind her. 'You've met Mrs Astor, I believe.'

Annie rose to greet the deputy head, who returned her handshake with a tentative grip.

'I thought I'd better come to see you as soon as I could,' Astor said.

'I'm very grateful. I appreciate things must be very difficult for you this morning.'

Once Bennett had poured them both drinks and left the room, Annie turned back to Diane Astor. Astor looked slightly crushed, Annie thought, as if she were literally taking on the weight of her new responsibilities. 'You must have a lot on your plate?'

Astor took a breath. 'It's not going to be easy. Lavinia's been the figurehead of this school for a good few years. It's hard to imagine it without her. We've cancelled lessons today, as a mark of respect. The governors are convening an emergency meeting this evening to determine next steps. Obviously, we'll do everything in our power to support your investigation.'

'I'm afraid it's bound to disrupt your normal routine, but we'll do our best to work constructively with you. Tell me about Ms Ellsworth. It sounds as if she was a popular figure?'

'She was very well respected. Everyone thought very highly of her.'

Annie noted that the response didn't quite answer her question. 'How long had she been head?'

'This would have been her seventh year. She's made quite an impact during her tenure.' Again, Annie thought she detected a note of ambiguity in Astor's words. 'It seems like hardly any time since her first day. I had the job of showing her round and introducing her to everyone. Even then, she struck me as quite a formidable woman.'

'Formidable in what way?'

'She knew her own mind. She seemed to have a clear vision for the school right from the start. I thought that was quite striking. People usually take a while to settle in, get a feel for the place. Lavinia wasn't like that. She was changing things almost from day one.'

On the surface it seemed like praise but, to Annie's ears, it sounded more like criticism. 'What sort of things?'

'Relatively small things at first. The structure of the senior team. The way we organised timetable planning. The schedule of the school day. It was quite refreshing, I suppose. New broom and all that.'

'How did the other teachers react?'

'It was mixed. Lavinia put a lot of effort into bringing everybody with her, but there are always the old guard who don't like any kind of change. One or two of the older teachers took early retirement at the next year-end. Lavinia did her best to talk them out of leaving, but I think she was happier they'd left than if they'd remained as continuing blockers.'

'Do you think any of the other staff here might have had cause to resent her behaviour?'

'You mean could any of the other teachers have…?' She stopped, clearly shocked even at the suggestion. 'I just can't envisage it.'

'What about outside the school? Did she have family or friends?'

'No family as far as I'm aware. As for friends, I really don't know. She kept her personal life private. Not secretive, exactly, but she didn't volunteer any information.'

'She didn't have a partner?'

'Not as far as I'm aware. I'd occasionally see cars parked outside her house. I've no idea who they were. As I say, it wasn't something that Lavinia ever talked about.'

'What about the pupils?' Annie asked. 'How did they see Ms Ellsworth?'

There was another brief but potent silence. 'I suppose I should be completely honest,' Astor said.

'We'd appreciate that, Mrs Astor. If we're to bring whoever did this to justice, it's important we have the whole picture, even if some of that might be uncomfortable.'

'To be frank, then, it was the same as with the staff. The girls respected her. Feared her almost. She was something of a disciplinarian. Not that there was anything necessarily wrong with that. It attracted parents to send their daughters to the school. We had a reputation for being well run.'

'I presume the governors also appreciated that?'

'I think opinions were more mixed there, just as they were among the staff. Some people thought her attitude to discipline was excessive. She proclaimed it as a zero tolerance approach, so even relatively minor infractions could attract major sanctions.'

'And that was seen as unfair?'

'My own view is that teenagers have a well-developed sense of what's fair and what's unfair. That doesn't mean they always behave responsibly or sensibly. But they're generally happy to accept the consequences of what they do, if they believe the punishment fits the crime. At times, Lavinia's approach distorted that sense of fairness, and I think the girls were smart enough to recognise that. It could be counterproductive, too. Sometimes girls would think, well, if I'm going to get punished anyway, I might as well take it a step further.'

'It must have worked, though? If the school had a good reputation.'

'It worked in pragmatic terms. But it sometimes fostered a sense of grievance. Girls who felt they'd been badly treated. It didn't necessarily create the healthiest culture. That affected the teachers too. They could see instances of what they took to be unfairness, but they knew they'd get short shrift if they tried to challenge Lavinia.'

Diane Astor was speaking with unexpected openness, Annie thought. Almost as if she'd been bottling up these thoughts for years, and Ellsworth's death had allowed her to release them.

'The other problem,' Astor went on, 'is that Lavinia could have favourites. Among both the girls and the staff, I mean. It was never particularly explicit, but every so often you'd get a sense that she'd taken a particular liking to someone and she'd treat them more leniently or generously than others.'

Annie thought it better to avoid any ambiguity. 'When you say "liking"…'

'I don't mean anything untoward. At least, I don't think there was anything like that behind it. It was more intellectual snobbery, I think. Members of staff she thought were of the right calibre. Pupils who were a little sparkier than the norm – not just academically bright but also with the kind of intellectual curiosity she thought was important.'

'Girls like Melanie Donnelly?'

'Melanie was a bit of a test for Lavinia's philosophy. She was undoubtedly a very academically able pupil, and she had a lot of energy and ideas. In some ways, the ideal exemplar of what Lavinia wanted. She was clever but also quiet and well-behaved. Which isn't to say she was in any way a shrinking violet. She was more than happy to express her views. That was the problem, really.'

'She seems to have had some strong views.'

'Lavinia was initially much more tolerant of her than she was of most pupils. I can't imagine she'd have allowed any other girl to set up the newsletter and the various campaigns. It was partly because she thought she could trust Melanie not to abuse the privilege. Lavinia was taken aback by all the school donations stuff that Melanie wanted to put in the last edition.'

'Tell me about that. I heard something about it from Melanie's parents, but I wondered what the school's position was.'

'I'm not sure the school had a position. This was more of a personal thing between Lavinia and Melanie. With a side order of Alice Cartwright.'

'I take it Alice Cartwright was one of Ms Ellsworth's favourites on the staff?' Annie thought she might as well ask the question directly.

'They were very close. Alice is another intellectual snob, if I'm being completely honest. She and Lavinia were among only a small group of the staff who went to Oxbridge. Alice tends to look down on those of us who went to what she thinks of as lesser universities. They'd known each other for years, and she saw herself as Lavinia's protégé. Very enthusiastically adopted her ideas, including her approach to discipline. So if Lavinia thought Melanie was the ideal pupil, Alice was going to think exactly the same. I'm not sure it was entirely fair on Melanie, and I made my views known more than once.'

'Why was it not fair on Melanie?'

'They gave her the impression she could do what she wanted. Melanie was bright enough not to take too much advantage of that. In that respect, I think she was probably more mature than either Lavinia or Alice.'

Annie had identified some of these dynamics during her previous interviews with Ellsworth and Cartwright, but Astor was expressing them much more bluntly. Annie had been expecting that today's interviews would be polite and deferential, with no one prepared to express a bad word about the late headmistress. It was as if Ellsworth's death had had the opposite effect on Diane Astor. As if she'd been freed from the burden of politeness and discretion that had previously held her tongue.

'I'm afraid Melanie had a rather romantic notion of investigative journalism. Saw herself almost as a teenage sleuth, digging out the truth. That was what led her to writing the article on donations. She thought she was exposing dark secrets, putting the world to rights—'

Annie sat up straighter in her chair. 'She actually wrote the article?'

'Yes, of course. I didn't see the whole thing. Lavinia showed me the opening section, which largely dealt with the historical donations. It was well written and very well researched, and I don't doubt everything in there was true. But even that section would have embarrassed the school. I'm sure the local media – perhaps even the national media – would have had great fun with it.'

Annie was only half listening to what Astor was saying. The impression she'd gained from both Melanie's parents and from Alice Cartwright had been that the offending article had never actually been written. That Melanie had done no more than discuss the idea with Ellsworth, and had been forbidden from proceeding. 'What about the rest of the article?'

'Lavinia wouldn't even show it to me. Apparently, it moved on to more recent donations and their sources, Lavinia reckoned that it was at least borderline libellous, though I've no doubt that Melanie would have researched it thoroughly. But obviously, the school couldn't endorse anything that might cause embarrassment to its benefactors.'

'What happened to the article?'

'I'm not sure. Lavinia made it clear to Melanie that it wasn't going to appear in the newsletter or anywhere else, and I believe she'd asked Melanie to delete the article and all her notes.'

'How did Melanie take it?'

'She was annoyed, as you'd expect. Angry with Lavinia because she thought the head was being hypocritical. Frustrated at the time she'd wasted in what she thought was good faith. Just generally filled with righteous anger. You know what teenagers can be like.'

Annie remembered all too well, and she also remembered something else. That in those moments of angst and fury – when you thought that the whole world was against you, and that self-evidently the whole world was wrong – even the smartest teenager was capable of doing something irredeemably stupid.

Chapter Twenty

Somercotes was a typical former mining town in the Amber Valley. It had once been ringed by five pits, but all signs of mining were long gone, except for the occasional self-conscious memorial to the industry that had once sustained the place. The heart of the town still recalled its history, with rows of terraced red-brick cottages straggling the road, but the place now felt more rural, as though the surrounding countryside had reclaimed its former hold on the place.

Entering the town from the A38 to the north, Zoe initially found herself driving through an anonymous and largely indistinguishable stretch of business and retail parks, dotted with the familiar logos of supermarkets and other outlets. This could be anywhere, she thought, any bleak stretch of suburban British road. 'Beautiful, isn't it?'

Andy Metcalfe shrugged. 'I'm a city boy, really. This feels like the worst of all worlds to me. But some people seem to like it.'

Certainly the retail parks looked busy enough even on a weekday morning. Zoe glanced at the satnav map, watching for the impending left turn to the care home. 'Peter Arnold's not moved very far in forty-five years, has he? But I suppose most people don't.'

'My mam and dad are both still in Nottingham,' Andy said. 'Same house I was brought up in. They keep saying they'll sell up and move out to the country somewhere, but I can't see them ever doing it. First, they were waiting for me and my brother to leave school. Then they were waiting till I'd finished uni. I don't know what the current excuse is.' He grinned. 'Mind you, it's not like I've moved far myself. Uni in Loughborough, then joined the force up here.'

'That's three different counties, at least,' Zoe pointed out. 'I'm the opposite, really. Not got any roots anywhere. Although I suppose I'm settled up here now, more or less.' She took the left turn and followed the road into a more residential area. The houses here were a little larger, post-war semis. Another few minutes brought them to the care home, a large single-storey building that looked purpose-built. The earlier rain and hail had died away, and the sun was making a half-hearted attempt to peer out from behind the heavy clouds. They climbed out of the car and stood for a moment looking at the building and its surroundings.

'Decent-looking place,' Andy said.

Zoe gave a mock shudder. 'I'm sure it's okay. I just have a dread of ending up in one of these homes, however good it might be.'

'You've got a few years yet before it's likely to be an issue, I'd have thought.'

'Was that supposed to be a compliment, Andy? If so, you need to work on your technique.'

'That's what my girlfriend keeps telling me.'

The rain had begun spotting again, and they hurried through the main doors into the entrance lobby. The interior of the building had the anonymous calm of an upmarket doctor's or dentist's surgery, replete with pastel shades and tastefully selected landscapes. The woman behind the reception desk looked up with a smile as they entered.

Zoe held out her warrant card. 'DS Everett and DC Metcalfe. I phoned earlier.'

'I'll let Mrs Tremain know you're here.' Her words were delivered with a singsong intonation which Zoe guessed was designed to make prospective residents and their relatives feel at ease. To Zoe's ears, the effect was like being buried under a mound of cotton wool.

After a couple of minutes, a woman appeared through the double doors beside the reception. 'DS Everett? I'm Clare Tremain. Delighted to meet you.'

She was younger than Zoe had expected from their earlier telephone conversation, probably no more than early thirties. She shook Zoe and Andy firmly by the hand, then led them back through the double doors and down the corridor to her office. 'I'll take you along to see Peter in a moment. But I thought it might be useful for us to have a short chat beforehand. Just so I can fill you in about Peter.'

'That would be helpful. It was you who called the police inquiry line?'

'I was in two minds about whether I should do it. I always feel uncomfortable when a resident can't give explicit permission for me to act on their behalf.'

'I'm grateful you did,' Zoe said.

'He's always been desperate to know what happened to his daughter. So I imagine he'd have been only too keen to talk to you, even if the news wasn't what he hoped to hear. But he's not really capable of making that decision for himself.'

'We understand he's suffering from dementia?'

'It's very variable. Some days he seems almost like his old self. He recognises who we are and he chats to us. He knows why he's here and something of his background. Then, almost in an instant, it can change. He doesn't know where he is or who we are. He keeps asking about his wife or even about his daughter.'

'Is his wife still alive?'

'As far as I'm aware he has no close relatives now. He divorced his first wife – that is, Jayne's mother – a long time ago. Thirty years or more, I believe. He remarried some years later but sadly his second wife, Maureen, died a year or so back. She'd been his sole carer, but she'd made arrangements for him to be moved here after her death.'

'It can't be good, to find yourself alone and vulnerable at that age.'

'The only saving grace is that, much of the time, he doesn't know he's alone and vulnerable.'

'What about powers of attorney?' Andy asked. 'Who takes care of him in that respect?'

'His wife had them assigned to their solicitor,' Tremain said. 'I don't think there was anyone else. Mostly things just run on in a routine way here, but if there's anything needed that requires Peter's sign-off, then I just liaise with the solicitor.' She paused. 'I have just let the solicitor know about your visit here today. I thought I'd better keep him informed, in case anything should result from it.'

'That's fine. If it does turn out that we have finally found Jayne Arnold's body we'll ultimately need to agree with Mr Arnold and his representatives as to how the remains should be dealt with. It's better if he's aware of what's going on.'

'I asked him if he wanted to be present when you saw Peter but he said it wouldn't be necessary.'

'It really isn't. Our main purpose in being here is to obtain a DNA sample from Mr Arnold. That will enable us to confirm whether the remains are those of his daughter.'

'I read up on the case when Peter first moved in here. It's a sad story, isn't it? From what I was told, I don't think Peter ever quite recovered from it.'

'Probably worse for having no clear ending.'

'I suppose it'll bring a partial closure if the body does belong to Jayne,' Tremain said. 'But probably too late for Peter. I don't know how much he'll take in of what you've got to tell him.' She offered them a faint smile. 'Let's go and find out, shall we?'

Chapter Twenty-One

Clare Tremain had suggested they see Peter Arnold in his room. 'He's most comfortable there, and it's more discreet than any of the public areas. Do you mind if I stay while you talk to him? It'll be easier if there's someone there he knows. He often mistakes me for one of his wives, but at least he doesn't get as agitated.'

When they entered the room, Arnold was sitting with his back to them, his gaze fixed on a television playing silently in the corner of the room.

'Peter, I've got some visitors to see you.'

He twisted in his chair and gazed at them, although his expression remained as blank as before. 'Is that you, Maureen?'

'Not today, Peter. These are two police officers. DS Everett and DC Metcalfe. They just want a chat with you.'

'We've come here about your daughter, Mr Arnold,' Zoe said. 'About Jayne.'

'Jayne. She's not here.' Arnold was silent for a moment, as if thinking. 'We don't know where she is. I don't think Chrissie does either.'

'That was Peter's first wife,' Tremain said quietly.

'We know that, Mr Arnold. We've been trying to find her.'

'She's missing, you know.'

'I'm afraid we may have some bad news for you, Mr Arnold.'

His expression suddenly changed, as if he'd registered the significance of what they were saying. 'Bad news?'

'We've found a body. Human remains. We think they may belong to your daughter. I'm very sorry.' She'd been in the position of breaking this kind of bad news on several occasions in her police career, and she'd generally managed it more tactfully than this. She felt oddly wrong-footed by Arnold's calm confusion.

'A body? I don't understand. Jayne's missing.'

'We think the body may be that of your daughter, Mr Arnold. It's possible she's dead.' She couldn't put it any more bluntly, but she expected the news simply to pass Arnold by, leaving him untouched.

It took her a moment to realise there were tears in his eyes. 'Dead? Jayne?'

'I'm afraid it looks as if that may be the case. We're not yet certain that the body is your daughter's. That's one reason we're here. We need to take a sample from you, so that we can match the DNA. That'll help us confirm whether the body is Jayne's.' She spoke the final sentences slowly, with no expectation that Arnold would understand what she was saying.

'Dead?' Arnold was crying now. 'We need to tell Chrissie.' He made it sound as if his first wife might be waiting in the next room.

'We'll do that, Mr Arnold. Once we've confirmed it is your daughter.' Zoe wondered what the chances were that Chrissie Arnold might still be living, might still reappear if the news of her daughter's death was confirmed.

'Where is she?' Arnold asked. It wasn't immediately clear if he was talking about his daughter or his first wife.

'We found the remains in Meresham,' Zoe said.

Arnold blinked, as if the name had stirred something in his distant memory. 'Where we live.'

'That's right.' Zoe decided she might as well use the opportunity to chance her arm. 'We found the remains buried, Mr Arnold. Beneath the foundations of the cottage opposite the school bus stop.'

Arnold frowned. 'Alan Harwood's place.'

Zoe exchanged a glance with Andy Metcalfe. 'You knew Alan Harwood?'

'I don't like him,' Arnold said firmly. 'Dodgy bugger.'

'Why do you say that, Mr Arnold?'

'I've seen him, watching the young girls on the bus. Watching Jayne. Nearly had words once.'

Zoe looked over at Clare Tremain, who offered only a slight shrug. 'When have you seen him doing this, Mr Arnold?'

Arnold looked back at her blankly. 'Who?'

'Alan Harwood, in Meresham. You said you'd seen him watching young girls. When did you see him do that?'

Arnold was looking bewildered now. 'Jayne's late. What time's she due back from school?'

It was gone, Zoe realised. The moment of lucidity, if that was what it had been, had melted away, and Peter Arnold was now lost in some other past. She considered telling him again that his daughter wasn't likely to be coming home. But she knew that would achieve nothing.

'She's not here yet, Peter,' Clare Tremain said from behind her. 'Don't worry.'

Zoe was happy to leave Peter Arnold in Tremain's hands. Tremain clearly knew how best to handle him, to deal with his confusion and agitation. Annie could see Arnold almost physically relaxing as she spoke to him.

They'd probably taken this about as far as they could. It was unlikely they would get anything more from Arnold other than the required DNA sample. 'We won't take up any more of your time, Mr Arnold. Thank you.'

'Is that you, Maureen?'

Clare Tremain had taken Arnold by the hand. 'She's not here at the moment, Peter. This is Detective Sergeant Everett. She just needs to take a swab sample from you. It's a routine matter.' She signalled with her eyes that they should take the sample while Arnold was calm. Andy Metcalfe stepped forward and carried out the task, taking care not to agitate Arnold.

'All done, Peter.' Tremain looked up at Zoe. 'If you go and wait in my office, I'll just take a few minutes to settle Peter.'

'What did you make of that?' Andy Metcalfe asked once they were back in Clare Tremain's office. 'Poor bugger.'

'I wonder what it's like for him,' Zoe said. 'I mean, I wonder what it's like to be in his head. What is it that he sees?'

'No way of knowing, is there? It was as if at some level he understood and took in what we were saying, and then it was just gone.'

'I was most intrigued by what he said about Alan Harwood.'

'Was Harwood a suspect at the time?'

'I'll need to go back and check the files. He was definitely interviewed, because we interviewed everyone in the village, and we'd have been particularly interested in anyone living near the school bus stop. I've no recollection of any specific concerns about Harwood.'

She recalled skimming through the interview notes with Harwood in case they'd provided any clues as to what might have happened to him in the intervening years, but from what she'd remembered they'd been brief and uninformative. Harwood had been a musician, who had played with various orchestras around the north of England. As far as she could recall, he'd been in a rehearsal at the time of Jayne's disappearance and had an unassailable alibi provided by his colleagues. There had been no suggestion the police had looked him particularly closely, or that any questions had been raised about Harwood's wider behaviour or reputation.

Peter Arnold was an elderly man with severe dementia. Most likely his utterances meant nothing. There were countless notes and records of discussions with and about Peter Arnold on the file, which Zoe had worked hurriedly through. Although Arnold had expressed mixed views of his neighbours, she could recall no mention of Harwood and no suggestion Arnold had mentioned any other individual as a possible suspect for his daughter's disappearance.

So why, four decades on, had he reacted like that to Harwood's name?

Chapter Twenty-Two

Annie had completed her initial interview with Diane Astor, and had then driven back round to the headmistress's house for a catch-up with Tim Sturgeon and the CSIs before returning to HQ to complete her preparations for the inquiry. This was going to be a big one, and Stuart Jennings would want to have everything meticulously planned, ideally before anything hit the media.

Except that, as she saw when she turned onto the track leading to the house, it was already too late for that. A van with the insignia of the local TV news was parked on the external road just beyond the house. If the TV news crew were already there, word would have leaked to the local print media as well. Their staffing resources were much more limited these days, but a story like this would be a big deal and they'd want to steal a march on the nationals.

She pulled into the side of the track, still some distance from the house, and dialled Stuart Jennings's number.

'Annie? How's it going?'

'Okay. Except that the local TV are already camped on site.'

'Shit. How did they get wind of it so quickly?'

'It's a boarding school, Stuart. The news would have spread round the place before I even got here. Anyone could have tipped off the media. One of the staff. One of the pupils.'

'Suppose you're right. I've just been talking to comms about it. We're putting together a statement to be issued later this afternoon. If anyone stops you, just tell them to talk to the media office.'

'Thanks for that, Stuart. I'd been planning to offer them a half-hour exclusive interview.'

To his credit, Jennings responded with a laugh. 'Just try not to give them anything they can run with. Given half a chance, those bastards can turn "no comment" into a front-page admission of police failings.'

'I'll do my best. I just want to have a quick catch-up with Tim, and then I'll head back to HQ to get everything up and running.'

'In the meantime, I'll warn comms that word's already leaked out. Always fun to be the bearer of good news.'

She started the car and continued up the track towards the house, pulling in as close behind the rows of marked cars as she was able, hoping to reach the house before she was waylaid by the reporters.

For the moment, there seemed to be only a couple of them, including a TV reporter Annie recognised from previous investigations. She was crouched under a large golfing umbrella clutching a microphone, with a miserable-looking cameraman, similarly protected, standing just behind her. It was one way to make a living, Annie supposed.

She pulled up the hood of her waterproof in the hope of remaining incognito. Even before she'd taken half a dozen steps towards the house, the TV reporter was waving frantically in her direction. 'Annie, Annie! Can you spare me a minute?'

It wouldn't be so bad, Annie thought, if these people didn't insist on behaving as if you were a personal friend, rather than someone they'd spoken to a few times during media conferences.

She nodded to the reporter. 'I'm sorry. I'm afraid we're not in a position to say anything at the moment. There will be a media statement issued later this afternoon. In the meantime, if you've any questions please contact the media office.'

Annie ducked past the uniformed officer controlling the perimeter of the scene. She'd called Sturgeon before she left the school, and he was standing in the tent entrance, waiting for her. 'You'd better come inside,' he said as she approached. 'We've set up an extra tent so you can keep dry without contaminating anything. See how thoughtful we are.'

'Thoughtful for your own comfort, Tim. You don't fool me.'

He looked mock-horrified. 'Never a thought for myself.'

She entered the tent to find a white-suited Danny Eccles also inside waiting for her. 'Thought it would be useful for us all to have a catch-up before you head back. It's an intriguing one.'

'They're always the most fun,' Annie said. 'Go on.'

'First of all, it looks as if, as we thought, the cause of death is asphyxiation caused by strangulation. Doc will have to confirm that there's nothing else, but that's what the bruising on the neck would suggest.'

'Tim said earlier that it looked as if she'd been strangled by bare hands. Do you still think that?'

'Looks like it. There's no sign of a ligature round the throat that would suggest anything else. Would take a bit of strength and determination, especially given that the victim wasn't a small woman.'

'Could another woman have done it? In terms of their relative strength, I mean.'

'I'd have said so. It wouldn't have been easy whoever did it, but then this isn't the sort of act that's carried out casually.'

Annie nodded, thinking about the implications of that. 'What else?'

'There's no sign of any break-in. We've checked that carefully. All the downstairs windows are sealed shut or have window locks, so it would have been very difficult for anyone to have broken in without leaving some sort of evidence. The rear door was deadlocked and bolted, so no one came in that way unless they were able to lock it again behind them. We found a set of keys upstairs in Ellsworth's handbag, but there could be spares somewhere. If so, we haven't found any.'

'Frank Garner had a set,' Annie pointed out, 'which makes him at least notionally a suspect. I guess there might be others floating around. As we discovered with the roof access, security here's not as tight as it might be.'

'If someone did have keys they could have gained access by either the front or rear doors. The front door wasn't deadlocked, which is maybe a little unusual given that Ellsworth lived alone in a fairly remote spot.'

'So someone could have come in that way and not re-locked it behind them,' Annie said. 'Or Ellsworth could have voluntarily let someone in, which would imply she knew her killer.'

'The third possibility is that she opened the door to someone who forced their way inside,' Eccles said. 'But there's a fairly sizeable chain on the door, which had been left unattached. If Ellsworth had opened the door late at night, she'd surely have put that in place first.'

'People can be careless. But, okay, we have the possibility that the killer was someone Ellsworth knew.'

'There's no sign of any protracted struggle,' Eccles went on. 'There are some items disturbed, but it looks as if that was only in the moments immediately before Ellsworth's death. There are plenty of other ornaments and other objects around the room that haven't been touched, so my feeling is that the attack came as a surprise and that Ellsworth had no real opportunity to fight back.'

'Which would reinforce the idea that this was someone she knew.'

'Potentially, yes. Though it leads on to the most intriguing thing. The bruising.'

'Tim mentioned that. On the face.'

'All over the body. Ellsworth was subjected to a very savage attack. It looks to me as if she was either given a literal kicking or beaten with some object. Repeatedly. The oddest thing is that it looks as if the attack happened after death.'

'After death?'

'It's something else for the doc to confirm, but she was already on the ground and seems to have made no effort to defend herself. She was either dead or profoundly unconscious. It's possible the blows contributed to her death, but that wasn't why they were administered. It's like an act of pure sadism.' He paused. 'Or fury, maybe.'

'Fury?'

'That's what it looked like to me.' Eccles's normally amiable face was as serious as Annie had ever seen it. 'As if the killer was venting their anger at Ellsworth.' He shrugged. 'Just an impression, for what it's worth.'

'Not a pleasant thought,' she said. 'If your impression's right, what might someone like Lavinia Ellsworth have done to provoke that kind of response?'

'She was a teacher,' Tim Sturgeon pointed out. 'People sometimes have strong views about teachers. But it's a weird one, all right.'

'We're checking for prints,' Eccles went on. 'Plenty of them, but the vast majority are Ellsworth's, as you'd imagine. We'll see what else we can get.'

'What about DNA?' Annie asked. 'If Ellsworth did struggle with whoever attacked her, even briefly, that's likely to leave some traces.'

'Again, we'll see what we can find.'

'Any CCTV?' Annie had noticed various cameras around the school buildings, but couldn't recall noticing any here.

'Sadly, no. The security here wasn't particularly strong, to be frank. Fairly standard domestic locks. A fairly low-spec alarm, which was deactivated with Ellsworth in the house. Couple of security lights at the back and front. That's about it.'

'Anything else I should know at this stage?'

'Not really. We're checking the rest of the house, although there's no evidence that the rest of the house has been disturbed in any way and there's no obvious sign of anything missing. If Ellsworth interrupted an intended burglary, it looks as if the intruders left without taking anything. Difficult to be certain, of course, but there are some potentially valuable items around the house that haven't been touched.'

'Most burglars would just be keen to get away if they were interrupted,' Annie said. 'We've had the odd stabbing or even shooting – though usually because the householder's produced the weapon rather than the burglar. I can't recall a case where the burglar's responded to an interruption by strangling the householder. Though I suppose if you were desperate anything might be possible.'

'I'll keep you posted if we come across anything else that's likely to be useful,' Danny Eccles said. 'But I think for the moment it's likely to be the usual detailed slog through the rest of the house.'

'Good luck with it. And good luck with the scrum outside,' she added to Tim Sturgeon.

'It was always going to be a big one, this,' Sturgeon said. 'Got all the elements, hasn't it?' He smiled. 'I'll just play my usual straight bat.'

Annie didn't doubt it. Sturgeon was the safest pair of hands she knew, not just in his ability to manage a crime scene, but also in his deadpan skills in handling the media. All the hacks knew him, and all of them knew they'd get nothing from him beyond a polite nod of acknowledgement. Most of them didn't even bother to try. 'You do that,' she said. She looked towards the entrance of the tent, already half dreading the gauntlet of questioning she'd have to face as she returned to her car. 'I'll do my best just to keep my head down.'

Chapter Twenty-Three

Stuart Jennings didn't so much come into the room as make an entrance, banging back the door and noisily dumping a stack of files on the table. 'Christ, what a morning!' He dropped himself into a chair. 'I don't suppose anyone fancies making me a coffee?'

Annie smiled back at him sweetly. 'If you mean "would someone be kind enough to make me a cup of coffee, please?", I'm sure you'll find a volunteer.'

Jennings glared at her for a moment as if genuinely about to lose his temper, then nodded wearily. 'Yeah, yeah, all that. Just somebody get me a cup of sodding coffee. Please.'

Andy Metcalfe was already jumping to his feet, but Zoe said, 'I'll come with you. Might as well get them for all of us if we're going. You want one, Annie?'

'Why not?'

Annie waited until Zoe and Andy had left the room, then said, 'I think that was Zoe being tactful. Bad time with the Chief?' Jennings had spent the latter half of the morning with the comms team, and he'd then been asked to provide an update as part of the Chief Officers' weekly team meeting.

'You know what they're like.'

'They gave you a tough time?'

'I've had worse. They're all showboating to each other. They weren't best pleased to discover the Ellsworth story had hit the media already.'

'There's nothing we could have done about that. It would have been all over the school before we even got there.'

'Feel free to go and have a word with the Chief. Oh, and just in case you were wondering, he wants a result on this as soon as possible.'

'Glad you told me. I was planning on putting my feet up for a couple of weeks.'

Jennings finally offered a smile. 'Not quite my response, but I think the Chief got the gist. Anyway, apparently we're supposed to treat it as the top priority.'

'I'll try to remember that. What are we saying to the media?'

'Just a holding statement. Confirming Ellsworth's name and occupation, and that we're treating the death as suspicious. We're not saying anything about the cause or nature of the death, though no doubt the rumour mill's churning, especially alongside the Melanie Donnelly death. That should hold them for a day or two. But this one's got real potential to go sour.'

'Tell me about it.'

'The nationals are already all over it. You can bet they'll be pestering the school staff, and quite probably the pupils to get an inside track. Two deaths in a week, and in a bloody girls' boarding school, too. You can imagine what the tabloids will make of that. Every variety of salacious bollocks, I don't doubt. The Chief's right, much as it pains me to say those words. We do need a result.'

'We'll do our best. We were talking about next steps before you made your grand entrance—'

He at least had the grace to look sheepish. 'I needed someone to vent my feelings at. You lot were just unlucky enough to come into my line of sight at the wrong moment.'

'No worries. I was also discussing with Zoe what we do with the Meresham Bones inquiry. I'm guessing it's a rather lower priority now than Ellsworth's murder.'

'Funny you should say that. You might be interested to know the Meresham Bones also made a guest appearance at the Chief's meeting. He hasn't forgotten about them.'

'Oh, great.'

'As far as he's concerned – and I more or less quote – the bones constitute a high-profile case with implications for public safety.'

'After more than forty-five years?'

'Yet again, it's the tabloid angle, isn't it? The bones have given the press the opportunity to regurgitate its coverage from 1976, so we've had all the "Is this Jayne Arnold?" stories back on the front pages.'

'Half their readers won't have a clue who Jayne Arnold even was.'

'Hasn't stopped them plastering her face all over the front page for the last few days. Along with reminders of the failings of the original inquiry. A mix of "will the police get it right this time?" and "is the killer still out there?" headlines. I don't really blame the Chief for getting twitchy. He'd like nothing more than to get a result where his predecessors didn't.'

Annie fell silent as Zoe re-entered the room, bearing two steaming mugs of coffee, Andy following behind with two more. 'Here we go.'

'Don't tell me you couldn't blag any biscuits. What do we pay you for?'

'Not to be your servant, Stuart. You want biscuits, go and source them yourself.'

'Okay,' Annie said. 'Let's get on. You okay to join us, Stuart, given how much you've disrupted us already?'

'There are times when I have to remind myself who's the senior officer here,' Jennings said. 'But, yes, I can spare you a few more minutes of my valuable time. Tell me where you're up to.'

Annie provided a brief update on her visit to the school. 'We've got a team kicking off first interviews with the staff, starting with the senior team and working downwards. Anything they might have seen last night. Not all the staff live on site, but some do. Anything unusual or suspicious they might have spotted around the school over the last few days. Anything at all to do with Lavinia Ellsworth.'

'Do we think her death's likely to be connected with the school?' Jennings said.

'Who knows, but it's the most straightforward place to start. Ellsworth was oddly secretive about her private life. So my instinct is that's most likely to be where the real story lies.'

'What about links to Melanie Donnelly's death?'

Annie shrugged. 'We have to keep an open mind on that. We can't ignore the fact that we have two unexplained deaths in the same institution within a week. On the other hand, the nature of the deaths is very different.'

Jennings nodded. 'Fair enough. And we don't think this was just a burglary that went wrong?'

'Again, it's possible. There've been burglaries at the school before. But it doesn't seem likely. No sign of a break-in. No sign of theft. It seems to me that the killer's most likely to be someone known to Ellsworth. I'm also hoping we may find some other clues to Ellsworth's private life either in the house or on her laptop or tablet. All that stuff's still ongoing. We've got to finalise the team, and there's still stuff we need for the MIR, but I can talk to you about that afterwards. So the next question is, what we do about the Meresham Bones?'

'Where are we up to with that?' Jennings said.

'We had a possible breakthrough while you were hobnobbing with the Chief. Zoe?'

'We've tracked down Jayne Arnold's father, so we've got a DNA match to compare.' She recounted the conversation she and Andy Metcalfe had had with Peter Arnold. 'He barely knew where he was. I don't think he really took in the news of his daughter's death at all.'

'Interesting comment about Harwood, though,' Jennings said.

'I don't know how much weight we should give it in itself,' Zoe said. 'It was odd. It felt like a short brief burst of lucidity, and then it was gone. Andy and I have rechecked the files since we got back in case I'd missed anything. There's only a short interview with Harwood. He was clearly seen just as another village resident, and there doesn't seem any suggestion that he was a person of interest to the inquiry at the time, even though his cottage was close to the bus stop. He had an unassailable alibi for the time Jayne went missing, so there'd have been no reason to treat him as a suspect.'

'What about Peter Arnold?' Jennings asked. 'Did he mention Harwood to the police at the time of the investigation?'

'Not that we can find. There were various interviews with Arnold, but we've not found anything that references Harwood. But it's possible he said something that wasn't recorded, especially if the police had already confirmed Harwood's alibi. There's no mention of Harwood in any of the other interview notes as far as we've been able to find. No suggestion he had any kind of reputation in the village.'

'So Arnold's comment may well be meaningless,' Jennings said gloomily. 'Maybe just some conflation of two people or two ideas.'

'It's entirely possible,' Zoe agreed. 'His mind seemed to drift backwards and forwards in time. He plucked Harwood's name out of nowhere.' She shrugged. 'On the other hand, Harwood owned the house at the time the body was buried there.'

'I take it we've had no luck in tracking down Harwood?'

'Not so far. There don't seem to be any likely matches on the local electoral roll, though we're following up some who might be relatives. The interview notes say he was a professional musician so we thought we might find some mention of him online, but we've not found anything that seems to relate to the Harwood we're looking for.' Zoe shrugged. 'I suppose the question is how much priority we give this.'

'We might be wasting our time with Harwood anyway, given he had a solid alibi,' Jennings agreed. 'Though it would be useful at least to know who carried out the building work in 1976.'

'I'm surprised the builders weren't interviewed at the time,' Annie said. 'Given the proximity of the cottage to the bus stop, I'd have thought the builders might have been treated as potential suspects.'

'It was raised in the interview with Harwood,' Zoe said. 'Various people in the village had mentioned that there was building going on at the cottage. Harwood reckoned that they hadn't been working on the day Jayne Arnold went missing. He said he'd been annoyed they'd dug the foundation and then disappeared for a couple of weeks to complete a job in Ashbourne.'

'Did anyone check that out or follow up with the builders?' Jennings was rubbing his temples again, as if in anticipation of an impending headache.

'If they did, there's no record of it. Just seems to have been taken at face value.'

'Brilliant,' Jennings said. 'And there's no mention of the name of the building firm?'

'Not that I've been able to find. The local authority records from the time leave a lot to be desired. It's been transferred to microfiche but they only seem to have kept the basic paperwork, so there are no plans or documents that might give us a lead.'

Jennings shook his head wearily. 'Doesn't sound to me like we're going to make progress easily. The Chief wants us to keep it ticking over for the moment, so we've at least got a story to tell the press if they keep pursuing it. I suppose the first thing is to confirm whether the remains really are those of Jayne Arnold. If they are, it might reignite media interest in the story. If they're not, we're back to square one with not much of a clue where to start. But the real focus has to be Ellsworth. That's a live case and, given the violence inflicted on Ellsworth's body, we have to consider the possible wider risk to public safety.'

'So what do we do with the Meresham case?' Zoe asked. 'Do you want me to stick with it?'

Annie looked at Jennings. 'I don't want to mess Zoe about, but I think ideally we need her on the Ellsworth inquiry. It's not as if we're overwhelmed with experienced detectives.'

Jennings nodded. 'I'm inclined to agree. What's your view, Zoe?'

Zoe was silent for a moment. 'Yes, of course that's sensible.'

'Okay, then,' Jennings continued. 'I'll continue as SIO on both enquiries for the present, but we'll scale back the resourcing on the Meresham case. Andy, are you happy to continue working on that for the moment, at least till we've had confirmation on DNA?'

Andy Metcalfe shrugged. 'If that's what you want.'

'You'll get your reward in heaven, Andy. Seriously, I want to be able to show the Chief that we've not given up on the Meresham case, so I want someone we all rate working on it, even if for the moment it's largely a paper exercise. It's a good opportunity to work on your own initiative. And tracking down Alan Harwood is still a major priority.'

'If you say so, boss. But no, that's fine.'

'That's good then. Right, I'll leave you to it.' Jennings was already on his feet, as always making no concessions to anyone else in drawing the meeting to a close. 'Thanks for the coffee.'

Annie watched the door close behind him before speaking. 'So who was that masked man?' She sighed and shook her head. 'Let's get back to the plan, shall we?'

Chapter Twenty-Four

Margaret Delamere closed the front door behind her, conscious of her rain-sodden hair and clothing. Sometimes wondered if she'd made a mistake moving here, though she'd never have admitted it to anyone, and certainly not to her daughter. Today, she had been grateful to be so close to the city centre.

If she was honest, at least part of her motive in selling the house and buying this place had been to wrong-foot Annie. What Annie wanted more than anything was for Margaret to settle into a quiet, dignified retirement. When Margaret had bought the house in the country following her divorce many years before, she'd assumed it was where she'd finally settle once her police career was over.

None of that had quite gone to plan. Her police career had ended earlier than she'd expected, and she'd quickly realised a discreet low-key retirement wasn't her style. She'd been offered a couple of non-executive posts which had kept her busy for a while. But attending a deathly dull board meeting every month wasn't going to occupy her mind for long.

The TV work had been a godsend. It had started slowly with the odd guest slot on programmes like *Newsnight* to pontificate about policing matters. The producers had quickly realised she was a TV natural, able to express her views in a way that resonated with viewers. She was an unashamed conservative in every sense. For a new editor seeking 'balance', her operational experience and seemingly pragmatic approach provided a counterweight to more liberal commentators and academics.

She'd expected her newfound TV fame to incur some resentment among her former colleagues, given the circumstances of her retirement. But, particularly in the early days, she'd made a point of championing the police cause. That had gained her some kudos within the force, and her past transgressions seemed largely forgotten.

Eventually she'd decided that, just as she wasn't cut out for a discreet retirement, so she also wasn't cut out for a quiet life in the country. The house she'd bought wasn't a large one but, once Annie had grown up and moved away, it was more than she needed. She was frustrated by the lack of amenities, and she had no interest in participating in the community activities that filled the lives of her neighbours.

She wasn't sure where the thought of moving back to the city had come from, but the idea appealed to her. She'd begun to look at property advertisements online, curious to see whether there was anything suitable available. It turned out that, even with city centre living becoming increasingly fashionable, the value of her detached house in the middle of nowhere would buy her a decent flat with a useful little lump sum left over. Almost before she knew what she was doing, she'd identified an attractive penthouse in a new development near the river opposite the Cathedral Quarter.

After that, everything had moved much faster than she imagined possible. Her own house had sold within days, she'd had her offer on the flat accepted, and within weeks she was moving in.

It had all happened so quickly she'd had almost no time even to think about what she was doing, let alone to have any regrets. It had only been on her first night here, as she'd sat out on her newly acquired balcony looking out over the cityscape in the evening sun, that she'd finally stopped to consider what she'd done.

Even now, there were moments when Margaret wondered if she regretted her decision. It was generally on the nights when, as she lay in bed trying to sleep, she realised the double-glazing didn't quite exclude all the traffic and other noises of the city. In those sleepless moments, she recalled the silence of her former house, the knowledge that she could walk out into the surrounding countryside often without meeting another living soul.

But those moments were few. For the most part, she enjoyed the fact that, as this morning, a few minutes' walk would bring her into the city centre. Today's visit had been yet another meeting about the impending television project. Margaret had originally been promised another lunch but at the last minute – or at least the previous day – Trevor Railstone's secretary had called to enquire if she could make a breakfast meeting instead. She'd been half inclined to say no, but this was supposed to be business rather than pleasure and a breakfast meeting might provide a better focus than another extended lunch.

The meeting, like most of the meetings with Railstone, could probably have easily been replaced by a phone call or an exchange of emails, but she wasn't sorry to keep things moving in person. She'd rejected the offer of the full English breakfast that Alastair Winters was wolfing down with alacrity, and had confined herself to a large espresso and a pastry. Railstone had worked his way through an impressive-looking bacon cob.

'I've been thinking about what you were saying, Margaret,' he said, through mouthfuls of bread and bacon.

'What did I say?'

'About your relative lack of experience doing this sort of stuff.'

'Well, all I meant was—'

'I think you're being hard on yourself. With Alastair's support you'll have no problem at all. But I can see that this is different from the work you've done before.'

She hadn't bothered to argue. She'd already learned that Railstone did what he wanted. He had his own ideas about how things should happen — even if those ideas often seemed to change from minute to minute — and it was easiest just to go with them.

'We're getting various guests and interviewees organised. So that's all looking good.'

'It all sounds tremendously exciting.'

'I thought that in the meantime you and Alastair could have a shot at recording some pilot segments. That'll give you an opportunity to get used to the presenting role. I'll email you both all the details.'

The meeting had come to an abrupt end with Railstone announcing in his usual manner that he was already running late for his next appointment. As they watched him hurry out to find a taxi, Winters pushed aside his empty plate and smiled at Margaret. 'A full English always tastes better when someone else is paying for it, I find. Especially if that someone is Trevor Railstone.'

'Do you think this programme's actually going to happen, Alastair? I've been down this way before. And Trevor seems a little — disorganised?'

'Trevor's walking chaos.' Winters took a final swallow of his coffee. 'But he knows what he's about. Nothing's guaranteed in this business, but he's got a better chance than most of making it happen. Just go with the flow.'

'Gareth Thomas is conspicuous by his absence so far.'

'Gareth's a busy boy. Or so he'd like you to think. This is his way of letting Trevor know he can't be taken for granted. But I've worked with Gareth before and, for all the political posturing, he's a pro. He'll be there when he's needed and he'll do a damn good job.'

'That's the other thing that worries me. Will *I* do a damn good job? This is all new to me.'

'You're born to it, Margaret. That's why Trevor wants you. You're integral to the whole project.'

Margaret was far from convinced – apart from anything else she knew flattery was Winters's default mode – but she'd gain nothing by debating the point. 'We'll see next week, I guess.'

'I'm sure we will.' Winters looked at his watch. 'Better be getting back. I've a couple more meetings this afternoon, so I need to do my prep.'

It hadn't occurred to Margaret that Winters actually prepared for meetings, though she suspected he was much less casual than he pretended. She'd noticed that at the event where she'd first met him. His relaxed manner belied the homework he'd clearly done on her and her fellow speakers.

The rain was falling harder than ever, the dark sky offering no promise of respite. Winters stood in the shelter of the doorway, looking out with an expression of distaste. 'I'm going to make a run for a taxi. What about you?'

She gestured over the river. 'I'm just heading over there. I'll probably brave the rain. I've got my trusty umbrella, and I'd probably get as wet trying to find a cab.'

'Well, if you're sure…' He turned up his coat collar and stepped out into the rain. 'See you next week, then.'

She watched him trot along to the end of the street before raising her umbrella and stepping out herself. Ten minutes later, as she finally arrived at the foyer of the flats, she was regretting her decision. The umbrella had afforded her some protection, but the wind-whipped rain had still found its way inside her raincoat and soaked the rest of her clothing.

As she passed, she paused to check the lockable pigeon-hole where her mail was delivered. There was nothing except a couple of marketing letters which she dropped into the communal recycling bin without bothering to open. Then she took the lift to her flat on the top floor.

Once she'd closed the door of the flat behind her she felt more relaxed. That was one of the reasons she liked this place. In just a few minutes, she could escape the stresses of dealing with the likes of Railstone and Winters, and step into a private space. From here she could see the world, or at least the centre of Derby, but feel utterly detached from it. Once she was here nothing could touch her.

She hung up her coat to dry out, then made her way through to the kitchen. She had no particular plans for the rest of the day, and she intended now to spend most of it trying to prepare herself for the proposed pilot filming. Despite what Railstone had said, she knew how limited her experience of this world really was. She needed to do some reading, try to get her thoughts in order, do her utmost to avoid making a fool of herself.

So she'd make herself another coffee, perhaps grab a quick bath, and settle herself down to some serious work.

She filled the kettle and then emerged from the kitchen intending to start the bath running.

She spotted the note only as she was crossing the hall to the bathroom. It had presumably been there when she'd re-entered the flat, but it had been pushed aside by the front door. It was just a single sheet, folded in half, slipped under the door while she'd been out.

There was no public access up here, and visitors had to be buzzed in from the entrance lobby by the flat-owners. She picked up the note and continued into the bathroom, leaning over to turn on the taps on the bath. It was only when she'd completed her preparation by pouring in some bath foam that she turned her attention to the note.

It was a sheet, apparently torn from a notebook, on which only a few words had been scribbled. The handwriting looked vaguely familiar, though she couldn't immediately place it. The note said simply: 'We need to talk. Call me tonight – after 7.00. Not before – I can't guarantee I'll be alone.' The words were followed by mobile phone number but no name or other clue to the sender's identity.

It took her another few moments before she realised. She supposed she should have expected it, though it was the opposite of what they'd agreed. She was also confident that, as yet, there was no reason to worry. That might change, but it was unlikely. The only real risk was if they allowed their own fears to gain the upper hand.

It was then that a second thought occurred to her. The note had clearly been hand delivered. Which meant that the sender had been here, standing outside her front door. How that was possible, Margaret had no idea, though the security was far from foolproof. Perhaps her visitor had slipped in while one of the residents had been leaving, taking advantage of the brief opening of the doors. The residents had requested a security control on the lift, but that hadn't yet been installed.

So the sender of the note had come here, presumably with the intention of seeing Margaret face to face. That worried Margaret. It was the opposite of what she'd always insisted on. As far as Margaret was concerned, it carried real risk. This place was stuffed with security cameras, installed supposedly for the reassurance of the residents. That meant that her visitor's presence here had almost certainly been recorded.

Margaret forced herself to think clearly. All of that was true, but the actual risk remained low. Yes, the visit would have been recorded, but no one would have any reason to look at the recording. The record would be held only for a limited time and would be of no interest to anyone.

Even so, Margaret was left with a dilemma. Her preference would have been to ignore the note. No good was likely to come of making contact.

But she knew that, if she didn't respond to the note, its sender would return, would continue to try to make contact. Each time that happened, it would further increase the dangers. The only option was to nip this in the bud immediately. That meant, against Margaret's better judgement, making the call.

She felt a clutch to her stomach. It took her a moment to realise that it was fear, a fear she hadn't felt, at least in this form, for a long time. She no longer wanted to take a bath. Even the thought of lying there, naked and alone, made her feel too vulnerable. She turned off the taps and, picking up her coffee, returned to the living room.

The rain was still falling, the rivulets running thickly down the windows. The city below was shrouded in haze, the streets filled with the white and red of car lights. There was a whole world of people out there, but Margaret felt desperately alone.

She slumped down on the sofa and turned on the television, switching to one of the news channels, as if seeking reassurance that life was continuing as normal. She was just in time for the main hourly bulletin.

It was only as the newsreader began to read the main headlines that she realised that all her assumptions about the sender of the note had been completely wrong.

Chapter Twenty-Five

Annie had spent the rest of the morning with Jennings completing the investigation plan for the Ellsworth inquiry. They'd decided, given the relative remoteness of the location, to establish a Major Incident Room in the school itself, and Annie had been liaising with Diane Astor to identify suitable accommodation. After some discussion, they'd selected a unit, away from the main school buildings and with its own external entrance, normally used for music and drama. Annie and Zoe had driven over in the early afternoon to determine what adaptations would be needed to suit their purposes.

It was still raining heavily, and Astor had suggested they drive directly round to the unit at the rear of the school. 'I'll wait for you over there. To be honest, I'll be glad to escape this madhouse for a few minutes.'

Astor was in the doorway waiting for them as they pulled into one of the parking spaces in front of the unit. She was already looking exhausted, as if struggling to cope with the stress of her unwanted new role.

'I'm sorry we've had to drag you away.' Annie and Zoe followed Astor into the building.

'I'm not sorry to get out for a few minutes. It might force them all to think for themselves for a change.' She shook her head. 'Sorry, that was unfair. Lavinia was such a dominant figure. Everybody's trying to second-guess what she would have done or wanted.' She led the two officers into a small hallway lined with closed doors. There was a further door at the end of the corridor ahead of them. 'I hope this is suitable. It sounded like the best fit for what you were looking for. It's what we call the music centre, but it's used for various purposes.' She opened one of the doors and peered inside. 'These are small offices we use for individual instrument practice, which you could use for interviews. Then you can use this as your main room.' Astor opened the final door. The room beyond was large, with high windows and an airy feel even on an overcast day. There were a few tables, stacks of chairs and some functional metal cabinets lined against one wall. 'We use this for orchestra practice and drama rehearsals mainly. I hope it's big enough for your requirements.'

The room was bigger than most of the open-plan offices and meeting rooms back at HQ. 'It's ideal. We just need space for our officers to get together, do interview write-ups, that sort of thing. I hope we'll only need it for a short period while the work's at its most intense.' She deliberately didn't specify how 'short' that period might actually prove to be.

'To be honest, it'll be reassuring to have you on site,' Astor said. 'This has left everyone jittery. It's not comforting to think that whoever did that is still out there. I want to make sure the girls take it seriously, but I don't want to create a panic. You know what they're like at that age. They're already coming up with all kinds of idiotic notions. Especially about Lavinia's death being linked to Melanie Donnelly's.'

'In what way?'

'All kinds of daft theories. That Melanie had shared some dark secret with Lavinia, or maybe vice versa. I'm not sure what sort of fatal secret they imagine a schoolgirl – or even a headmistress – would be party to. Incidentally, you said you wanted to look at Lavinia's work laptop and tablet. They don't seem to be in her office. She must have taken them over to the house last night.'

Annie nodded. 'I'll speak to the CSIs then, but thanks for checking. And thanks for the use of this place. It looks perfect for our needs.'

Astor looked at her watch. 'I'd better be getting back. Goodness knows what might be happening over there. I've got to start planning for tonight's governors' meeting too.'

'Good luck with that.'

'I'm not looking forward to it. It was one of the tasks I was generally only too happy to leave to Lavinia. That was one of her strengths. She always had them eating out of her hand. I'd better go and try to prepare for all the impossible questions they're bound to throw at me. I'll probably see you in the morning, assuming I still have a job.'

Annie waited until she'd heard the outer door closed behind Astor before she turned her attention to Zoe. She hadn't moved in the time Annie had been talking to Astor and had made no effort to join in the conversation. 'Penny for them, Zo?'

Zoe's vacant expression cleared, and she appeared as if surprised that Annie was still present. 'Sorry. Not even worth that. It's just this place.'

'Go on.'

'It's funny. I hadn't realised till I drove through the gates how much it would bring back memories.'

'Don't tell me you went here too.'

Zoe finally smiled. 'God, no. But it's just schools, isn't it? All different, but all the same. This even feels like the music room in the place I went to. Where I played the viola really badly. Not exactly the happiest days of my life.' She shrugged. 'Don't get me wrong. Looking back, I don't think here was anything particularly awful about it. It was just that I hated almost every minute.'

This was the most open Annie could recall Zoe being. She'd never been exactly secretive about her background, but she didn't talk about it much either. Annie knew Zoe had been brought up somewhere in the Home Counties by relatively elderly parents. Her father had been some sort of administrator in local government. Zoe had rarely mentioned her mother.

'So this place brought back a few memories?'

'More than I expected. I still have dreams about my schooldays sometimes. The usual anxiety dreams about having to do an exam you haven't prepared for. That kind of thing.' She turned away from the window. 'Sorry, this isn't helping us get on with the job, is it? But it just made me wonder how this place might affect you if you never managed to escape it.'

'Like Lavinia Ellsworth?'

'I suppose she did go off to other schools. But yes, someone like that.'

It was a good question, Annie thought. She was still staring out at the dark bulk of the school building. How *would* this place affect you?

Chapter Twenty-Six

DC Andy Metcalfe was feeling sorry for himself.

During the first part of the morning, following the early briefing, the office seemed to have emptied around him. There were still a couple of the administrative and support team in the next room tapping assiduously away at their computers. But most of his fellow officers had been designated tasks on the Ellsworth inquiry, and were now up at the school either getting on with the first round of interviews or helping to set up the local incident room.

Only Andy was left, almost the last person standing on the already depleted Meresham Bones inquiry. He'd tried to tell himself this was a vote of confidence in his abilities. He was a relatively inexperienced DC, and he'd been left in effective charge of what he supposed was at least potentially a major inquiry.

But he knew that was an overstatement of his role. At best, he was just seen as a safe pair of hands who would keep things ticking over while the rest of the team focused on the real work of the Ellsworth investigation. He wasn't expected to do much except continue reviewing any information received from the public while they awaited the results of the DNA match. Stuart Jennings had told him they'd review the status of the inquiry once they knew whether the body was that of Jayne Arnold. All Andy could do for the moment was wait to see how matters panned out.

The only thing he could do was make the best of it. He was conscious that, in the face of the other priorities, very little work had been done on the Meresham case to date. If he could manage to make some progress, however minor, that would surely be evidence of his abilities.

He'd checked again through the various public responses to the media reports of the discovery of the skeleton. The police had explicitly sought information from anyone living in the village in 1976, but so far the results had been disappointing. They'd had a handful of relevant calls but none of the callers had anything new to offer.

Andy's primary interest, for the moment, was in Alan Harwood. Prior to their visit to Peter Arnold, they'd arguably paid too little attention to Harwood himself. They'd inevitably seen him as a person of interest in the investigation, given his ownership of the house at the time the body had been buried. But it occurred to Andy that, despite Jennings's scathing words, they might so far have fallen into the same trap as their 1970s predecessors. Perhaps they should have been looking more seriously at Harwood's own history.

A file note indicated that one of Andy's colleagues had conducted an initial cursory search on Harwood's record, but had found nothing of significance. Andy decided to approach the matter more rigorously, working system-atically through the records. It took him longer than he expected, but eventually he found the information he needed. It seemed that one Alan Robert Harwood did indeed have a police record, although this name was recorded only as an alias against the nominal Kenneth

McRae. The conviction was from just over ten years ago, and at the time Harwood had been living in West Yorkshire.

McRae had been found guilty on multiple charges of serious sexual assaults on females largely in their early teens, and had been sentenced to five years in prison. His occupation was recorded as musician/teacher, and it appeared he had been using the name Kenneth McRae officially for both personal and professional purposes for over thirty years prior to his conviction. This explained why Andy had found no online reference to Harwood's musical career. More pertinently, it might mean that Harwood had assumed this new identity not long after Jayne Arnold's disappearance.

The reported assaults had taken place over a period of several decades, but there were none from as far back as 1976 and none from Harwood's time living in Meresham. No one had spotted that Harwood had previously been interviewed in the Arnold inquiry, but again that was unsurprising. He'd been interviewed only as a possible witness, along with dozens of others from the village.

There were only the basic details of the story available, and it would no doubt take time to obtain the relevant files from West Yorkshire Police. Andy's first thought had been to break his news to Stuart Jennings immediately, but ideally he wanted some more information before he made too much of this. The last thing he wanted was to approach Jennings with a supposed breakthrough only to discover there was some very good reason why no one had pursued this particular line before. The PNC record suggested that the trial would have been a relatively big deal, so would presumably have been widely reported.

Andy returned to his computer and conducted an internet search on Kenneth McRae.

The coverage was more limited and less lurid than Andy had expected. The trial had taken place before the death of Harwood's West Yorkshire neighbour Jimmy Savile and the spate of high-profile trials and convictions that had followed from Operation Yewtree and other investigations. The reporting carried a slightly more sceptical tone than might subsequently have been the case, as if the media had been reluctant to question the integrity of a supposedly respectable elderly man. As Kenneth McRae, Harwood had established a career as a well-regarded classical musician playing with a number of major orchestras, including the Hallé and the Liverpool Philharmonic. He'd supplemented his professional income, at various points in his career, by teaching violin and piano, both through association with local schools and on a one-to-one basis at his home.

The story was depressingly familiar. Harwood had groomed a succession of teenage girls, mostly during the teaching sessions in his home, though there was evidence he'd engaged in similar practices in a number of the schools where he had been employed. This behaviour had continued over several decades, and the successful prosecutions had related to incidents stretching from the early 1980s until only a few years before Harwood's arrest.

As so often, one lingering question was how Harwood had been able to escape the consequences of his behaviour for so long. He had clearly been devious and manipulative, but there was an implication that at least some of his employers had turned a blind eye rather than risk losing the services of a supposedly distinguished teacher. At various points, complaints against him had been dismissed as malicious attempts to damage his career or reputation.

Harwood's abuse had finally been exposed only by determined campaigning by the mother of one of his last and youngest victims, a gifted thirteen-year-old who, at the recommendation of his school, had been receiving additional tuition from the now retired Harwood. The girl had been bewildered by Harwood's behaviour and told her mother, who'd immediately removed her daughter from his tuition and complained to the school. When the school failed to take the matter seriously, the mother had not hesitated to make a complaint to the police. Harwood had vehemently denied the accusations, claiming that the mother's complaint was a vexatious response to his criticisms of her daughter's ability and application.

In the meantime, the mother had been painstakingly gathering accounts, not only from the parents of other students but also from former pupils at the schools where Harwood had taught. In the face of this mounting evidence, the police had commenced a formal investigation which finally resulted in Harwood being arrested and charged.

From that point, an increasing number of complainants had come forward to report abuse at Harwood's hands. It became clear very quickly that there was a pattern of complaints, many almost identical in their descriptions of Harwood's behaviour, across his career. Harwood, who had protested his innocence since his initial arrest, pleaded not guilty but was ultimately convicted on all but one of the charges.

Andy pieced together this narrative from the accounts in the newspapers of the time, which ranged from the comparatively factual reports in the broadsheets to the more sensationalist later coverage in the tabloids which focused on the courage and tenacity of the mother in pursuing Harwood. There were hints, even in these stories, that Harwood's record of abuse had been more extensive than the limited number of cases for which he had been convicted.

It seemed quite possible, therefore, that Harwood's abuse had already begun at the time he was living in Meresham. The question was whether that abuse might have extended as far as killing Jayne Arnold.

Beyond the trial and its aftermath, there seemed to be little further media coverage. Andy found a subsequent report claiming Harwood was considering an appeal, and another stating that police were considering bringing new charges against Harwood relating to further victims. Neither claim appeared to have been followed up, and there were no further reports on Harwood's case following his conviction.

The final report that Andy was able to find was from a year or so later, when a couple of the broadsheets reported that Harwood had been found dead in prison. The stories hinted that Harwood had taken his own life, but Andy could find no subsequent detail or confirmation of that.

He sat back and thought about what he'd just read. If the bones really were those of Jayne Arnold – or even perhaps if they weren't – Harwood had to be a prime suspect. Whether they would ever be able to prove his guilt was another matter.

At a pragmatic level, that might suit everyone. The police could tacitly accept Harwood was the likely killer and the case could be quietly closed. There would be no benefit in pursuing a dead man. No one was likely to challenge the decision. They had so far failed to track down Jayne's mother, and her father was in no state to question the outcome. Any officers who'd worked on the original inquiry, even at a junior level, would be retired. Many of the older officers would no doubt be deceased. In any case, no one was likely to volunteer information that might cast further doubts on the rigour of the original investigation.

Andy knew he ought to be feeling pleased with himself. This could easily be a major breakthrough in a case that had remained unsolved for more than forty-five years. Even if his own contribution had involved little more than following up a passing comment from an elderly man lost in the haze of dementia, Stuart Jennings would be pleased with the outcome. Particularly if it satisfied the Chief and allowed Jennings to focus all his energy and resources on the live inquiry.

But even as he picked up the phone to speak to Jennings, he still felt uneasy. Something didn't feel right. It wasn't that he'd necessarily got the story wrong. It was more that he felt he didn't yet have had the whole story.

But that was for later. For the moment, he might as well enjoy his moment of glory. He finished dialling Jennings's number and waited for Jennings to answer.

'It's Andy Metcalfe. I just wondered if you could spare me a few minutes. I think I might have something on the Meresham case.'

Chapter Twenty-Seven

It was slightly disconcerting to see Danny Eccles without his clothes on, Annie thought. That is, without his usual white protective suit and helmet. She'd always assumed he must be wearing ordinary clothing underneath all that paraphernalia, but couldn't recall the last time she'd seen him other than at a crime scene. That was most commonly where their paths crossed, and their subsequent communications would generally be by phone, email or through Danny's rigorous reports.

Now he was sitting opposite her in the newly established incident room, wearing an open-necked blue shirt and a pair of black trousers. Almost like a normal human being.

'Nice set-up you've got here.'

'It'll do the job,' Annie agreed. 'Better than the glorified broom cupboards we sometimes end up in. What's the news on the laptop front?'

'Still nothing. Which is definitely a bit odd.'

'We know she had a school-issue laptop and tablet, both of which she normally kept in her office here. But they're not there now, and her secretary assumed Ellsworth had taken them home to use there.'

Eccles shook his head. 'I checked again. There was no way we could have missed them in the house, but I don't like to take anything for granted.'

'That's never been one of your failings, Danny.'

'It goes with the territory. But they're definitely not there. What's maybe even odder is that there's no sign of any other laptop or tablet either. No personal mobile phone. Her school-issue phone was on the coffee table in the living room.'

'Her secretary reckons Ellsworth definitely had a personal laptop and phone, and she thinks she had a tablet too. You think whoever killed her took the laptops and tablets?'

'That's your area, there were no other signs of theft. There were some obviously valuable items left untouched, and there were cash and bank cards in Ellsworth's handbag,' Eccles said.

'Could be amateurs who just grabbed the first thing they saw that they thought might have any value. There've been previous break-ins at the school, apparently. Maybe got freaked when Ellsworth interrupted them.'

'Amateurs who managed to break in without leaving a sign? And who, having been panicked into killing her, waited around to give her a good posthumous kicking? I'd have thought any amateur who'd got themselves into that mess would give be keen to make themselves scarce. And a second-hand laptop's worth peanuts on the black market.'

'I thought you said that was my area, smartarse. But, no, you're not wrong. Doesn't sound a likely scenario. So the alternative is the killer was either interested in what might be on the devices, or keen to stop us finding out what was on there.'

Eccles grinned. 'Again, your area. But I'd have said so.'

'We can check if there's any backup of the material on Ellsworth's school laptop. Her personal stuff will be trickier, I'm guessing. The real question is, what's a head teacher likely to have on her laptop that's worth killing for? Anything else from the scene?'

'Lots of stuff. None of it obviously useful. We'll check out the prints we've got. We've a decent collection of forensic samples, though obviously the vast majority will relate to Ellsworth herself. Beyond that, not much. No signs of any disturbance other than in the sitting room. My gut feel is that the killer was someone Ellsworth knew. But it was a savage attack – both the strangulation and what was done afterwards.'

'I look forward to reading the report.'

'We'll see what the doc has to say. It all seems so out of place somewhere like this.' He pushed himself to his feet. 'Right, I'll let you get on. I've left the lads packing everything up in the rain, so they'll think this meeting is just an excuse to be inside.'

'You never do that sort of thing, Danny.'

'Given half a chance I do. I don't usually get half a chance.'

After he'd gone, Annie looked around the room, taking stock of their progress over the last twenty-four hours. At least the basics were in place. The incident room was established, lines of tables topped with laptops, a printer chuntering away in the corner. All in all, a better result than she'd feared the previous day.

The team was also now more or less in place back at HQ – not just officers, but exhibits managers, analysts, administrators. Annie always felt a mild sense of exhilaration during this initial phase of any major inquiry, when the building blocks were falling into place, the evidence and intelligence were still coming in thick and fast, and there was the sense that a breakthrough might come at any minute.

Their next task would be to work through the papers and documents the CSIs had found in Ellsworth's house. Most of these appeared uninformative – standard domestic bills and similar documents. But there was the possibility that somewhere among them there might be something of interest. There had been no sign of any written address book or diary or any private correspondence that might shed any light on Ellsworth's life outside school.

Annie had asked the forensic IT team to take a closer look at Melanie Donnelly's laptop in the hope of tracking down the missing article on the school's benefactors. Annie had no idea whether the article was likely to be significant even in the context of Melanie's own death, but for the moment any lead, however tenuous, seemed worth pursuing. She took out her mobile and dialled Robbie Handsworth, the team leader.

'Robbie? Annie Delamere. Just wondered if you've been able to make any progress with Melanie Donnelly's laptop.'

'We've just got round to it. Been a bit hectic down here.' This was notoriously Handsworth's response to any unprompted query – to the point where, among Annie's colleagues, he'd become known as 'Hectic' Handsworth. It wasn't that he wasn't efficient, but he did things in his own way and at his own pace. He'd committed to providing Annie with a report within the next couple of days. This was his way of saying that, if she wanted the information early, she'd have to accept an imperfect summary.

'What have you got so far?'

'It's interesting. When we first looked at it, we focused on checking what was actually there, because you were looking for clues as to her state of mind. I was struck at the time that there wasn't much. Most of the content related to Donnelly's schoolwork. There were files of essays and assignments, the school's internal software with her timetable and all that sort of stuff. But nothing personal.'

'She had a tablet,' Annie said, 'but you looked at that too.'

'Nothing much on there, either. It looked as if she mainly used it for watching movies and listening to music. Same with her phone. She didn't have email on there, and there were only a few texts to schoolmates about school stuff. And only a handful of names in her address book – again, mainly school friends and contact numbers for her parents.'

Annie remembered all this from Handsworth's original report. It had been uninformative but, at the time, largely unsurprising. Melanie had been an assiduous and serious student, so it was perhaps understandable that there'd been little personal or frivolous on her school laptop. 'So what have you found this time?'

'It's more about what isn't there. For a start, she has no real internet history. It also looks as if, on the tablet, she used a VPN. That's a virtual private network—'

'I know what a VPN is, Robbie. That would enable her to override safeguards the school might impose on its own internet connection, right?'

'Among other things. Of course, there are countless reasons why she might have done that.'

'Including a simple teenage desire for privacy.'

'Exactly. I wouldn't be surprised if a lot of her school-mates did the same. But it also looks as if there was a mass deletion of data not long before her death. Files, applications, addresses, all sorts of stuff. Quite possibly some of her call log. All within a day or two.'

'Can you retrieve any of it?'

'We're trying. That's why I wanted an extra couple of days before getting back to you.'

Annie ignored the familiar jibe. 'How successful do you reckon you're likely to be?'

'Difficult to say. It's partly a question of how much time and money you want to throw at this.'

As usual, Annie thought. 'Let's see what you come up with on the first pass. Then we can decide if it's worth pursuing. I'm particularly interested in seeing an article that Melanie apparently wrote. About benefactors to the school.'

'Benefactors?'

'Financial benefactors. People who donated money to the school.'

'I know what a benefactor is, Annie. IT geeks can use words as well as initialisms, you know.'

'Touché.' Her conversations with Handsworth tended to go like this, a series of gentle jibes that she assumed concealed either mutual respect or mutual contempt. She was never quite sure which.

'Why are you interested in a schoolgirl's article?'

'She wrote it for this newsletter she edited. It linked the school to some dubious historical figures and raised similar questions about more recent benefactors. We were originally told Melanie was ordered not to pursue the idea, but it looks like she did write the article and the head banned it. It may be nothing, but it's the one blot on her school record. If nothing else, it might give us another clue as to her state of mind. We know she was frustrated that her writing wouldn't be published in the newsletter.'

'I can have a look.' The doubt was evident in Handsworth's tone. 'Anything else?'

'The only other thing I'm interested in is any contacts she might have had, particularly outside the school. You say she'd deleted some of her call log.'

'It looks like it. And contact addresses and numbers.'

'Anything you can retrieve there could be useful.'

'We'll see what we can do. She'd done it quite expertly. Not to a professional standard, but she's done a thorough job for a schoolkid.'

'She was a bright one, Robbie. That's one of the things that worries me. That she might have been bright enough to get herself tangled up in something risky – but not quite mature or experienced enough to deal with the consequences.'

Chapter Twenty-Eight

Stuart Jennings looked at his watch. 'He's late.'

Andy Metcalfe looked at the clock on the wall, which still showed two minutes to the hour. He wasn't about to tell Jennings his watch might be fast. 'He said he might be a minute or two late,' he lied. 'He was finishing off another meeting.'

'I've already put off another meeting for this. He'd better not be too late. What's his name again?'

'DCI Ken Smailes,' Andy said. 'He was the SIO on the Harwood inquiry.'

'You've told him what this is about?'

Andy had already told Jennings all this, but he knew Jennings liked to make sure his proverbial ducks were fully lined up before he joined any meeting. 'Yes, I said—'

He was interrupted by the phone ringing on the table in front of them. Jennings pressed the call button on the conference phone. 'Stuart Jennings.'

'Morning.' The voice was jovial, with the air of someone keen to discuss last night's football with his mate in the pub. 'Ken Smailes. Understand you wanted a chat.'

'That's right, Ken. Thanks for getting back. I'm on conference and I've got DC Andy Metcalfe here with me. I understand you've already spoken to him.'

'Sounds a good lad. On the ball. You want to talk about Kenneth McRae?'

'Or Alan Harwood, as we know him.'

There was silence for a moment. 'You're going to tell us what we missed?'

'I wouldn't put it like that—'

'Neither would I, son. Just so's we're clear. Not at all like that.' The joviality had momentarily dissipated. Smailes's flat Yorkshire vowels seemed to have become more pronounced.

Jennings raised an eyebrow to Andy, his expression articulating the words 'old school' more clearly than if he'd spoken them. 'That's not what this is about, Ken. It's just that with potential new evidence—'

'About the Arnold kid. That was always a black mark against you lot down there. You reckon this is her body you've finally stumbled across?'

Jennings showed no inclination to rise to the bait. 'We think it's likely. We've got a potential DNA match but we're still waiting for confirmation. But whoever the body is, Harwood's now in the frame.'

'Sounds like it, if he owned the cottage where the body was found.'

'Two questions, then. First, do you think it's possible Harwood was up to his tricks as far back as 1976? And second, would he have been capable of killing Arnold, or whoever this is?'

'I'm not sure why you care. This was forty-six years ago. If you can pin the Arnold case on Harwood, I'd jump at the chance. Removes the stain on your force's reputation. Closes the book. Who's going to ask any questions?'

'Jayne Arnold's father's still alive. Her mother may be too.'

Smailes was silent for a moment. Andy could see Jennings had no intention of telling Smailes that they hadn't yet tracked down the mother or that Peter Arnold was lost in the wilds of dementia, and maybe that was irrelevant anyway. Jennings might be happy to close the case, but Andy knew he wouldn't do it at any price, particularly if there was a chance something might come back to bite him later.

'Okay,' Smailes said. 'The answer to the first question is yes. We didn't have any doubt Harwood was a prolific offender. We brought to trial the cases we felt most confident would result in a prosecution. But there were others on our books. In some cases, the victims were reluctant to testify. In others, we or the CPS didn't think the evidence was strong enough. But the cases that came to court were the tip of the iceberg. And we're fairly sure, just from hints that Harwood let slip, that there were cases that predated anything we were dealing with.'

'Harwood pleaded not guilty to all the charges?' Jennings asked.

'He was deluded. Right to the end, he couldn't believe he'd done anything wrong. He'd persuaded himself it was all consensual, even though some of the kids were as young as thirteen, for Christ's sake. He really thought they were in love with him. But that meant he sometimes said more than he intended. So, yeah, I'm pretty sure he'd been behaving like this for most of his adult life.'

'Did you look at his past?'

'What do you think? But in the end there wasn't much point. We had more than enough evidence from the women who'd come forward. We didn't have the time or resources to delve back into the past in the hope of finding more.'

'You didn't register a possible connection with Meresham and Jayne Arnold?'

There was a longer silence this time. 'No. Why would we? The Arnold case was more than thirty years before. Harwood had led a pretty mobile life, which is probably one reason he was able to get away with what he did for so long, but the Meresham link never came up. If we'd thought it worthwhile to dig further back into Harwood's past, I dare say we'd have made the link eventually.'

'I dare say.' Jennings's tone was neutral. 'What about my second question?'

'Whether Harwood would have been capable of killing? I'm not sure, to be honest. He was an odd character, and not just in the obvious way. His personality was a strange mixture. I've seen clips of him performing, and he looked like a different person. Almost – I don't know, imperious. Totally in control. In his element. That's what he was like as a teacher, I believe. Someone lording it over his students. Outside of that he just seemed – ineffectual, I suppose. Timid, quiet. Jayne Arnold was – what? Fifteen?'

'Sixteen,' Andy contributed.

'I just can't see the Harwood I met as having the initiative or the bottle to kidnap and kill someone of that age. That wasn't his style. He got them young and groomed them gradually. There were one or two instances where he'd used threats or violence, but only in a teacherly kind of way, when he felt there was a challenge to his authority. Mind you, I encountered Harwood in his seventies. He might have been a different character in his younger days.'

'But none of the cases you dealt with were anything like Jayne Arnold?'

'Nothing like that. These were all students, mostly ones who'd come to him for private tuition. He worked on them slowly, over months or years. He was a manip-ulative bastard and he made them believe what he was doing was normal...' He trailed off. 'I've dealt with some nasty buggers over the years, but Harwood was one of the worst. Partly just because he was so low-key. When you first met him, he struck you as Mr Ordinary. You'd have pigeonholed him as a junior clerk or a bookkeeper or something. I was startled when I first saw footage of him playing. He looked like a man possessed. No, that's not quite right. It was more that it was the only time he looked on top of things.' There was another prolonged silence, as if Smailes was thinking about what he was saying. 'I think that was how it worked for him. He was clearly a very bright man, but he seemed to struggle with everyday life. He couldn't relate to other people the way most of us do. It was all about gradually taking control. To the point where he could play his victims the same way he played his violin.' Smailes laughed. 'You've probably guessed I'm not a psychologist. But that's the way it seemed to me.'

'So that wouldn't fit what happened to Jayne Arnold,' Jennings said.

'People don't always play to type, do they? Maybe he tried a different approach. Maybe he was a different person back then. I can't say no. It just doesn't fit the person I dealt with.'

Jennings looked more morose than at the start of the conversation. 'Thanks, Ken. That's been really useful.'

'You don't sound as if you mean that. Sorry if I've thrown a bit of a spanner in the works.'

'No, it's what we needed to know. I mean, you're right. If we can put this one to bed, so much the better. But I reckon we owe it to Jayne Arnold to make sure we get it right. After all these years.'

'Aye. You've got a point. We'll get the files sent over so you can judge for yourselves.'

'Thanks, Ken. I look forward to the read.'

He ended the call and leaned back in his chair, looking at Andy. 'What do you think?'

'I don't know. It sounds as if grabbing Jayne Arnold off the street would have been out of character, but...'

'But Smailes only saw Harwood as an old man, and they obviously didn't want or try to delve too far back into his past. And, if Harwood wasn't involved, it would be a hell of a coincidence that the body ended up under his cottage. But it feels as if there's a piece or two of the jigsaw missing.'

'What do you want me to do?'

'We can't do anything till we've got the DNA confirmation. Once you get the Harwood files, go through them as rigorously as you can. It wouldn't remotely surprise me if those buggers missed something significant. Once you've done that, we can have another chat about where we take it.'

Andy had been half hoping that, as Smailes had suggested, Jennings would use this as an opportunity to put the cold case to rest. But Jennings was too cautious to do that without making sure his backside was well and truly covered. That would mean at least going through the motions to determine whether they'd fingered the right man, even after four decades.

It was frustrating but, even discounting Jennings's caution, Andy felt it was the right thing to do. Jennings had been right about that, even if his sanctimony had mainly been intended to wind up Ken Smailes. Jayne Arnold's disappearance had remained unresolved for nearly twice as long as Andy had been alive. They owed her something.

Chapter Twenty-Nine

'Margaret! You found us okay, then?'

'Eventually.' She allowed just a trace of frost to creep into her tone. She'd had an awful drive over, compounded by further difficulties first in finding the place and then in finding somewhere to park. She felt nervous and not in the best of tempers.

All this was on top of the nagging sense of anxiety she'd felt since receiving that note. When she'd first received it, she been disturbed but thought she'd known what was going on. But the subsequent news had raised questions she couldn't begin to answer, questions she didn't even want to think about. All she knew was that she wanted to be as far away from it as possible.

'What do you think of the place?' She was brought back to the present by Trevor Railstone's booming voice. She made the effort to calm her nerves and looked around her.

She wasn't sure what she'd been expecting, but it was undoubtedly something more salubrious than this. Somewhere with a bit of style, and with groups of eager young people running around doing the bidding of the likes of Trevor Railstone. This place was simply a small unit in a tired industrial estate on the edge of Nottingham city centre. The businesses around them, at least in the units that had been taken, were print-shops, small engineering companies, accountants. The whole place looked as if it had seen better days.

Still, that was understandable. At this stage, they were only working on a pilot that might well never be shown. As Railstone had said, just something to show the network what they were capable of. He was clearly not a man to waste money, so he'd no doubt picked the cheapest place he could find. She just wished he'd picked somewhere with a little more parking. Margaret had parked several streets away, and she was fairly confident that even if her treasured little BMW survived till the end of the day, its paintwork would have been keyed and its wheels removed.

'It looks very – suitable,' she said to Railstone.

Alastair Winters was already present, standing at the far side of the room clutching a mug of coffee. As Railstone moved away to engage in intense discussion with the cameraman and sound engineer, she walked over to join him. Winters waved an empty coffee mug in her direction. 'Let me get you a drink, Margaret. It's not exactly artisanal but it is instant. We even have little pots of fake milk.'

It was only as she drew closer that she realised that the man standing facing Winters was the elusive Gareth Thomas. 'Good morning, Gareth. Nice to see you here.' The final words came out more pointedly than she'd intended, but Thomas didn't seem to notice.

'Hi, Margaret. Geared up for the big debate?'

'Is that what we're doing? I didn't…' She'd read carefully through the various materials Railstone had sent her over the preceding days, but it had been largely background on the various guests Railstone had suggested they might involve in future programmes. There'd been nothing on the purpose or format of today's filming, and she'd assumed it would be something low-key and informal.

Thomas was grinning, as if at some private joke. 'I think today's just about getting to know each other. A little gentle sparring on suitable topics. Work out the chemistry between the three of us. Should be fun.'

Fun wasn't quite the word in Margaret's mind. She accepted the coffee gratefully from Winters and turned to look around at the room. 'Nice place.'

'It's a dump,' Winters said. 'But that's Trevor for you. Never spends more than he has to. Still, it'll be fine for our purposes today, as long as they can get those lights sorted out.'

Margaret couldn't see anything wrong with the lights, but she knew she wouldn't have been able to see anything right with them either. She was more than happy to leave that stuff to the people who pretended to know what they were talking about.

She stood in silence, drinking her coffee, while Winters and Thomas blethered behind her. She still didn't feel entirely at ease with these people. It still wasn't a world she fully understood, even though she seemed gradually to be becoming part of it.

'Margaret? Are you ready?'

She'd been lost in thought, and she realised Winters and Thomas had already taken their seats under the lights. The three chairs had been arranged in a triangle around a low table containing a jug of water and glasses. 'Sorry, just coming.'

She took her seat facing Winters and Thomas. There were two camera operators standing on opposite sides of the triangle, Railstone standing just behind them. 'Thanks, Margaret. Now, this is a little experimental. I want to try this with a kind of live news feel, which is why for the moment I haven't bothered with make-up. I want it to feel as if we – the viewers – are intruding on an ongoing discussion, as if we're just overhearing the next table in the pub—'

'A very distinguished next table,' Winters added.

'Quite, Alastair. A very distinguished next table in a very upmarket pub,' Railstone continued. 'I want a different feel from the usual panel discussion. When we do this for real, we'll obviously have to structure it rather more to ensure we cover the right topics, but for the moment I just want you to extemporise.'

'Extemporise.' Gareth Thomas echoed the word with an edge of sarcasm.

'Chat away as if you were talking in the pub, agreeing, disagreeing, just letting the conversation go where it wants.'

'This would be a lot easier if we could actually do it in the pub,' Winters pointed out. 'Ideally with a few pints inside us.'

'It's not a bad thought for later in the series.' Railstone seemed oblivious to Winters's irony. 'Film it in a pub for real. Get the crowd involved.'

'That's sure to be edifying,' Winters said. 'Okay, what do you want us to talk about?'

'Anything you like. As long as it's political. What about something on standards in public life? Cronyism. Corruption. That's all very topical.'

Winters groaned. 'If you insist. I thought we were all about breaking new ground.'

'It's just a test, Alastair. I want to see how the idea works, and then you're welcome to come up with something more inspired. Give it a go.'

Winters gave a surreptitious wink to Margaret and kicked off. To give him his due, Margaret thought, he was very good at this. She had no idea whether he really was improvising what he was saying, but it sounded remarkably fluent. She couldn't begin to match that, but she supposed she didn't have to. She just had to sound – to use Trevor Railstone's favourite word – natural. At the moment, she felt even that was going to be a challenge.

'…The question,' Winters was saying, 'is whether anything has really become worse, or if it's always been that way. Scandal and cronyism have always been with us. The Marconi scandal, Lloyd George selling honours, Profumo, Back to Basics, every generation has its share. Are things really that much worse now? Gareth, I understand you're currently researching a book on standards in public life. Do you believe standards really are lower now than they've ever been?'

Thomas gave his usual knowing smile before responding. 'I've never had a particularly high regard for politicians of any variety, as you know, Alastair, with a very few honourable exceptions. There've been rogues and scoundrels throughout the ages. It's probably not helpful to debate whether things are better or worse than they've been in the past.'

'And yet…?' There was a touch of mischief in Winters's tone.

'And yet corruption and cronyism are probably more endemic than at any time in my admittedly relatively short life. They're taken for granted, priced into our views of the great and the good. If the scandal's exposed, those involved just brazen their way through it. If they're forced to resign, they just wait a few months and then reappear as if nothing ever happened.'

'What's your view, Margaret? I hope it's not ungallant of me to point out that you're a little older than Gareth. Do you think things are worse now than they've ever been?'

Her mind had been elsewhere and she was a little caught out by the question. 'I'm not sure about that. As Gareth said, it's probably not helpful to draw comparisons. But for once I do broadly agree with Gareth in that there's a shamelessness about current behaviour which does seem new. I'm old enough to remember that John Profumo had the dignity to retire from public life and devote himself to public works.' She wasn't really old enough, or only barely, but no one was likely to challenge her. 'That just doesn't happen now.'

'It's not just politicians,' Thomas said. 'It's public servants generally. The whole notion of public service has become debased. The public sector's been infected by private sector values that themselves have become ever more corrupt. It's one of the legacies of Thatcherism—'

'I should have known you'd get round to blaming her before too long. It's thirty years since she left office.' Margaret shook her head.

'I'm afraid your namesake still casts a rather long shadow,' Thomas said.

'You're being unfair,' Margaret said. 'Look at the police, for example. We've had a number of senior police officers resign in recent years because their conduct has been judged inappropriate to their office...'

Too late, she saw Thomas exchange a glance with Winters. Not for the first time in her dealings with these people, she felt there was some private joke that hadn't been shared with her.

'It's interesting you should say that, Margaret. I'm right in thinking, aren't I, that you left your role in the police rather unexpectedly?'

The question took her by surprise. She'd assumed Thomas might have lined up some instances of police corruption to wrong-foot her or undermine her arguments. She hadn't envisaged he might reference her own circumstances. 'I'm not sure what relevance my career has to this debate.'

'I believe you took early retirement?'

Her first instinct was to refuse to engage, but she felt any attempt to dismiss Gareth's questions would only strengthen his cockiness. 'I retired a little early, though I really don't think that's pertinent—'

'Can I ask why you retired early?'

She'd always expected that this question, or some variant of it, might come up at some point in her media career, and she'd given considerable thought to possible answers. Now, when she was put on the spot, those answers felt thin and unconvincing.

'It just felt as if it was the right moment. I'd completed some major projects which had been taking up the bulk of my time, and I wasn't sure I wanted to take on any more. I'd had a good career and achieved everything I'd wanted to.'

Thomas nodded thoughtfully. 'Does the name Ryan Challis mean anything to you?'

It was only then that Margaret realised she'd been ambushed. She'd felt like the outsider in this project, but she'd put that down to her inexperience, knowing the others understood this business much better than she did. Now she realised that this was something more. She wasn't part of a collective. She'd been set up as a target.

She turned to look at Trevor Railstone, who was watching the scene with something like amusement. His smile widened as he saw her expression.

At another time, Margaret might well have just gone along with this charade. It was what she did. Try to ingratiate herself by playing along with the bullies and the tricksters, pretend she didn't mind. It was what had always got her into trouble. She guessed Railstone or Winters had seen that trait in her, and had organised this accordingly.

'What the hell is this, Trevor?' she said. 'I didn't expect this to turn into some kind of inquisition. This is supposed to be a discussion.'

Gareth Thomas's familiar smirk had returned. 'Are you saying you didn't know Ryan Challis?'

She told herself she should just get up and walk out. But the two camera operators were continuing to film, and she realised a walk-out would be used as an admission of guilt. 'I really don't see what this—'

'My information,' Thomas went on, 'is that Mr Challis is an influential businessman. I've been looking into him as a case study in my research into standards in public life. He seems to be a man with his finger in many different commercial pies, as it were. The common factor is that he's not been afraid to buy influence to further his business interests.'

Margaret looked up at Railstone. 'I hope you've got your lawyers well prepared. Gareth's claims seem to be verging on the libellous.'

'Only if I can't evidence their accuracy.' Thomas smiled. 'I've amassed some very interesting documentary evidence, and we also have covert footage of Challis himself boasting about some of the people he claims to have bought over the years. That was why we thought you might appreciate the opportunity for a right of reply. A chance to refute Challis's claims.'

Margaret looked over at Alastair Winters as if hoping he might help her out. But his smile matched Thomas's. For them, this was clearly a job well done.

'I've really no idea what Mr Challis might be claiming. From what you're saying, I assume he isn't the most reliable of witnesses.'

'But you do know him? Or at least you knew him at the time of your retirement.'

She hesitated. If she had to lie, she wanted to keep it as close to the truth as possible. 'I came across him a few times during my time in the force, yes. As you say, he's an influential figure locally.'

'Our information is that you did rather more than come across him.' Thomas's intonation made the words sound like an innuendo.

'I'm not sure where you've obtained this so-called information.'

Thomas's smile widened. 'From various sources. Including our filming of Mr Challis himself. He claims that you were – well, let's say friends. And that for a number of years you were effectively on his payroll.'

'You can look at my record as a police officer. There was never any suggestion of inappropriate conduct. I took early retirement voluntarily at a time of my own choosing.'

'That's why I found this case study so interesting. Challis claims a number of public officials, including other senior police officers, were on his payroll. He claims an investigation into his activities at the time was discontinued because its findings would have been too embarrassing to the great and the good in the region.'

'This is ridiculous,' Margaret said. 'As far as I'm aware, Challis is just some two-bit builder. I don't know the circumstances in which you've filmed him saying this nonsense, but I'm assuming it's nothing more than him mouthing off in his cups. He's not even a has-been. Just a never-was trying to pretend he once had some influence.'

'You seem to be protesting a bit too much, Margaret. Challis is a very successful businessman, with considerable influence. I'm interested in how he acquired that influence. I assure you that the sources of our information are impeccable. Are you denying that you were, to use Challis's own words, on his payroll?'

She had been well and truly stitched up. She realised that now. There had never been television programme, or at least not one of the kind that Railstone had described to her. This was some investigative documentary that Railstone, Thomas and Winters had cooked up between them. They'd known she'd never agree to be interviewed on this topic if they'd approached her straightforwardly.

That wouldn't have stopped them cobbling together something based on whatever evidence they had, but it would have lacked the dramatic impact of this interview. Her guess was that their substantive evidence was thin or non-existent, or they'd have ambushed her with something more damning. By throwing these questions at her in an interview recorded as live, they'd capture her squirming and looking guilty. She could imagine how that could be made to appear.

She couldn't control how this would be edited, but she was damned if she was going to make it easy for them. 'I'm afraid I'm not prepared to take this nonsense any further. I've been invited to this studio under false pretences by individuals who clearly care nothing for integrity or truth.

That includes you, Mr Thomas, as well as Mr Winters and Mr Railstone, the so-called producer of this travesty. The three of you have lied to me, wasted my time, and now have the audacity to pontificate about standards in public life. I suggest you in the media look at getting your own house in order before you start lecturing to others. With that I'll wish you all a not remotely fond goodbye.'

She made every effort to maintain her composure as she rose and walked from the room, remembering to pick up her handbag and overcoat from the pegs by the door as she passed. She was pleased that the door slammed satisfyingly behind her.

Outside, it was still raining, a dull, seemingly endless drizzle from an iron-grey sky. Inevitably, she had left something behind after all – the umbrella she'd propped up in the corner of the entrance lobby – but she had no intention of returning for it. She turned up her collar, ducked her head, and walked, slowly but purposefully, back to her car.

It hadn't been a bad speech on the spur of the moment, she thought. It would never be shown, of course, unless they managed to edit it to make her look even more foolish. At least it had given her a few moments of satisfaction and denied them the look of guilt or embarrassment they'd no doubt been hoping for.

She still couldn't believe they'd gone to these lengths to set her up. But then how much effort or expense had really been involved? A lunch, a few coffees. The whole phoney edifice had been constructed round her own vanity and stupidity. They'd known how to suck her in, and she'd jumped at the opportunity. She wondered how many others they'd lured in and what tricks they'd used.

It didn't matter, she told herself. She'd maintained her dignity in the face of the most shameless provocation. She'd probably kiboshed whatever burgeoning media career she might have had, but she'd most likely been deluding herself about that anyway. It was one thing to appear as a talking head on panel shows and news reviews. It was another to believe you were about to embark on a full television career at an age when even experienced presenters might struggle to find work.

The more important question, she thought, was what information they really did have about Ryan Challis. She still felt confident that there was unlikely to be anything of real substance. Challis wasn't a careless man. And if they'd had anything really damning they'd have used it to stop her walking out.

Nevertheless, they clearly had something. Gareth Thomas had sounded too confident to have nothing up his sleeve. Normally, she might not have bothered too much. The force had been content to bury the truth at the time. She couldn't imagine it would be in anyone's interest to start digging it up now. But too much was happening all at once. There was always a risk that somewhere, somehow, someone would start fitting some of the pieces together.

She finally reached her car. It was only once she was inside that she finally felt able to drop the steely demeanour she'd maintained since leaving the studio. Then, as the rain drummed steadily on the car roof, she finally allowed herself to cry.

Chapter Thirty

'Anything new?'

Zoe slumped down on the seat opposite Annie's desk and took a large swallow of her coffee. 'Well, we're making good progress in the sense that we've interviewed a lot of people. Less so in the sense that we don't seem to have much to show for it.'

'Usually the way.'

'Suppose so. The main thing that seems to be coming through is that Ellsworth seems to have been a bit of an enigma. She clearly had a big impact on the school, and most of the staff we've spoken to seem broadly positive about her. But no one seems to have had much of a sense of her as a person.'

'If I worked in a place like this, I might want to keep my private life just that. Can you imagine the gossip?'

Zoe gave a shiver that didn't seem entirely feigned. 'Tell me about it. To be honest, this place still gives me the creeps. It feels horribly claustrophobic to me.'

'What about Ellsworth's life outside school? Anything there?'

'She just seems to have kept it very private. She doesn't often seem to have invited any of the staff or pupils to her house, other than these organised get-togethers. Those almost feel like a deliberate attempt to keep curiosity at bay. As if Ellsworth was just allowing sufficient access to her domestic life to demonstrate she had nothing to hide.'

'What about the pupils?' Annie said. 'They can sometimes have more of an insight into these things than the supposed adults.'

'Can't argue with that. We're making slower progress talking to the pupils because of the safeguarding issues, but we've talked to a few who, for one reason or another, were perceived as Ellsworth's favourites.'

'Anything in that? The favourite thing?'

'Difficult to say. It's not something that the girls in question seem to have been particularly conscious of. Ellsworth just seems to have been interested in the pupils – and maybe the teachers – who had something more to offer. She seems to have devoted a bit more attention to them.'

'Hence her interest in Melanie Donnelly?'

'Funny you should say that,' Zoe said. 'I got an interesting perspective on Donnelly.'

'Go on.'

'From Samantha Challis. The head girl.'

Annie felt the mild unease she always experienced at the mention of the Challis name. 'Challis? We interviewed her during the inquiry into Donnelly's death. She didn't seem to have much to offer.'

'I read through the previous interview notes before I spoke to her. Don't think the guy who interviewed her warmed to her too much.'

'"Snooty and supercilious", I think were the words.'

'He wasn't wrong about that. But I thought there was more to her than met the eye. Maybe she responded better to a female interviewer.'

'Or maybe you're more skilled at interviewing than some of your colleagues.' Annie smiled.

'If you say so. Anyway, it seemed to work with Samantha. We spent a bit of time initially dancing round each other. She was keen to have her status recognised—'

'As head girl?' Annie raised an eyebrow.

'As a generally superior human being from a much higher social class, I think. I was happy for her to believe that, if it meant she relaxed a bit. Anyway, eventually she did, and she began to talk much more openly. She didn't seem to have much time for Ellsworth. I suspect Samantha rather despises anyone who would allow themselves to do anything as mundane as teaching.'

'I hope Samantha never loses her privileged lifestyle. The real world might come as a bit of a shock to her.'

'I suspect it will anyway at some point. But she didn't see herself as a favourite of Ellsworth's. The interesting thing is that she didn't really think that Melanie had been a favourite of Ellsworth's either.'

'I thought Samantha didn't have much of an opinion of Melanie. The impression I'd got was that Melanie was rather beneath her contempt.'

'I had the feeling she was more interested in Melanie than she wanted to let on.'

'In what way?'

'I think she was intrigued by Melanie. Melanie was a much more complex and interesting individual than Samantha will allow herself to be. Melanie wasn't defined by her wealth or social standing. I don't think Samantha can quite compute that. She made a few half-hearted attempts to dismiss Melanie as some kind of geek but it didn't quite ring true to me. And she made a few disparaging comments about champagne socialists, but that just sounded like a line she'd filched from somewhere else. If anything, I had the sense that Samantha almost admired Melanie. Not that she'd ever use that word.'

Annie nodded. 'I can see how that would work, yes. But she didn't think Melanie was really a favourite of Ellsworth's. Why did she say that?'

'She agreed Ellsworth did have favourites, but that they were generally more predictable than Melanie. She wasn't exactly a troublemaker – she was too smart for that. But she stirred things up. Samantha reckoned Ellsworth didn't like that.'

'I thought Ellsworth was keen on those with a spark of originality.'

'Not the way Samantha tells it. She thought that Ellsworth was initially impressed by Melanie but had begun to see her as a pain in the backside. Samantha reckoned that, if Melanie's parents hadn't been who they were, she'd have got into a lot more trouble than she did. Melanie recognised that and decided to push the boundaries with the benefactor stuff.'

'How does Samantha know all this?' Annie said. 'I thought she and Melanie had nothing to do with each other?'

'I reckon there might have been more of a relationship between them than we'd thought.'

'I can't imagine they had much in common.'

'No, me neither. When I asked Samantha about that she was very vague. It felt almost as if I'd caught her out, or at least as if she'd shot her mouth off more than she'd intended.'

'You think she's hiding something?'

'Maybe. It feels as if there's something more there.'

'Something pertinent to Melanie's death?'

'That's where I'm hesitating. I reckon if Samantha genuinely knew something about Melanie's death, she'd relish being the centre of attention. She wouldn't be able to keep quiet.'

'Unless it's something that incriminates her.'

'Maybe not even then. But I don't think so. She seemed to be talking too openly for that. It was more as if there was something she and Melanie had shared. To be honest, I'd wondered if it was just that Melanie had written about her father's donations to the school.'

'Samantha wouldn't have liked that, surely? Apart from anything else, isn't that why she was made head girl?'

'That's not how Samantha sees it. It's another thing she's permanently embarrassed about. She thinks she's there on her own merits, and she's not keen on suggestions that her dad just bought it for her.'

'Heaven forbid.'

'I didn't get the impression there was much love lost between Samantha and her father.'

'What's the problem? Father too common for her?'

'Exactly that, I'd have said. We know what sort of reputation Ryan Challis has around these parts. I don't imagine Samantha would want to be associated with that.'

'I can see that. Even Challis's best friends — assuming he has any — would describe him as a rough diamond.'

'It's not going to get any easier for her,' Zoe said. 'I understand Challis has just been appointed Chair of Governors.'

'Really? Who'd vote for Ryan Challis? And why would be want the job anyway? He's never exactly struck me as the public-spirited type. I can only see Challis taking on that kind of role if he thought there was something in it for him.'

'I don't get the impression the governors are a notably democratic institution. Challis has apparently been a governor for a few years, presumably as a result of his donations, but he's never been very active. Last night was apparently his first night in the chair.'

'Interesting coincidence. So the first issue he'd have been dealing with was what they do after Ellsworth's death.'

'And how they should go about finding Ellsworth's successor.'

'I wonder what the other governors make of Challis. He probably isn't exactly their type.' Annie rose and walked over to the window. From here she could see the rear of the dark gothic bulk of the school. In the distance, past the building, she could see the edge of the school's playing fields. The rain was still coming down, as if the weather might continue like this forever. The same sheeting drizzle, the same leaden skies. Like Zoe, she was beginning to find this place oppressive. 'It's quite a place this, isn't it? How are you coping, Zo? Not getting to you too much?'

Zoe looked unsurprised by the question. 'I'd rather be somewhere else. I won't hide that. But I'm doing okay.'

'I can get you moved on to something else if it would help, Zo. It sounds like Andy might have made a bit of a breakthrough on the Meresham case. Stuart might be amenable to shifting some resource back to that.'

'I don't want to be treated as a charity case, Annie. I'm either up to this job or I'm not. And for the avoidance of doubt,' she added, 'I think I am.'

'I didn't mean—'

'I know you didn't. I know you've got my best interests at heart and all that. But I don't want anyone – not Stuart, not even you – thinking I'm not up to it.'

To Annie, Zoe sounded more brittle than she'd ever done, but it wasn't the moment to offer that observation. 'I know you're up to it, Zo. I just don't want to put you in a difficult position.'

'I'm fine. In any case, the Meresham case is going nowhere. You know that as well as I do. All credit to Andy for following up on that comment of Peter Arnold's, but most likely he's just confirmed it's a dead case. If the bones are confirmed as Jayne Arnold's, or even if they're not, it just gives Stuart an excuse to shut the whole thing down. Case effectively closed, with Alan Harwood pinned as the killer. Harwood's dead and no one's going to shed any tears for him.'

'Okay. I'd much rather have you working on this. But if you do find it's becoming too much, just say. We've all got our own histories to deal with. I know that better than anyone.'

That was all too true. Her mother was always there as a reminder of their joint histories, and it was something Annie would never entirely put behind her. Now, like a ghost from that past, Ryan Challis had appeared to stir up the memories still further. Perhaps, she thought, it was time she confronted that history.

Chapter Thirty-One

There was a phrase for it now, wasn't there? What did they call it? FOMO. Fear of missing out. It was the idea – which admittedly Andy Metcalfe had felt for most of his teenage and adult life – that everyone else was off having more fun than you were.

He was stuck here in an empty office while most of his colleagues were off participating in a major inquiry. This time he really was missing out. He was missing out on the invaluable experience, the opportunity to build stronger relationships with his workmates, the chance to involve himself in a full-scale murder inquiry. He'd tried out these arguments on Stuart Jennings the previous afternoon, raising the issue as tactfully as he could.

He'd felt that he was making some headway with Jennings, but yet again Jennings had promised only to revisit the situation once they'd had confirmation of the identity of the human remains. Andy couldn't really see that it made much difference whether or not the bones were those of Jayne Arnold or some other poor teenager. But with any luck the information would come through today and Jennings would be forced to make a decision.

In the meantime, Andy had been dutifully ploughing his way through the files sent over from South Yorkshire Police. He couldn't really imagine what they were likely to gain from this material, but at least for the moment it gave him a way of filling his time.

As he'd expected, the files didn't add enormously to the narrative he'd already pieced together from the various newspapers of the time. There were some disturbing – in some cases, harrowing – transcripts with Harwood's victims. Andy sensed from the interviews that many of the victims had kept this secret bottled up for many years, manipulated by Harwood into believing the shame was theirs rather than his. Once the first victim had spoken out, it was almost as if a spell had been broken. In the weeks after Harwood's arrest, the police had received a stream of similar complaints from girls and women who had been Harwood's students over the years. It was clear that, in preparing their evidence against Harwood, the police had selected several cases where the victims were credible and articulate, and where there was a pattern of consistent behaviour reported by individuals who'd had no previous contact with each other. The picture that emerged was damning.

Alongside those, there were numerous other cases which, for one reason or another, had not been prosecuted. It was evident that Harwood's behaviour had continued over many years, and that, with minor variations to reflect the different contexts and circumstances, his manipulative techniques had been systematically refined over that time. Andy wondered, bleakly, if there were parallels with Harwood's musical career – a similar dedication to a set of well-practised skills.

Smailes had been right, though. There was nothing in any of the case files to indicate Harwood would have been capable of kidnapping a victim off the street. He came across, both in his own interviews and in others' accounts, as an oddly passive figure. It was clear from the way he spoke that, grotesquely, he saw himself more as victim than as perpetrator. Although he largely avoided saying so explicitly, he gave the impression that he saw his acts as consensual, as if he believed that his victims had been complicit in, or even responsible for, his behaviour.

Harwood had needed that veil of illusion. He'd needed to persuade himself, as well as his victims, that he wasn't the monster others might imagine. It was an illusion that, in each case, he'd built up gradually, painstakingly working on each girl to change her understanding of reality. It was difficult to imagine this man simply snatching a victim off the street. Andy was no psychologist, but that didn't seem to fit the profile of the man he'd been reading about.

The associated question was whether Harwood would have been capable of killing Jayne Arnold. There were very few instances in the case files of Harwood engaging in any physical violence, although he had clearly lost his temper on a few occasions when his victims had proved resistant to his blandishments. But the anger came across as tetchy and schoolmasterly, rather than as anything that might lead to overt violence.

The case files revealed little at all that seemed pertinent. In preparing their evidence against Harwood, the police had devoted some time to trying to piece together a picture of Harwood himself. Reading between the lines of the police statements, one of their major concerns had been to cast doubts on Harwood's apparent respectability. There had clearly been a fear that, faced with the lack of corroborative evidence that almost inevitably characterises an accusation of sexual assault, a jury might choose to believe the word of an apparently respected and distinguished elderly man rather than the potentially faulty memory of his past students. In the end, the sheer volume of the evidence against Harwood had been sufficient to allay that concern. But in collating the material, the police had sought to establish an image of Harwood that would counter his public profile.

The picture that emerged, fairly or unfairly, was of a man perceived by his colleagues as an oddball. He was seen as a loner, with little time for social interaction with his fellow musicians. Those who'd worked with him had a high regard for his professionalism and dedication, and most were highly complimentary about his abilities. But there was a general sense that Harwood had little or nothing in his life beyond music.

There was little in the files about Harwood's earlier life. His father had apparently died when Harwood was still a child, and Harwood been brought up by his mother and grandmother in Ashbourne. His musical talents had been obvious from a relatively young age and he'd won a music scholarship to a local independent school, and eventually obtained a place at the Royal Northern College of Music.

There was no reference in the files to Harwood's time in Meresham, and no clue what might have brought him there. He had lived at various points in the 1970s and 1980s in Manchester, London and Newcastle, presumably following the progression of his professional career. At some point in the late 1970s, for reasons unknown, he'd begun using the name Kenneth McRae in both his personal and professional life.

From the mid-1980s onward – that is, from the time of the first case for which he was prosecuted – he had settled in Manchester, having bought a house in Didsbury which had remained his base until his retirement. During those years, he'd supplemented his career by teaching, both at various schools across the city and, supposedly for those he perceived as particularly 'promising', through personal tuition. Andy shuddered slightly at the thought of what 'promising' might have meant in this context, and how Harwood would have presented that to the child's parents.

To his colleagues, Harwood had remained an enigma. He'd been pleasant enough in his day-to-day dealings with his fellow musicians and was perceived as easy to work with. But he'd never participated in any of the social activities which some of his colleagues had enjoyed. No one had seemed to have any knowledge of his private life, but some had echoed the sentiments expressed by Ken Smailes, commenting that Harwood had always seemed slightly overwhelmed by the demands of everyday existence. 'He always looked uncomfortable when he had to interact with others, and I had the sense he was intimidated by stuff that most of us see as routine – shopping, paying bills, organising his life. The only time he really looked at ease was when he was playing.'

Andy turned wearily through file after file, hoping to find some detail that might help open up his understanding of Harwood or, more importantly, of what might have happened in Meresham all those years ago. Finally, with a growing sense of futility, he turned to the packages prepared for the trial itself. He couldn't envisage that these were likely to add much to what he already knew. The prosecution files would be little more than an appropriately condensed version of the mass of material he had already waded through. The defence files would most likely relate to the specific cases that had been prosecuted, along with more generic character statements.

As Andy had expected, the defence case had rested largely on demonstrating Harwood's respectability and

235

apparent trustworthiness. There were statements from distinguished figures in the music world extolling Harwood's virtues. There were statements from the head teachers of leading schools confirming that they had employed Harwood without any reported complaints. There were statements from Harwood's fellow musicians commenting on his professionalism and his dedication to his art.

Andy was left with the impression that Harwood had groomed his associates as skilfully as he'd groomed his victims. He was seen as an eccentric, certainly, but no one had imagined him as capable of this kind of act. Most had assumed, if they assumed anything at all, that Harwood was essentially sexless, just not interested in anything much beyond his beloved music.

It was only towards the back of these testimonials that Andy finally found something potentially interesting. The bulk of the character statements had been obtained from individuals who had known Harwood during the years relating to the various charges. But the defence team had clearly recognised that this parade of Harwood's professional associates provided a limited perspective on Harwood's character – the public face he presented to the world rather than whatever reality might lie behind it.

It was evident that the defence had cast their net widely in their efforts to counter this, but with limited results. Harwood's mother and grandmother, the constant presences in his childhood, were both deceased. He had no other close relatives and no close friends.

In their efforts to track down someone who had known Harwood outside a work context, they had finally identified a cousin who had known Harwood, albeit from something of a distance. Even here, despite the close family connection, the link was a tenuous one and the cousin had had no real contact with Harwood for many years. 'I can't claim to know him well,' the cousin had explained unhelpfully. 'The real contact was between my dad and Alan's mum. My dad's first wife and Alan's mum were sisters, and even after they both married they stayed close. My dad's wife died unexpectedly of cancer not long after Alan's dad had also died. The sisters and their husbands had always spent a lot of time together, so I guess my dad and Alan's mum looked to each other for support. I really don't know if their relationship was ever anything more than a friendship but my dad became a kind of surrogate father to his nephew by marriage, Alan. This was long before I was born so he had no children of his own. He was in awe of Alan's talents, but always reckoned Alan needed a hand dealing with everyday life. For years, my dad acted as a guardian to him, helping to sort out all the practical stuff Alan struggled with. Not in his professional career – Alan had an agent for that, though I think it was my dad who helped him sort all that out in the first place – but day-to-day stuff like finding accommodation. He even helped Alan buy his first home and did all the work to do it up. He was a builder, like me.'

It had been the word 'builder' that caught Alan's eye. Was it possible that, quite by chance – or at least by the kind of chance that occurs when you've spent two days working systematically through a mass of files – he had come across the identity of the man who had worked for Harwood on the cottage in Meresham?

'By that stage,' the interview transcript continued, 'my dad had remarried and his contact with Alan's mum had gradually decreased. But he kept up his support for Alan for a good few years after that, much to my mum's annoyance. I've sometimes wondered if there might have been more to Alan's parentage than my dad's ever let on – he's not normally that generous in throwing his time and money about – but that's his business. Things changed after I was born. My mum became less tolerant of Dad spending time helping Alan. By the time I was aware of things, he was more like a family friend. To me, he was just another adult. Pleasant enough, a bit shy, obviously obsessed with his music above all else. For what it's worth, he always seemed a bit awkward with children. He never seemed to know what to make of me, and he certainly never tried anything on...'

'Bloody hell, Andy. You've been busy.'

Andy looked up from the file to see Stuart Jennings standing in the door of the office, looking around at the heaps of documents filling the floor. It was difficult to tell whether his expression was one of admiration or pity.

'Just thought I might as well try to make as much headway as possible before—'

'Before I gave you something useful to do? Probably a good idea.' Jennings grinned. 'Don't worry, Andy. I know this isn't the kind of cutting-edge, vital stuff you expected to be doing when you joined the team, but it's all part of the job. And, credit to you, you've been doing it well.'

Andy decided to accept the compliment at face value. For once, Jennings sounded sincere enough. 'Thanks.'

'And I come bearing news. We finally have the white smoke.'

'White smoke?'

'On the DNA tests. There's no doubt. Our bones are definitely those of Jayne Arnold. After forty-six years, we've finally found her.'

Andy felt as if the discovery ought to be accompanied by some sense of achievement. But he felt the opposite. Having read the news reports and case notes from the time, he was conscious only of the wasted years. The years in which Jayne Arnold's parents must have sat, still hoping for some positive news – that their daughter might be sighted somewhere, safe and well. Then, after the hope had finally died, perhaps longing for nothing more than an answer. An explanation as to why their daughter had never come home.

'So what does that mean?' Andy asked.

'It means that, at least to some extent, the media are going to run with this. So we have to decide how we're going to handle it. I can't really imagine that anyone other than Alan Harwood is responsible for Jayne Arnold's death. It's all just too much of a bloody coincidence otherwise. And that would get us off the investigative hook, given that Harwood's already popped his proverbials.' He paused. 'But.'

'But?'

'I'm with you on this, Andy. Something doesn't feel right. There's something missing. Although it's not likely after forty-six years, I don't want that something reappearing to bite us on the bum. I think for the moment we need to continue working on this.'

Which means, Andy translated for himself, you want *me* to carry on working on it.

As if reading Andy's thoughts, Jennings continued, 'I'll try to bring in some further resource, but it's not easy with the Ellsworth case ongoing, so in the meantime...'

'That's fine.' Andy tried hard not to allow any note of annoyance creep into his voice. He gestured to the room at large. 'It's not as if I'm short of material to work on.'

'Any luck with any of this?'

'Most of it's just the same old stuff, only in more detail. But there's one thing...' He opened the file of character statements and pushed it across to Jennings. 'Transcript of an interview with one of the few people who seems to have known Harwood in his younger days.'

'And?'

'It's not terribly informative. It looks as if this guy's father became a kind of surrogate father to Harwood after Harwood's real father died. Harwood's uncle – married Harwood's mother's sister.'

'I'm just about keeping up. That was generous of him. The uncle, I mean.'

'It was, wasn't it – to the point where the son wondered about Harwood's paternity.'

'Ah. So where does this get us?'

'Nowhere, in itself. But the uncle helped Harwood to buy his first house and carried out building works.'

'Building works?'

'I mean, it may be nothing. It may be a different house entirely. But it's worth exploring.'

'If this guy was working on Harwood's cottage in 1976, he'd be pretty elderly or even dead by now. We're going to have as much trouble tracking him down as we did Peter Arnold.'

'Except that we have the name and contact details for the son. From ten years ago, admittedly, but that's better than forty-six years. And the son was also working as a builder, so he's quite likely still operating. We should be able to track him down.'

'Now that sounds a lot more promising. What's this guy's name?'

Andy looked back down at the file. 'Challis,' he said. 'Ryan Challis.'

Chapter Thirty-Two

Margaret Delamere stood at the large window looking down on the city. When she'd bought this place, one of the attractions had been the balcony. She'd envisaged sitting out there in the summer evenings, glass of wine in hand, a book on her lap, some appropriate classical music playing gently in the background, while the city continued its business below. Or being out there with a group of friends, sharing drinks and canapés, chatting about whatever it was groups of friends chatted about when they got together.

It had never happened, or at least not like that. Yes, there'd been some fine summer evenings, and she'd sat out there reading a book or a magazine. But the traffic was noisier than she'd hoped, the wind stronger and more blustery than she liked, and she'd never felt entirely comfortable. The friends had never materialised, mainly, she now realised, because she didn't actually have many friends.

She'd always thought of herself as the sociable type, able to chat comfortably with anyone of any background or social standing. She'd seen herself as having a wide circle of contacts. She'd enjoyed feeling part of whatever in-crowd applied to people of her age.

All of that had been true. It was just that none of those people had ever really been *friends*. She'd had real friends among her colleagues in the force, but she'd left most of those behind on retirement. Once she'd retired no one had made much effort to try to contact her, and she'd politely rebuffed those who had.

Since her retirement, she'd built up a new set of contacts, but none of them were what she'd really call friends. For the most part, they were people like those she'd been faced with today. People like Trevor Railstone, Alastair Winters and bloody Gareth Thomas. People who glad-handed her when it suited them, while preparing to stab her in the back. Journalists who called her only when they wanted a quote. Radio and TV researchers who were eager to invite her on to their programmes as long as she could be available down the line in the next fifteen minutes. Organisers of events who were keen for her to give a talk, as long as she was willing to do it free of charge, for her 'profile'.

She'd even become estranged from her own daughter. Annie called dutifully a couple of times a week and still popped round occasionally for a coffee. But they couldn't talk without ending up sparring, each trying to score points off the other. Margaret couldn't pretend this was a new development. Their relationship had soured over the years, through Annie's rebellious teenage years, her subsequent decision to join the police herself, Margaret's quietly ignominious departure from the force, and then Annie's relationship with Sheena Pearson. Each of those, in its different way, had driven a wedge between the two of them, and Margaret wasn't sure the breach could ever now be repaired.

Somehow Margaret had sailed through all that, unaware how much her isolation was increasing. With so much going on in her life, she'd fooled herself into thinking she was at the heart of things. Today's events had brought home to her that for the most part she was simply being used.

Suddenly everything was going wrong at the same time. Everything she'd held together for decades, even under the most severe of tests, was splintering, slowly breaking apart. She supposed that had been inevitable, even though she'd persuaded herself otherwise. At each stage, she'd cobbled together some sort of solution, but each time she'd put a little bit more of her soul into hock. She'd signed the proverbial deal with the devil, and sometime soon he'd be coming to collect.

Now the balcony in front of her just looked bleak. It had been raining all day and it felt as if it might rain forever. On a clear day, you could see from here all the way to the fringes of the Peak District, the blue hills lining the horizon like the distant memory of something better. Today there was nothing but haze, the grey fog of drizzle ringing the city.

She turned and walked into the kitchen. She hesitated a moment and then opened the cupboard she used as drinks cabinet. Margaret had never been much of a drinker, and the cabinet was filled with a motley selection of half-empty bottles of spirits she'd acquired over the years. On the shelf above, there was a small wine-rack containing a selection of wine – her more usual drink – which she received quarterly from a wine club she'd subscribed to years before.

After a moment's thought, she pulled out a bottle of a single malt she'd bought, mainly as a souvenir, on a visit to the Highlands a couple of years before. She knew nothing about whisky, but it was a taste she enjoyed when she was in the mood and, just at this moment, she felt very much in the mood. She poured a large measure and returned to the living room. She forced herself to sit down on the sofa and to take a sip of the Scotch, enjoying the smoky taste, the burn at the back of her throat.

She had to face this on her own. There was literally no one she could talk to about this. Annie – perhaps, despite their differences, the one person who might listen to her troubles – was out of the question. The only way she could involve Annie was by compromising her in the same way Margaret herself was compromised. Annie – righteous, straight-as-a-die Annie – would never be prepared to accept that. Even if she was, it wasn't a price Margaret could ask her to pay.

She'd dealt with this before, so surely she could find a way of doing it again. Another way of kicking the can further down the road, at least. She'd tried to fool herself that one day, somehow, this would all go away. She knew now that was unlikely to happen. All she could do, yet again, was find another way of staving off the consequences. She took another mouthful of the whisky, trying to use the alcohol to kickstart her thinking.

The first question was how much trouble she was really in. Gareth Thomas's verbal attack today had been full of suggestion and innuendo, but she suspected there was little of substance behind it. The circumstances of her retirement had been kept very quiet, in line with the agreement she'd reached at the time, but she didn't doubt that they'd leaked more widely than the small number of people who'd been privy to that agreement. It probably wouldn't have taken any particularly persistent investigative journalism to find someone prepared to share the rumours. The question was whether Thomas actually had any hard evidence. The real problems would arise if

Thomas's programme was ever made and broadcast. If that encouraged people to start digging more deeply into her case, the consequences could be severe – and not only for her.

The worst part of this was that that particular can of worms was now being opened from both ends. Gareth Thomas was delving into the more recent consequences. At the same time, someone, for whatever reason, seemed determined to disrupt the uneasy equilibrium they'd established over all this time.

She couldn't fully understand what had disturbed that balance. Perhaps it had just been anxiety or conscience, prompted by the recent discovery. But they'd always known that that might happen, and they'd known that it would almost certainly make no difference. All they had to do was keep their heads down, keep on as they'd agreed, and all would continue to be well.

But now something had gone wrong. Whatever had prompted it – a sudden panic, a slowly mounting sense of guilt – it had unleashed something more disturbing than Margaret could ever have expected. The horror was no longer behind her. It was with her now. It might, even at this moment, be waiting for her. It might, conceivably, be waiting outside the door of her flat.

She had pieced that thought together slowly, not wanting to believe it. They'd all made different decisions over the years – some, in Margaret's view, less than wise – but she had assumed they were all in this together, protecting themselves by protecting each other. She had clung to that idea even when she'd seen the news, not wanting to face the implications of what it might mean.

There might be other explanations, she tried to tell herself. Perhaps Challis was even more ruthless than she'd imagined. But that made no sense. Challis was many things, but ultimately he was a pragmatist. He'd do what needed to be done – and she'd sometimes felt uneasy at quite what he was prepared to do – but he didn't take unnecessary risks. If he'd wanted to take action, he'd have done it discreetly, quietly, in a way that wouldn't have attracted anyone's attention.

After that, as she'd sat thinking in the long hours that had passed since her humiliation at the hands of Gareth Thomas, she concluded there was only one possibility.

There was no one she could talk to about this without risking dragging them all even further down into the mire. That might in the end be unavoidable, but in the meantime she needed to take one more shot at salvaging everything.

She couldn't stay hiding forever. There was only one thing she could do. And that was to confront this head-on.

Chapter Thirty-Three

'I feel as if Andy Metcalfe should be doing this,' Zoe Everett said. 'He's earned it.'

'We're only going for a chat,' Annie Delamere pointed out. 'That's how Stuart wanted to play it, given how little information we have. If we're eventually in a position to turn this into something more formal, Andy'll get his moment of glory.'

'I hope so. I still feel guilty for leaving him dumped with the Meresham case.'

'That was Stuart's decision. Anyway, he's done a good job with it. It won't do his reputation any harm.'

'I guess you're right.'

'He's bright *and* dogged. It's a good combination. He'll go far.' Annie glanced over at the satnav. They'd just passed through Ashbourne heading north and were due to turn left in the next quarter mile. 'I suggest we play this on the basis that we're here mainly to talk about Lavinia Ellsworth. That was what I indicated to Challis when I contacted him. He reckoned there wasn't much he could tell us as he hadn't really known Ellsworth personally. I played to his ego. Told him we'd be wanting to talk to all the governors in due course so I thought it was important we spoke to him first as the newly appointed Chair.'

'He's got a high opinion of himself, then?'

'He's your archetypal self-made man. Rough diamond, as they say. He's obviously relishing lording it over the posh types on the board of governors. This looks like the turn.' She followed a B-road up into the hills. Moments later, the satnav directed them to take a further left turn up a single-track road. Ahead they could see an imposing former farmhouse perched on the brow of the hill.

Annie turned off the road into the sweeping driveway. Challis's house was imposing and had clearly had money spent on it, mostly in ways that seemed designed to impress visitors or passers-by. Another householder might have worried about the risk of attracting burglars with such a display of external ostentation, but Annie guessed any clued-up thief would think twice before trying his luck on Ryan Challis's house.

She pulled up beside what she took to be Challis's large Mercedes. The rain had shown no sign of lessening during their drive from the school, and Annie was grateful for the porch that provided them with partial shelter as they waited for Challis to respond to the doorbell.

The door opened and a large shaven-headed man peered out at them. Annie had seen various photographs of Challis, but the reality was more intimidating than she'd expected. He was well over six feet, with a broad, slightly overweight body to match. He wore a single earring in his left ear, and he stared at them with an expression Annie characterised as amiable belligerence, as if he might be looking forward to getting into a fight with you. 'Yes?'

'DI Delamere and DS Everett. I called earlier.'

'Oh, aye.' He blinked as if trying to retrieve the memory. 'You'd best come in. Pissing down still, I see.' He had a strong Derbyshire accent, which Annie could imagine him exaggerating when it suited him.

He led them into a large hallway and then through into a living room. The room was as tastefully decorated as the exterior of the house, though Annie imagined Challis hadn't had much of a hand in it. 'Nice place.'

'Thought it was better to meet here than at work. All hard hats and gravel there. I'd offer you a coffee but the wife's away. Down in London giving the credit card a hammering.'

Annie was mildly impressed that Challis had managed to sum up his character and approach to life so well in just a couple of short sentences. 'We shouldn't keep you long. We just wanted to talk to you about Lavinia Ellsworth.'

He threw himself down into one of the armchairs, inviting them to sit on the sofa opposite. 'Nasty business. Sooner you catch the bastard the better. String him up.'

'Can I ask how well you knew Ms Ellsworth?'

'Not particularly well. We'd met a few times at school events and suchlike, what with our Sam being head girl and all. Then obviously I've had a few dealings with her since I joined the governors. I'm not sure what to say, really. Capable woman. Always presented herself well at the meetings. Seemed on top of things. I'd no complaints.'

'Did you get the impression she was well liked in the school?'

'By the girls? Can only go by what Sam's told me – and she doesn't tell me a lot these days. Not sure "liked" was the right word, but I'm not sure it should be. I'm a believer in old-fashioned discipline. I'd say Ellsworth was well respected. Firm but fair.'

'What about among the staff?'

'Couldn't say, really. Never saw any signs of any problems.'

'You're not aware of anyone who might have reasons to harm her?'

'Reckon you're barking up the wrong tree, lass, if you think one of the other staff did this. Most of that lot wouldn't say boo to a goose. This'll be some little toerag off his tits on drugs, something like that.'

'We obviously have to look at all possibilities, Mr Challis.'

'Aye, I just know where I'd be looking if I was in your shoes.'

'Rest assured, we'll be exploring all avenues.' It was true that, despite the absence of any evidence of a break-in, they were looking at all the local housebreakers as a routine part of the investigation. Most of them were small fry, though, and in Annie's view would most likely have fled the scene rather than commit a murder of that brutality. 'We'd also like to know more about Ms Ellsworth's life outside the school. Are you aware of any friends or other contacts she might have had other than the staff and governors?'

This time, Annie thought she detected something different in Challis's response, as if his former casual manner had been overlain by a new wariness. 'You're asking the wrong bloke. I've no idea about Ellsworth's life outside the school. She always struck me as a woman who didn't have much in her life except work.'

'I just wondered if she might have mentioned anyone or any interests. You must have chatted to her at the governors' meetings.'

'She wasn't one for idle chat,' Challis said. 'If we chatted, we were talking shop.'

'Yes, of course.'

'I'm sorry, lass. I feel I'm wasting your time here, but I did warn you. There's not really anything I can tell you about Ellsworth.'

'Can I ask you about another topic? We understand you've made a number of sizeable financial donations to the school?'

'Aye. What of it?'

'I just wondered what had prompted you to do that.'

Challis laughed. 'I wasn't trying to buy my way into Ellsworth's knickers, if that's what you're thinking. There was nowt between me and her.'

Annie was struck by his need to deny something that hadn't even been implied in her question. She also guessed Challis was accustomed to using crudity to distract attention from what he might really be thinking or feeling. She made a mental note to delve more deeply into whether Challis might have known Ellsworth better than he was letting on. It was an unlikely pairing, but stranger things had happened.

'I was just intrigued as to your motivation for making the donations.'

'It's a good school. It's done all right by my lasses. I can afford to splash a bit of money about, and where I splash it's my business. I don't see what this has to do with Ellsworth's death.'

'Just my interest, Mr Challis. There's nothing else you can tell us that might be relevant to our inquiry?'

'I'm afraid not, lass. Like I say, probably just wasting your time.'

Annie turned to Zoe. 'Anything else you want to ask, Zoe?'

Zoe took her cue. 'There's just one other thing, Mr Challis, on a slightly different topic.'

'Aye?'

'I just wondered if you knew a man called Alan Harwood?'

This time the change in Challis's demeanour was instant and unquestionable. He sat back in his seat almost as if struck a physical blow. 'What's this have to do with Ellsworth?'

'It doesn't. Not directly,' Zoe said vaguely. 'His name's come up in connection with another case. We understand you knew him?'

'Harwood's dead.'

'We're aware of that, Mr Challis,' Annie said. 'But you did know him?'

'Aye, I knew him. I didn't know what he was, though.'

Zoe offered an unthreatening smile. 'We're just trying to build up a picture of his early life, and we'd been told you knew him. I wondered if you might be able to help us.'

'I don't see what this has to do with Ellsworth. Directly or indirectly.'

He was clearly too smart to be bamboozled, Annie thought. Smarter than he wanted you to think. Annie guessed a few of Challis's business rivals had suffered as a result of underestimating him. 'It doesn't. As Zoe said, we're looking at Alan Harwood as part of another investigation. We just thought it would be useful to take this opportunity to raise it with you rather than wasting your time with further interviews.' With the concluding words, she allowed an undertone of threat to creep into her voice. She guessed that, given that Challis's business practices, he'd rather get any questions out of the way now rather than have the police prying further into his affairs.

'Only too pleased to help. But again, I don't know what I can tell you. Harwood's been dead for years, and I hadn't seen him for even longer before that.'

'You gave a character reference at his trial?'

'They approached me. The defence was desperate to talk to anyone who knew Harwood in a personal capacity. They seemed to be hoping someone would vouch for Harwood as just another bloke. Well, good luck with that, as I told them at the time. Man was a nonce, simple as that. Just wish I'd known earlier.'

'How did you know him?'

'If you've read the notes of the interview, you'll already know the answer to that.'

'We understand he knew your father.'

'Aye, well, that was my dad's weakness. He liked lame ducks.' There was something in the way Challis said the final two words that made Annie wonder about the nature of his father's relationship with Harwood.

'He was your cousin?'

'Aye. Family. That was the reason Dad helped him out. None of us knew what he was capable of. That all came later.'

'You saw no sign of Harwood's – proclivities when you knew him?'

Challis seemed to hesitate a second too long before replying. 'Do you think I wouldn't have stopped him if I had?'

'You said he was family. We sometimes give family the benefit of the doubt even when we shouldn't.'

Challis shook his head firmly. 'I saw nowt. He was just a pathetic little man, for all his musical talent.'

'You didn't like him?'

'I wasn't allowed not to like him. My dad thought the sun shone out of his arse, so I was supposed to think the same.' Annie had the sense that if Challis had been outside, he'd had spat on the floor in disgust. 'My old man was dazzled by anything he thought was posh. He'd come from a poor background and he wanted to prove he'd made it. So he pretended to like classical music and opera and ballet, and all that bollocks. He couldn't believe he had his own virtuoso musician in the family.'

'He gave financial support to Harwood?'

'Aye, far too much.'

'He helped Harwood buy his first house?'

Challis's eyes were fixed on the rain-sodden decking through the window. 'I don't know about that.'

'You mentioned it in your interview for the trial.'

'Did I? You must be right then.'

'Can you tell us where that house was?'

Challis had been growing visibly tense during the exchange, and now Annie could sense his body almost physically tightening. Finally he turned back towards her. 'Right. That's what this is about, is it? What was found in Meresham.'

'You're aware of that, are you, Mr Challis?'

'Only what I've seen on the news. You notice stories like that when they're local.'

'Was that the house your father helped Harwood to buy?'

She could see Challis hesitate. 'Aye, that was the one. Dad gave him the deposit.'

Annie exchanged a glance with Zoe, who said, 'This hasn't been formally announced yet, but we've now had confirmation that the remains belonged to Jayne Arnold.'

'There was never much doubt about that, was there?' Challis said.

'We needed confirmation.'

'Aye, I can see that. What I don't see is what this has to do with me.' Some of his previous belligerence had returned.

'We're just looking for information, Mr Challis. We're talking about something that happened forty-six years ago, so information hasn't been easy to come by. In particular, we've been keen to identify the builder who was working on the house at the time the body was deposited there.'

Challis was staring out of the window again. The weather had closed down even further, the further reaches of the garden lost in drizzle and mist. 'Aye, that was Dad.'

'He laid the foundations under which the body was buried?'

'You'd have to ask him. Except you can't. What with him being dead for ten years or more.'

Annie had been half expecting this. It meant another source of possible information was closed to them. But that was the way with cold cases. All you could do was keep digging until there was nowhere left to dig. 'I'm sorry to hear that.'

'I don't think the old bastard's been much missed. And, no, we didn't get on. Not once I grew up.'

'Any particular reason for that?'

Challis was silent for a long moment. 'A million and one. I just didn't want anything to do with him.'

'But you followed him into the same line of business?'

'What else could I do? The Hallé weren't prepared to offer me the post of first violin, but I knew how to lay a brick. I'd no desire to go into business with Dad, so I set up on my own. Got the last laugh, though. Made far

256

more out of it than he ever managed with his tin-pot little firm. Mind you, I've diversified. He wouldn't know the meaning of the word.'

'What about other people who worked on the cottage? People who worked for or alongside your father. Any of those still around?'

'Christ knows. Dad had a couple of labourers he used regularly, but I'm buggered if I can remember their names. Anyway, they'd be long gone. They were getting on even then. There were other specialists he worked with – sparks, plumbers, plasterers – but again I can't remember who they were. I can have a think and let you know if any names pop into the brain, but don't get your hopes up.'

He could easily be lying, Annie thought. Whatever he'd thought of his father, Challis wouldn't be keen to offer any information that might be incriminating. Either way, there was probably little point in pursuing it. Even if any of these possible witnesses were still alive, it was unlikely they'd be able to provide anything useful. 'See what you can come up with, Mr Challis. Even the smallest of leads might be useful to us.'

'I'll see what I can remember,' Challis said grudgingly. 'But it won't be much.'

'Can I ask you a different question?' This was Zoe, sounding even more 'butter wouldn't melt' than usual.

Challis regarded her with weary disdain. 'It's a free country, lass. Knock yourself out.'

'The Alan Harwood you knew. Do you think he'd have been capable of snatching Jayne Arnold off the street?'

Again, Challis was slow to reply. 'Christ knows. He was a pathetic little man, but I don't what he was capable of. She was what – fifteen? Sixteen?'

'Sixteen. Putting aside the question of taking her off the street, do you think he'd have been capable of killing her?'

Challis was still staring through the window. Annie wondered what he was seeing. Something other than the gloomy landscape, she suspected. 'I don't imagine he'd have intended to kill her, but if he'd tried something and she'd fought back...' He shook his head, as if trying to remove the thought from his mind. 'Maybe it's a pity you lot didn't look at Harwood at the time.'

'He was interviewed. But there was no reason to treat him as a suspect. You've said you didn't get on with your father. What sort of man was he?'

Challis finally looked back at her and gave a mirthless smile. 'You mean, was he the sort of man capable of burying a body? Aye, maybe. That old bastard was capable of anything.'

Annie thought about Challis's own reputation, and wondered how different father and son actually were. 'Including being an accessory to murder?'

'I've no idea. If it was a question of getting Harwood out of the shit, I reckon it's possible.'

She had the sense that there was something more, something Challis was still holding back. 'It might have helped us if you'd come forward with the information about Harwood when you saw the news stories about the remains.'

'What would have been the point? Harwood and my dad are both dead. I assume there's no way of proving or disproving their involvement after all this time. You can draw what conclusions you like, but you'll never *know*.' The final words sounded oddly like a challenge. 'In any case, this is just a question of putting a tick in a box for you, isn't it? After forty-odd years, who actually cares?'

'Jayne Arnold's father is still alive. Her mother may be alive.'

'Aye, I suppose.'

'Is there anything else you want to tell us, Mr Challis? About Harwood or your father? Or about Jayne Arnold?'

Challis had returned to staring out of the window and didn't look back as he replied.

'I've told you all I can.'

Chapter Thirty-Four

Annie's phone rang as soon as she'd sat back down at her desk in the incident room. She groaned and looked at the screen. 'No peace for the wicked. It's Hectic Handsworth. I'd better take it.'

'I'll get you a coffee,' Zoe said. 'Then at least you won't have to face him uncaffeinated.'

The supposedly short journey back from Ashbourne had taken much longer than they'd expected following a major collision on the A515. They'd sat motionless in a queue of traffic until Annie, having taken advice from the operations room, had U-turned and found a much longer alternative route back to the school, crawling behind a trail of drivers who had obviously had the same idea. Annie and Zoe had arrived at the school to find all the parking near the incident room taken and had had to leave the car on the far side of the school, necessitating a rapid scurry round the building in the still pouring rain. The last thing Annie felt like right now was another sparring session with Handsworth, but there was always the possibility he might have something useful to tell her.

'Robbie. How's it going?'

'Full report's on its way to you. Melanie Donnelly's phone and laptop.' His tone suggested he expected congratulation for meeting his own deadline. 'Thought you might want a heads-up.'

'Thanks, Robbie. Anything useful?'

'Depends what you're looking for. First, we've managed to retrieve the list of contacts she'd deleted.'

'That's good. Anything significant in there?'

'I've sent you the full list. Some interesting ones, though, and a lot with fairly cryptic names.'

'Cryptic?'

'Just initials, or what look like code words. I did a search on a few of the numbers, just out of curiosity. The ones I looked at were newspapers. Newsdesks. National and local.'

'She had ambitions to be a journalist, and she seems to have had quite a lot of initiative. Maybe just looking to build up her contacts list.'

'We've also managed to retrieve her call log, at least for the weeks preceding her death. So you'll be able to check any incoming or outgoing calls over that period. There are a fair number of them.'

'Thanks, Robbie. Sounds useful.'

'And you sound patronising. Anyone ever tell you that?'

'Mainly you. Sorry if it came over that way. It's been a long day already. Seriously, it does sound useful. If nothing else, it might give us more of a clue as to her state of mind in those final weeks.'

'Okay, forgiven.'

'What about texts?'

'Retrieved those as well, but there's not much in there. Don't know if young people really do texts any more. Think that's more for the fogies like us.'

'Speak for yourself, Handsworth.'

'Oh, believe me, I was. I'm surrounded by bloody *wunderkind* here. Child prodigies who could code at the age of five but still can't string a coherent sentence together. Anyway, that brings me on to the laptop.'

'Anything interesting there?'

'I'd say so. First, among the material she deleted there were a couple of confidential messaging apps.'

'Ah. Hence the lack of texts. No chance of accessing what was on them?'

'Not easily. There are routes we can go down to access some data, but it takes forever and we'd generally need some evidence of likely criminality. I'm guessing that's not the case here.'

'We don't even know if we have a crime. Just an unexplained death, unless there's somehow a link with Ellsworth killing.'

'Not much chance of getting anything useful then. The better news is we did manage to retrieve a number of files Donnelly had deleted. She'd done a smart job, but luckily my *wunderkind* are slightly smarter.'

'You love them really.'

'If you say so. Anyway, we found some interesting stuff on there. Including what looks like the article you were looking for. Stuff about donations to the school. Quite incendiary stuff, I'd have thought.'

'Incendiary in what way?'

'You'll have to look at it for yourself. I'll send it over with the report. It's in two sections. The first part deals with historical donations to the school, and that's interesting if you're into that kind of thing, I guess. Usual stories about money from dodgy sources, including some payments that are still funding scholarships and bursaries today. Mildly controversial in a conservative environment like that, I suppose, but nothing very startling. It's the second one that's more interesting. It's a series of fairly large-scale donations made to the school over the past few years by someone called Ryan Challis.'

'We'd understood that. What makes the article so incendiary?'

'Your reading skills a bit rusty too, Annie? I've said I'll send it over.'

'I thought you'd be desperate to spill the beans, Robbie.'

He laughed. 'Okay, the main point of the article is that Challis has donated some substantial sums to the school over the past few years. There's some innuendo about his reasons for being so generous, with the implication that it's not entirely altruistic. For a start, it looks as if Challis has got more than his share of building work from the school.'

'The school's not a public body,' Annie said. 'There's no obligation for them to follow rigorous procurement standards. I guess the Charity Commission might be interested if the action contravenes any charity regulations, and fee-paying parents could have a concern about how their money was being spent. I can't see it's likely to concern us unless there's evidence of something like—'

'Like fraud or money laundering?'

'Donnelly was implying that?'

'It looks like it. It takes a bit of disentangling because Donnelly had obviously been through a series of drafts – again, I'll send you all the documents. There's what looks like a sanitised version which she'd presumably prepared to send to Ellsworth for vetting for the school newsletter, and then there's a longer version with the really damning stuff in it.'

'So what was she intending to do with that?' Annie asked.

'Your guess is as good as mine. Maybe she was hoping to blindside Ellsworth with the sanitised version and then publish the full version somewhere else.'

'Publish and be damned? What exactly are her allegations?'

'That Ellsworth had taken too much control over the school finances. There's supposed to be a school bursar, but the job's been vacant since shortly after Ellsworth became head. Ellsworth basically ran the school finances on her own.'

'What about the governors? They must have had some oversight, surely.'

'You'd think, wouldn't you?' Handsworth said. 'But Donnelly suggests Ellsworth could wrap the governors round her little finger. There's been some churn among the governor membership, and those who've left had typically been the ones with some financial nous. Donnelly's implying that there are inconsistencies between the formal school accounts and the actual ins and outs of money through its accounts.'

'How could she possibly know that?'

'That's the most interesting thing about this. She clearly doesn't have any access to the school accounts, but she does seem to have evidence relating to Challis's accounts and what he's paid to the school.'

'That seems even more incredible.'

'You'd have thought so. But we also retrieved a file which looks to be PDF downloads of several of Challis's business accounts.'

'So what was she suggesting? That money was paid through the school for money-laundering purposes?'

'That seems to be part of it. Quite smart, if it's true. If you were checking out possible money-laundering vehicles, a long-established independent girls' boarding school would be low on the list.'

'I see what you mean about incendiary. So she thought Ellsworth was in cahoots with Challis?'

'Donnelly leaves that as an open question. What was in it for Ellsworth? She's the one taking the real risks here. Donnelly concludes that Ellsworth must have been receiving a cut, but she also implies that there may be some other motive for Ellsworth's involvement. Interesting stuff, eh?'

'You might say that. Blimey, Robbie, well done.'

'I might ask you to repeat that, so I can record your words. Better still, you could put it writing.'

'I'll do that. Though I know the *wunderkind* have really done the heavy lifting here.'

'Only with inspired leadership. I'll send you all this stuff over, shall I? There are various files of background material as well. All interesting stuff.'

'Thanks, Robbie. And again, just for the tape, well done.'

She ended the call and sat for a moment, thinking through what Handsworth had told her. It raised as many questions as it answered. It would provide a motive for Melanie Donnelly's death and perhaps also for Lavinia Ellsworth's murder, though that was harder to untangle. But there were other questions. For example, how had Melanie gained access to Ryan Challis's bank details? The only thing that was clear was that they needed to talk to Challis again, as a matter of urgency.

It occurred to her that Zoe still hadn't returned with the coffees. Annie rose and looked around the incident room. A few officers were tapping away at their computers, inputting data, but most were engaged elsewhere. Most of the smaller rooms had been trans-formed into interview units but the smallest room, just by the entrance, contained a sink with running water and so had been commandeered as a makeshift kitchen, with a kettle and a microwave. Annie pushed open the door and peered inside.

Zoe was sitting at the small table at the side of the room, her head in her hands. Two mugs stood by the sink, but it was clear that Zoe hadn't yet made the coffees.

'Zo?'

Zoe looked up and stared at Annie as if not recognising her.

'You okay?'

'I'm not sure.'

'What is it?'

'I don't know. I – I nearly fell over.' She was silent for a moment. 'I don't know what happened.' She looked blankly around her.

Annie found a glass in one of the cupboards and filled it from the sink before handing it to Zoe, who sipped it gratefully. 'Tell me about it.'

'I'm not sure how to explain it.' She took a breath and continued. 'I came into here to make the coffee. Then the feeling just swept over me. I was standing there by the kettle, and then suddenly I felt as if my balance had gone. I thought I was going to fall over. Eventually, I managed to get over here and sit down.' She looked up with a faint smile. 'Sorry you had to wait for the coffee.'

'Is this the first time this has happened?'

Zoe said nothing for a moment. 'No, it's happened a couple of times. Not quite as bad.'

'You need to get this checked out, Zo. Whatever the cause, you need to get it sorted.'

'I know. I've been telling myself it's nothing. At first I thought it was just some kind of minor panic attack, but who knows?'

'You need to find out, Zo. Whether it's a physical or psychological issue, you need to know. Do you think you're up to work?'

'At the moment, yes. The whole thing just feels like a bad dream. I feel – well, not perfect. I still feel a bit shaken. But I don't feel ill. What worries me is not knowing when it might hit again.'

'I'd rather you took some time off, Zo. Apart from anything else, I don't know if it's safe for you to continue at work. What if this happens to you at some critical moment?'

'I'll contact the GP in the morning and see what he says. I've got some leave owing so I can take a few days off if you think that's best. I'd feel bad taking sick leave. To be honest, I feel bad taking time off at all. Not with all this on.'

'It won't help anyone if you try to push yourself too far, Zo. It certainly won't help me, much as I'd like you here. Take a few days off. We'll sort out the admin side of it later, once you've spoken to the doctor.'

'I don't think I've got a choice, have I?' She shook her head, her face bleak. 'Christ, what's Stuart going to think?'

'He's going to think you need to take a bit of time off, just as we all do. He knows you're good at the job.'

'He thinks I'm brittle. Fragile.'

'No, he doesn't.' In truth, Annie had little idea what Jennings really thought about Zoe or indeed herself. He'd made all the right 'duty of care' noises after Zoe's traumatic involvement in a couple of recent cases, but she sometimes suspected he hadn't quite shaken off the ingrained sexism that was still too much a part of the police culture. She'd do her best to ensure he did the right thing by Zoe.

'Anyway, what did Hectic have to tell you?'

Annie forced her mind back on to the details of the case. 'A hell of a lot, actually. And a surprising amount of it was about our old friend Ryan Challis.'

Chapter Thirty-Five

When Margaret reached the road up to the house, she pulled into the side and turned off the engine. If nothing else, she needed a few minutes to gather her wits. Everything was telling her this was a very bad idea. She was here only because she had no real alternative. She needed to do something, and this was the only thing that made any sense. Even if it didn't make much.

What she ought to do, she told herself, was sit tight, hope all this would somehow blow over. But there was no guarantee it would, and if it didn't it would get a hell of a lot worse.

She couldn't pretend Challis would be pleased to see her. Even her presence here would be an embarrassment to him. It was one of the agreements they'd made all those years ago. Any contact was strictly at his instigation and on his terms. He'd no doubt object to her turning up when his wife was in the house, but then he'd not cared much about messing up her life to get what he wanted, and she knew he'd done the same to the others.

The main question was what she wanted from him today. Above all, she wanted to know what was going on. She wanted to know why and how things had gone awry. And she wanted to know what he was doing to get things back on track. She hoped he could handle this, just as he'd handled most of it over the years. He had a cool head and nerves to match. Maybe too much so at times. He'd taken a few risks that she wouldn't have countenanced, and sometimes it had come horribly close to going wrong. But he'd always pulled though, even if he'd left casualties in his wake.

She was about to restart the engine when she saw the flash of lights on the road ahead of her. A vehicle coming away from the house. She turned off her own headlights and waited, hoping that in the late afternoon gloom her car wouldn't be noticeable to whoever was driving in her direction. Moments later, a vehicle flashed past, taking the narrow track at an excessive speed.

Had that been Challis heading out somewhere? The car hadn't been Challis's preferred large executive saloon, but something much smaller, though she hadn't caught the make. It might be Challis's wife, or Challis using his wife's vehicle for some reason. She was almost tempted to use the departing car as an excuse to turn back. But if it had been Challis's wife, it might give Margaret the opportunity to see Challis alone. If his wife was in the house by herself, Margaret would come up with some excuse for her visit.

She restarted the engine and continued up the track. The converted farmhouse was at the top of the hill, lights showing in all the windows. A large Mercedes was parked in front of the building, and there was no sign of any other vehicle.

The rain had eased slightly, although there was still a fine drizzle in the air. Margaret hurried over to the front door and pressed the bell. There was no answer, and after a few minutes she tried again. It was only then that she realised that the door wasn't fully closed. It had been left slightly ajar, not quite catching on the latch. She gently pushed it open. 'Ryan?'

There was silence. She took another few steps forward. All the lights in the house were on, but the whole place felt eerily quiet. 'Ryan? It's Margaret Delamere. I'm…' I'm what, she thought. I'm here because I want you to dig us all out of another hole? I'm here because I want to know what the hell's going on? I'm completely out of my depth? The last was the answer that felt most true, as it had for a very long time.

She took another few steps forward and looked into the living room. It was empty, the television set playing silently in the corner.

She ought to leave now, she told herself. She had no right to intrude in someone else's house, even if they'd inadvertently left the front door open. There was no justification for her just wandering in.

She reached the door to the kitchen and pushed it open.

Challis was lying on the floor, a slowly spreading pool of blood around him, a large kitchen carving knife protruding from his stomach. Margaret had seen plenty of dead bodies during her career, even one or two like this. She walked forward and pressed her hand to Challis's neck, seeking a pulse. There was none.

Margaret knew exactly what she ought to do. She ought to take out her phone, dial 999, call the emergency services and wait here till they arrived. But then she'd have to explain who she was and why she was here, and how she knew Challis. That would open up the whole bloody can of worms, just at the point when she most wanted to shut it down.

But Challis's death would do that anyway.

It was only then, oddly, that it occurred to her even to think about who might have killed Challis. The same person who had killed Lavinia Ellsworth, presumably, and that left a decreasing number of possible suspects.

She leaned forward and took another look at Challis's body, and saw something that she'd missed when checking his pulse. He was lying on his back, his face turned away from her, but she saw now that the skin on his face had been broken in several places, as if someone had struck him violently and repeatedly.

No longer thinking clearly, Margaret hurried out of the house, almost running back to her car, leaving the front door wide open behind her. Moments later, she was heading down the track away from the house, at the same speed as the car she'd witnessed earlier.

This was stupid. All she was doing was further incriminating herself, perhaps even putting herself in the frame for Challis's killing. She couldn't remember if she'd touched anything in the house, and she had no idea what kind of evidence she might have left. She didn't even know, it occurred to her now, whether Challis had had any CCTV that might have recorded her arrival and departure. If so, the real killer might have been smarter at avoiding it.

She drove another half-mile, not even sure where she was heading, until she saw a farm gateway that provided her with an opportunity to pull off the road. She killed the engine and sat, breathing heavily, trying to force herself to think clearly.

She could no longer rely on Challis to help her. This time, he wasn't going to be the one to drag her out of the mess. And it was worse than that. This time there was no one she could rely on but herself.

She told herself again what she ought to do. She should call the police, return to the house and wait there till they arrived. She should tell them the truth. If necessary, the whole truth. Every last painful, sordid detail.

But she knew she couldn't do that. There were only two things she could do. She could turn round and drive back home, lock herself in the flat and try just to keep herself safe till, somehow, this resolved itself. But how was that likely to happen? Two people were already dead, and there was no saying Margaret wouldn't be next on the list.

The whole thing was a massive shit-show, and there wasn't much she could do about that. The police would, at the very least, start investigating Challis's past, and all that history would be dug up again. The whole thing would be brought back into the light just in time to give Gareth Thomas the impetus he needed to promote the results of his muckraking. That was assuming that the police didn't also try to put her in the frame for Challis's killing.

Whatever the outcome, more and more people would be crawling over all this, scrutinising every inch of it. Eventually someone would start wondering about her history with Ryan Challis, and about where and how it might all have started. Once they pulled on that thread, the whole messy tapestry – already beginning to unravel from other directions – would begin to fall apart and they'd discover the sordid truth that lay behind it.

If she turned to drive home, she'd be doing nothing but forcing herself to sit and wait till that happened. If she turned the other way – well, she really had no idea what she might achieve. It was probably too late now to stop it all falling apart. But she might at least find out exactly what was going on, what had provoked this mess now, and whether there was any chance of salvaging anything, at least for herself.

The one chance, she thought, was for Challis to become the scapegoat. There were plenty of people – powerful people – who had a vested interest in making sure the true scale and scope of Challis's crimes didn't come to public light. There were plenty of people who'd be prepared to dump endless tons of ordure on Challis's reputation if it meant their own involvement was never exposed. That was the only reason she'd been able to leave the force with her reputation and her pension largely intact. If she'd gone down, she'd have taken plenty of people with her.

Now Challis was dead, he'd make a very convenient whipping boy. Everything could turn out to have been Challis's fault, and everyone else was just a dupe or a victim. That would suit a lot of people, and it would certainly suit Margaret.

This was the only way she might keep a lid on the whole mess. There'd be fallout, but it would be in everyone's interest to minimise it, and with luck no one would be too interested in Margaret Delamere's part in events. Even Gareth Thomas might be persuaded that Ryan Challis, all-powerful criminal kingpin, was a bigger story than a few backhanders paid to an ACC.

Margaret couldn't yet envisage the entire route that might take her from her current predicament to that more enticing future, but she could at least see a glimmer of light ahead. There was only one major obstacle in her way.

There was one person here who was out of control. There was one person who hadn't played by the agreed rules and who, for whatever reason – panic, fury, guilt, perhaps even cold, belated revenge – had taken matters into their own hands. One person who seemed determined to drag everything, all the history, out into the open air.

There might still be time to prevent that. Ellsworth's and Challis's deaths could be tied back to Challis's business corruption rather than to anything else. But only if she could get everything back under control. Restore, one way or another, the old discipline.

Margaret knew she wasn't thinking clearly, but it seemed her only hope. She started the car and pulled back on to the road, heading north, away from home.

Chapter Thirty-Six

'You sure you're up to this, Zo?'

Zoe looked weary, but much more herself than she had back at the school. She was even managing to look mildly irritated at Annie's repeated question. 'I'm fine, Annie. Really. I'm happy to take a few days off if that's what you want, and I'll get myself checked out, but I'm okay at the moment.'

'I won't ask again then. At least not today.' Zoe's car was back at HQ anyway, so she'd need a lift back. It made sense for Zoe to travel back with her and use this opportunity to complete their unfinished business with Ryan Challis. Apart from anything else, she wanted to keep an eye on Zoe.

Under the leaden sky, it felt as if night had already fallen, though it was only late afternoon. The landscape was lost in mist, the hills little more than eerie presences occasionally swimming into view as the car headed south.

'What I don't understand,' Zoe said, 'is why Ellsworth would have done this stuff for Challis in the first place. Assuming there's any truth in what Donnelly was claiming.'

'I suppose the first question is whether Donnelly was actually right. The stuff that Hectic sent over looks convincing, especially the bank statements, but we'll have to get its provenance checked out. Even if the material's legit, it's all a bit opaque. It might be that Donnelly put two and two together and made something rather more than four. We'll need to get the forensic accounting people working through all that. But it looks solid enough on the face of it.'

'So why would Ellsworth have taken the risk? Especially for someone like Challis. It's hard to imagine they were exactly soulmates.'

'I suppose people can surprise you. But I take your point. That seems to have baffled Donnelly as well. She assumed Ellsworth was taking her cut, but I'm not sure she was entirely convinced by that as a sole motive. It's something to check when we get access to her bank records.'

'It'll be interesting to see how Challis responds to all this, anyway.'

'I imagine he'll complain of harassment and threaten to call the Chief Constable.'

'Would be do that?'

'He might. He's Ryan Challis. But it's a murder inquiry. We harass anyone we need to. But we do need to be careful how we handle this. Fairly low-key at this stage. Just push him harder on the donations to the school. I don't want him to know how much information we actually have.'

'And keep Melanie Donnelly out of it?'

'I'd have thought so. We can play it by ear when we see how he responds.' She glanced across at Zoe, but the other woman's face was turned away, her eyes apparently fixed on the now barely discernible passing landscape.

Another five minutes brought them to the narrow track leading up to Challis's farmhouse. The place looked unchanged from their former visit, though Challis's Mercedes had now been joined by a smaller, sporty-looking vehicle. The front door of the house was standing open.

'Looks like he might have company. That might work in our favour if he's keen to get shot of us.' Annie pushed open the door and climbed out, grimacing as the cold drizzle struck her skin.

It was only as she approached the front door that she began to feel a degree of unease. She couldn't even have said why. Just the familiar copper's instinct, she assumed, that inexplicable sixth sense that accrues through years of attending incidents and crime scenes. She stepped up to the door and called, 'Mr Challis?'

For a moment, she thought the house was silent. Then she realised that she could hear a sound – a muted sound, as if someone was trying to suppress it – from somewhere inside the house. Annie glanced over her shoulder to ensure Zoe was close behind, then stepped into the hallway. 'Mr Challis?'

The woman was almost on top of her before she realised. Annie staggered back against the wall, almost falling. She raised her arms to defend herself. The woman was looming over her, brandishing a kitchen knife. 'Get back. Stand against the wall.' The woman nodded to Zoe. 'You too.'

The woman continued to wave the knife in their direction, though her hand was now looking less steady. 'Who the hell are you? And what are you doing in my home?'

Annie spoke as slowly and calmly as she could. 'We're police officers. DI Delamere and DS Everett. We're here to see Ryan Challis.'

'Ryan? But now—?' The woman tensed again, still pointing the knife towards them. 'Show me some ID. Slowly.'

Annie reached into her coat and withdrew her warrant card. She flipped it open and held it out towards the woman. 'There. DI Annie Delamere.'

The knife dropped from the woman's hand, and she fell back against the wall opposite Annie. 'How did you know? Did someone call?'

'Know what?'

The woman was gesturing towards the kitchen doorway. Annie followed her gaze to see Ryan Challis's body spreadeagled on the floor. She looked back at the woman, then down at the knife on the floor. 'Did you…?'

The woman shook her head vehemently. 'No, I swear! I just got here. I saw him lying there, then I heard you outside and I thought… I just grabbed the knife from the kitchen to defend myself…' She was hunched over, crying, a long way now from the angry-looking woman they'd encountered moments before.

Challis was lying on his back on the floor, his body surrounded by congealing blood. Whether or not the woman was telling the truth, it was clear that the knife in the hall wasn't the murder weapon. A similar, larger knife was protruding from Challis's stomach. As Annie turned back, she was already dialling back to the operations room to call the incident in.

She nodded to Zoe, and together they led the woman into the living room, placing her carefully on the sofa. 'Are you Ryan's wife?'

The woman looked up, her eyes red-stained, and nodded. 'Megan Challis. I just got back. I swear. I didn't—'

'Just tell us what happened.'

'I've been in London for the last couple of days.' She seemed to hesitate. 'Do you need to know the truth?'

'It's probably best you tell us the whole truth, Mrs Challis. If you conceal something now, it won't help us.'

'Ryan thought I was going shopping with a couple of girlfriends. Or that's what he pretended to think. I was never sure…'

'But you weren't?'

'Ryan and I live…' She stopped. 'We lived separate lives. That suited us. I've been seeing someone in London. A man.'

'It's better you told us now. We'll need to get all this checked out.'

'Will you be discreet? It's just that – well, he's married…'

'We'll be as discreet as we can.' Annie didn't add that discretion was unlikely to be a major priority in a major murder inquiry. 'Go on.'

'I'd just got back, a few minutes before you arrived. The front door was wide open, which wasn't like Ryan. He's normally obsessive about security. I came inside – hadn't even taken my luggage out of the car – and I found him in there…' She'd begun to cry again, sobbing more gently this time. Annie was unsure whether her reaction showed a genuine sorrow at her husband's death or merely shock at its circumstances. Either way, it didn't seem feigned. 'I was just terrified. Then I heard you arrive outside and I thought – well, I didn't know what to think. I just grabbed a knife from the rack in the kitchen and hid myself in the hall…' She looked up suddenly and stared at Annie. 'What were you doing here?'

'We wanted to talk to your husband about an inquiry we're conducting.'

Megan Challis nodded wearily. 'You lot have talked to him a good few times over the years. I hope you're going to put in as much effort into finding out who killed him.'

'We'll do our best, Mrs Challis.' The front door was still open, and Annie could hear approaching sirens. 'We'll need to talk to you in some detail about your husband's associates, when you feel up to it.'

'You think he shared any of that stuff with me? He just told me to keep my mouth shut and enjoy the proceeds. But, sure, I'll tell you what I can.'

Through the window Annie could see the pulse of blue lights in the evening gloom. She pushed herself to her feet. 'I'd better go and greet the assembled troops.'

She walked out into the hall, glancing back at the hunched figure on the sofa. Annie supposed that, for the moment, Megan Challis had to remain a suspect in her husband's death. She'd been found by the body with a knife in her hand, and, with a lover in London, she had at least some kind of motive for her husband's killing. But it didn't ring true to Annie. It was too much of a coincidence, given everything else Challis was involved in.

The answer to this lay somewhere else. In the school, alongside the deaths of Lavinia Ellsworth and possibly Melanie Donnelly. In the issues that had brought Annie here in the first place, and that had brought them back here tonight.

She stepped out on to the doorstep, waving to the first marked car that had just pulled up beside her own. Behind it, she could see a trail of further vehicles heading up towards the house.

It was going to be a long evening.

Chapter Thirty-Seven

Margaret Delamere ignored the main school gates, and followed the road round the school perimeter until she came to the less ostentatious side entrance. It was well over forty years since she'd been a pupil here and she'd been back only a handful of times since, but she still knew the layout of the place almost intuitively.

There'd been changes over those years, of course. New buildings erected, layouts altered, the number of parking spaces increased. But the fundamentals remained the same, and she still felt the same mix of excitement and mild fear as she drove into the school grounds. Tonight she perhaps had more reason to experience those emotions than ever before.

She'd chosen to use the side entrance because she didn't want to advertise her arrival. It wasn't that she necessarily wanted to be secretive, but she did at least want to be discreet. Driving through the main gates and along the road through the sports fields towards the school always made her feel as if she was being watched by every girl standing behind each of those windows. It was nonsense, of course. Lessons would be long over for today, and most likely no one would have noticed her arrival. Even so, she felt more comfortable arriving unobserved.

She was conscious too that the police team would still be here. Most likely none of them would know or remember her, but better not to take any more chances than she had to. She found an unobtrusive place to leave her car, then made her way around the school to her destination, hoping this was an area that had been left unchanged since her time here.

The teachers who lived on site were housed mostly in a small row of terraced cottages, lined around a small courtyard at the rear of the school grounds. The cottages themselves had been part of the original legacy that had founded the school, and the buildings were of the same vintage as the main school building. In Margaret's day, these had been prized accommodation, occupied by the longest-serving staff, the remainder relegated to a newer hostel on the other side of the grounds. Margaret hoped that the pecking order had remained the same.

Sure enough, she found the name she was looking for listed on a sign at the entrance to the courtyard. Number 3. She passed through the stone archway into the courtyard itself, hoping the murky rain and gloom would conceal her presence, and was startled by the sudden glare of a motion-sensitive security light. She walked over to the door of cottage number 3 and pressed the bell.

She hadn't thought about what she should do if there was no one in the house. She couldn't simply leave a message. If necessary, she'd have to find somewhere to wait. She glanced up at the rain-soaked sky, wondering where she was likely to find anywhere suitable in this place.

She glanced over her shoulder, trying to see whether anyone might be watching her from the surrounding houses. There were lights showing in several windows, just as there were in the house in front of her, but no sign of movement.

It was only now that she really considered the risk she might be facing. Someone here – most likely the occupant of this house – had already killed at least two people. Margaret didn't know what had provoked those acts, but the apparent logic would suggest she should also be on that list. It was madness for her to turn up here as a willing victim.

But what was the alternative? If she turned away, the risk wouldn't disappear, but would most likely be doubled. It would only be a question of who reached her first – the killer or the police. At least this way there was a chance she might be able to restore some stability, put the lid back on all this.

Behind her, the security light had been extinguished, throwing the courtyard back into gloom. Margaret was sheltered by the small porch over the front door, but she could hear the rain had returned, spattering on the paved path behind her.

It was then that she heard a noise from within the house. She couldn't immediately work out what the sound had been – the choked-off sound of human voice, perhaps, then something else. A thump or bang, perhaps of a heavy object being dropped. She tried to rationalise the sounds as something falling in the house, but something about the suddenness and sequence of the sounds left her uneasy.

Margaret peered into the window beside the front door. The room beyond was in darkness, but she could see through an open doorway that lights were showing further inside the house. She could see nothing that provided a clue to the source of the sounds she'd heard.

She pressed her ear against the front door, trying to work out what might be happening inside. Another thump. Then another, louder. Finally, a sequence of bangs, not loud, but growing more frequent and seemingly more intense. Then the sounds ceased and the silence returned.

Margaret pulled her phone from her pocket, and skimmed through her address book for a name. If she was smart, she would just dial 999 and have done with it, but that would just take her back where she started. There was only one other alternative, and that wasn't what she wanted, not least because it probably wouldn't make any difference. But, if things really did go wrong, she might at least be able to buy herself a little time and space before everything hit the fan.

Her finger hovered above the doorbell, wondering whether to press it again. Then, as if on instinct, she tried the door. She somehow wasn't surprised when the handle turned and the door opened.

The house was small, designed as a functional living space for a single individual. The front door opened on to a small hall, with the living room she'd peered into on the right. Stairs led to the upper floor, and ahead of her Margaret could see a kitchen. There was a light in the kitchen, and a further light from upstairs. 'Hello?'

She heard a movement above her and, as she looked up, a figure appeared at the head of the stairs.

Not the figure she expected. Not even a figure she recognised.

Margaret thought at first she must have made some kind of dreadful mistake. Come to the wrong house. Walked in on a complete stranger.

She was about to attempt some kind of apology and explanation, when she realised that the person descending the stairs was smiling. A smile of apparent welcome.

As if, even though Margaret didn't know her, she very much knew Margaret.

Chapter Thirty-Eight

'Am I glad to see you, Tim.'

'I don't remember you ever saying that before.' Tim Sturgeon climbed out of his car and looked around. 'Normally you seem only too glad to get rid of me.'

'We're always delighted to see your cheery face. But I'm happier today, having spent the last forty-five minutes trying to keep control of a crime scene in the pouring rain.'

'You look to have done a decent job,' Sturgeon said. 'Considering.'

'Considering what?'

'Considering you're not me. But nothing a professional can't put right.'

'Kept this lot under control at least.' She gestured to the apparent army of uniformed officers milling around them.

'Half the battle. Okay, fill me in.'

She provided Sturgeon with a brief update on what had been done, the location and condition of the body, and various other details she thought would be useful to him.

'Where's the wife?'

'We took a statement from her, then had her driven over to her sister in Belper. She's been seen by the CSIs, so we can get the forensics sorted. But she was in a real state. Anyway, she's there if we need her. I'll leave you the contact number in case you need any info about the house.'

'Is she a suspect?'

'She has to be, at least notionally, until we know better. She found the body, and when we arrived she was brandishing a knife.'

'Sounds open and shut.'

'Not really. It wasn't the murder weapon. She was waving it around because she thought we might be the killers. Which was understandable given that she'd apparently only just got back and found the body when we walked in on her. The CSIs checked her out. No trace of blood on her or the knife. As you'll see from the state of the body, it's unlikely the killer would have got away from this with no trace of blood on their person. But we've taken fingerprints and DNA samples, and we'll make sure her alibi checks out.'

'CSIs all here then?'

'Danny is, along with a couple of others. More on their way.'

'Everyone's keen to join the party. I'll take over then. You heading home?'

'As if,' Annie said. 'Sheena's already told me that supper's in the bin. Poor Zo's been trying to get home for the last two hours. But we've apparently got another little mystery to look into.'

'No peace for the wicked.'

'Just wish I'd been wicked enough to justify it. Feel I've missed out.'

She walked back over to the car, where Zoe was sitting waiting for her. As she climbed in beside Zoe, she said, 'I could get someone else to drive you home, Zo, if you preferred.'

'Might as well stick with you now.'

'This may be a wild goose chase anyway, but Stuart's concerned about the PR. Whereas I'm mainly concerned about ensuring we don't have another killing on our hands.'

Annie had called Stuart Jennings to break the news about Challis's death, but he'd been tied up in a meeting with the DCC. He'd called back as the first contingent of uniformed officers had been arriving, and their initial conversation had been disjointed and mildly chaotic. When they'd finally had a chance to talk clearly, he'd said, 'This is all getting out of hand, Annie.'

'Tell me about it. I'm the one trying to herd uniformed officers. Give me cats any day.'

'I mean the whole thing. DCC's just been bending my ear, because the tabloids at making a big thing about the Ellsworth killing. Murder of the head of an exclusive girls' school presses all their buttons, especially alongside the Melanie Donnelly death.'

'I bet it does.'

'He's going to be over the moon when he hears about Challis. Especially if we think there's a connection. As for the idea of money laundering through a boarding school...' He'd trailed off as if he couldn't think of anything to top that.

'You do know I'm aware of all this, Stuart? We're doing everything we can.'

'There's one more thing you're not aware of.'

'Oh, great. Go on.'

'We've apparently had a call from Diane Astor's husband—'

'Astor? The deputy head?'

'So I understand. She's gone missing. Or at least he's concerned she has.'

'What?' Annie could feel an uneasy chill in the pit of her stomach. 'Gone missing how?'

'It's almost certainly something and nothing,' Jennings had said. 'I mean, it's not surprising they've all got the jitters up there. He was concerned because she didn't come back from the school this afternoon.'

'It's not that late, even now. She'll be up to her ears at the moment.'

'I know. But she apparently always makes a point of calling him to let him know if she's going to be late. He called the school and they hadn't seen her since earlier in the afternoon. They were keen to track her down because – well, as you say, she's a lot on her plate. She's not answering her mobile, and hasn't responded even though they've left her several messages.'

'This isn't sounding good, Stuart.'

'There's probably some perfectly—'

'We've already got Ellsworth dead, and now Ryan Challis. We don't know whether Melanie Donnelly's death is linked to all this. Enough to make me nervous if someone goes missing.'

'I think we need to speak to Astor's husband anyway. Whatever has or hasn't happened to his wife, we need to show we're taking this seriously.'

'We'll head up there, then, and keep our fingers crossed that she turns up in the meantime.'

Annie entered the address Jennings had given her into the satnav, and they headed down the track back towards the main road. It was beginning to feel as if they'd already made this journey too many times today.

After twenty minutes they were directed off the main road. Jennings had given them only a house number, street name and postcode, and it was a few moments before Annie realised they were following the road back towards Meresham. They found themselves passing the cottage where Jayne Arnold's remains had been found, and then turning right through the village. The same route that Jayne would normally have followed on her walk home from school.

Then they were directed to take another right-hand turn, this time into the estate where, forty-six years earlier, Jayne Arnold had lived with her parents.

'What the hell is this?' Zoe was staring out of the car window at the passing houses. 'What number did Stuart say?'

'Thirty-seven.'

'Shit.' Zoe shook her head. 'It's like some grotesque cosmic joke. I don't understand.'

'Me neither.' Annie pulled up in front of the house in question. 'But if it's a cosmic joke, I don't know who the hell's laughing.'

She climbed out of the car and surveyed the building in front of her. There was no doubt about it. Zoe had shown her the pictures from the reports at the time. The same house where Jayne Arnold had lived. Annie looked back at Zoe, who gave a baffled shrug.

The front door was opened even before they'd reached it, and a worried-looking middle-aged man nodded to them as they approached.

'DI Annie Delamere and DS Zoe Everett,' Annie said. 'We thought it best to come ourselves as we're leading the inquiry at the school.'

They followed him through into a tidy, slightly fussy living room. 'I'm worried that I'm going to make myself look stupid. When she comes breezing in, I'm going to feel such a fool. But it's just not like her not to call.'

'You've tried her mobile?'

'She's got two. A school one and a personal one. I've tried them both but they're just going straight to voice-mail. Again, that's not like her, unless she's teaching or in a meeting or something like that.'

'There's probably some perfectly straightforward explanation,' Annie said. 'She must be a very busy woman with everything that has been happening at the school. When did you last speak to her?'

'This morning. Just for a couple of minutes. I was going to ask her about a couple of domestic things, but she seemed distracted.'

'In what way?'

'At the time, I just thought I must have caught her at a bad moment, so I didn't keep her on very long.'

'How's she been generally lately?'

'Similar, I suppose. As if she's had a lot on her mind – which she must have, to be fair – or as if she was anxious or nervous for some reason.'

'And that was unusual?'

'She's always been the nervous type. Highly strung, my mother used to say. There's always something worrying her. Sometimes it's just something personal. Sometimes it's the state of the world.' He gave an awkward laugh, as if his words had shown a disloyalty to his wife.

Annie sometimes wondered what brought people together in a relationship. In the Astors' case, she guessed that it was the attraction of similars. Astor had the same slightly troubled, slightly anxious air he was describing in his wife.

'What was her usual routine at the end of the day?'

'It varied by the day, and there'd sometimes be meetings in the evening and suchlike. I'd normally have expected her home by around six today, but I realise everything's up in the air while they deal with the impact of the head's death. I was mostly worried that she hadn't called to let me know what her timing was likely to be. That's not like her. Eventually, I felt anxious and called the school. They told me they hadn't seen her since early afternoon...' He still hadn't sat down himself, and now he walked over and peered through the uncurtained window, as if hoping his wife's car was about to turn into the drive. 'They seemed as worried as I was. That's why I thought I should call you.'

'You did the right thing, Mr Astor. Better to take no chances. Is there anywhere else she's likely to have gone? Friends, relatives, anyone like that?'

'I honestly can't think of anyone.'

'Okay, Mr Astor. We'll go and make some enquiries at the school. We'll need you to provide some basic inform-ation about your wife – car registration, a recent photo-graph if you have one—'

'A photograph? You don't think...'

'Just routine at this stage, Mr Astor. I'm sure we won't need to use it. But if we do need to make wider enquiries, it'll be useful to have.' She tried to maintain the reassuring note in his voice. 'Most likely your wife will turn up safe and sound.'

She waited by the door while Zoe took down the necessary information, watching as Astor fumbled with his phone trying to find a suitable photograph of his wife.

After he'd transferred the image across, Zoe asked casually, 'Have you lived here long, Mr Astor?'

'Six, seven years. Why?'

'I just wondered what had brought you here.'

'To the village? It was Diane's idea. We had a place some distance away, almost up near Buxton. Diane was finding the commute a bit much. Didn't really worry me as I work in Ashbourne and my hours are more flexible anyway, but I could see her point. She spotted this place when it came on the market and was bowled over by it.' He shrugged. 'To be honest, it wouldn't have been my choice. I prefer a place with a bit more character. But it was what she wanted, and I was happy to go along with that.'

They said their farewells to Astor, promising to keep him updated on developments, then stepped back out into the damp evening air. As soon as Astor had closed the front door behind them, Zoe said, 'Weird.'

'He didn't give the impression he knew anything about the history of the place.'

'I don't think he was trying to pull the wool over our eyes. I genuinely think he doesn't know.'

'It's pretty bloody odd. Something for us to talk to Diane Astor about, assuming we can find her.'

'You think there's a chance we might not?'

'None of this feels good to me. Astor doesn't sound like the type who'd just go AWOL. Let's get up to the school and see what we can find out.' She was opening the car door when she felt her mobile phone buzz in her pocket. She pulled it out and stared at the screen. 'Oh, God. That's all I need right now. My mother. Well, for once, Mum, you're going to have to wait. I've actually got something more important to do than waste time listening to you.'

Chapter Thirty-Nine

'You don't recognise me at all, do you?'

Margaret stared back at the woman on the stairs, trying to place her face. There was undoubtedly something familiar about it. At the same time, Margaret had found the woman's smile of recognition disconcerting.

The woman was at the bottom of the stairs now, still smiling amicably. 'No? Not after everything I did for you?'

It was only then that Margaret finally made the connection. 'Eleanor? Eleanor Mason?'

The woman softly moved her hands together in mock applause. 'I'm impressed. Lavinia and Alice worked alongside me for years and never made the connection. I wasn't surprised. I look very different now.'

That was very true, Margaret thought, and yet somehow it wasn't. Without prompting, she would never had recognised the woman standing in front of her. Now she knew, she couldn't imagine how she hadn't recognised her immediately. 'It's been a long time.'

'Forty-six years.'

Margaret sometimes asked herself where that time had gone. A supposedly glittering career that ultimately had fizzled out to nothing but mild notoriety and a pension. A family life that had never really happened. There were times – including the nights when she woke bathed in sweat from some nightmare she couldn't quite recall – when that baking summer seemed more real than anything that had happened since.

'Where did you go, Eleanor? Where have you been?'

Margaret could still recall the initial terror when Eleanor had disappeared from their lives. There'd been countless lurid rumours in those days after she had first been removed from the school – that she'd been taken just as Jayne Arnold had, that she'd been expelled for some unspecified offence, that she'd had a mental breakdown and been taken away. Only Margaret and her friends had known the truth, or at least a part of the truth, and had recognised that each of those explanations held a fragment of the story.

For the first couple of weeks, they'd feared that something worse had happened to Eleanor – that she'd been arrested and the full story would now be leaking out. They'd spent each day glued to the radio news, following the detail of the Jayne Arnold story and expecting that, at any moment, the police would announce that they'd made an arrest and were charging the culprit with Arnold's killing. They'd known that, once that happened, it would be only a brief time before they too would be joining their friend.

But it had never happened. The hot days had ticked by. The school had broken up for the summer and they'd returned to their respective homes, maintaining their anxious vigil in isolation. They'd made an agreement not to contact each other during the holiday, as if in some superstitious belief that the truth would remain concealed as long as they remained apart.

For Margaret, it had been an agonising period. She desperately wanted to talk to someone, to share her burden, and she'd felt painfully alone. She was an only child, and her parents were elderly and had increasingly little in common with their teenage daughter. She clearly couldn't talk about what had happened, and now she found herself trapped in a place where she lacked even more trivial human interaction. Her primary memory of that summer had been lying in the garden trying to focus on *Wuthering Heights* – an A-Level text for the forthcoming sixth-form term – feeling a permanent knot of anxiety in her stomach.

The breaking of the weather, late in August, had felt like a turning point. It had seemed as if the tension that had been building over the summer had finally been released. She'd sat indoors, watching the teeming rain, suddenly feeling more at peace. Nothing had really changed, but the summer had passed and the worst hadn't happened. The new term would be starting soon, and they could finally put the past year behind them.

That was how she remembered it, anyway. Even then, she'd known she was deluding herself. It was true that each passing day was likely to make them more secure, but it was also true that what had happened would always be there. She hadn't realised then how much it would return to haunt her.

They'd half expected Eleanor might return for the new school year, but she hadn't. They'd heard on the grapevine that she'd been moved to another school, though no one seemed to know why. Margaret had wondered if Eleanor might try to make contact with them, but it had never happened. At least, she added to herself, not until now. 'Where were you?' she asked again.

The woman was still smiling. 'Here. I've been here.'

'*Here?*'

'Not all the time, of course. Not quite.'

'We never knew what happened to you. We assumed you went to another school…'

'I did, eventually. I had a breakdown after – well, after it all happened. I just couldn't cope. I remember making my way to the school sickbay, just a whimpering mess.'

'Why didn't we hear about any of this?'

'My parents made sure it was kept quiet. Threatened the school with legal action.' Her smiled had widened. 'The funny thing is that, if I'd been in a state to talk coherently, I'd probably have told everyone the whole story, but I just couldn't manage it. By the time I was able to say anything, I'd come up with some cock-and-bull story about being bullied. Although, I suppose, looking back, that wasn't too far from the truth, was it?'

'We never—'

'Bullied me? No, that's true. But only because I tried so hard to be one of you. I knew if I didn't play the game, I'd become one of your victims too. So I went along with it all, even if you never really accepted me.'

Margaret offered no response. She told herself that this was a misrepresentation, an exaggeration of what had happened, but she knew she didn't really believe that. 'So where did you go after that?'

'My parents took me back home. I was being hassled to say who was bullying me, but I said I was too scared to name names. They didn't press it because my mental state was so fragile anyway. In the end, I took a term out sick and went off to do my A-Levels elsewhere.'

'We were so worried that summer. We didn't know what had happened to you.'

'You were worried for yourselves. Worried I might talk. You don't need to tell me. Don't you think I was terrified too? Terrified about what the rest of you might say. I've been terrified every day since. The dead don't stay buried forever.'

'You said you'd been here all along. What did you mean?'

'Just what I say. I scraped through my A-Levels, managed to get a place at university, went into teaching and, after a couple of jobs elsewhere, I applied for a job back here. That was nearly thirty-five years ago, and I've been here ever since.'

'They must have known you were an old girl of the school?'

'When I applied for the job, yes. That was one reason I was offered it, I suspect. But that was a long time ago, and I've never made anything of it. I imagine no one even realises now. Certainly, Lavinia and Alice never guessed, and I assume no one ever bothered to check my file.'

'They must have recognised your name?'

'I haven't been Eleanor Mason in a long time. I started using my middle name when I changed schools. It felt symbolic, as if I was trying to start a new life. Then I married. By the time I came here I was a different person.'

'So why come here?'

'I had to. It was like a penance. I've devoted my life to this. Trying to make amends for what I could never talk about.'

'You were the one who saved us. All those years ago.'

'I paid the price for it then and I've paid the price every day since. I did everything I could. She still wouldn't stay buried.'

There was something in the woman's tone that sent a chill down Margaret's spine. She looked around the tiny hallway. 'I don't understand. Why are you here? I mean here in Alice's house. Where's Alice?'

The woman was watching her, unblinking. 'That's the extraordinary thing, isn't it? We all came back here. In the end, none of us could tear ourselves away. First Alice. I knew her from the moment I saw her, even though she never recognised me. Then Lavinia. Now even you, Margaret. The ringleader. The one who was always in control. Even you, finally, couldn't stop yourself from returning. It's as if we all needed to bring this to a close.'

'Where's Alice?' Margaret said again.

'She's resting now.'

Margaret looked past the woman towards the kitchen. 'Where is she?'

'We can be together in a moment. You remember that day, Margaret? Forty-six years ago.'

'Of course I remember.'

'How you encouraged us to taunt that poor girl? How we did for weeks, every time we saw her. She wasn't even scared of us, really, was she? She wasn't scared of you. That was what you hated. That there was someone you couldn't control.'

Margaret remembered that only too well, and she felt the emotion now rising in her, as potent as it had been on that afternoon. Jumped-up little cow. How dare she ignore them? Despite everything that had happened – her own agonies, the pain she'd felt on behalf of Jayne's parents, everything she'd had to suppress during these decades of waiting – she could still taste the anger and resentment she'd felt on that sweltering afternoon.

'I remember you grabbing her, and then you lost it. You dragged her down, and just started kicking her and kicking her. And we joined in.'

'You didn't join in.' Margaret's voice was toneless. 'You just watched.'

'I didn't do anything. I didn't try to stop you. I just let you do it.' There was silence for a moment. 'Then I helped you sort out the whole bloody mess out.'

'Your uncle—'

'He wasn't my uncle. I just told you all that because I didn't want you to know who he really was.'

'I thought—'

'None of you really believed that story. You didn't care. You just wanted it all to go away. There was no uncle. There was just a dirty old man with a thing for school-girls. It was all the rage in those days, wasn't it? Jailbait. We giggled about it, without really knowing what we were giggling about. He'd been pestering me for weeks. He'd seen me walking past there. It started with the usual wolf whistles and catcalls. I was flattered, to be honest. I mean, God knows how old he was, but Pat was fit and decent-looking. I suppose every day's a workout if you're a builder, isn't it?' The woman was staring at Margaret, her face expressionless. 'I've told each of you this story now. Because I wanted you to know. I wanted you to know how much I paid.'

'I don't understand.'

'Do you remember what you did to that poor girl?'

Margaret didn't, not really. She remembered losing control, the proverbial red mist descending. She could barely recall what she and the others had done. She didn't want to think about that bruised, unconscious body lying on the hot cobbles. She hadn't been dead, then, Margaret told herself. We didn't kill her. That must have come afterwards. 'What did you do?' Her voice was little more than a whisper.

The woman shook her head. 'It was almost funny, looking back. Suddenly, you didn't have a clue, and I was the only one with the bottle to sort it out. I got you all to drag her into the garden of the cottage by the bus stop. Just to get her off the street before anyone saw. And because that's where he was working. My so-called uncle.'

That was the last Margaret remembered. She recalled that somehow, by some miracle, Eleanor had taken control, had told them all to go and that she'd deal with it. She'd almost resented it at the time. Who was this upstart, hardly even part of the gang, telling them all what to do? But they'd been terrified and had no alternative, and had just wanted the whole mess to go away. So they'd done what they were told. 'What did you do?'

The woman was silent for a moment. 'I went to find him, at the back of the house. Luckily, there was only him and his teenage son there. I don't know how I did it, but I told them what had happened and asked him to help. They both just seemed to find it funny, him and the son. Mind you, the son was a pathetic thing. He wasn't going to do anything except what his father told him to.'

Ryan Challis, Margaret thought. He might have done what he was told, but he'd extracted his own price for it later. A formidable price over many years, from her and from Lavinia Ellsworth. She'd never discovered how he knew or what his own involvement had been, and she'd never known how much evidence he really had. He'd claimed to have witnessed the assault and that he knew the body was buried under the cottage, but he'd never revealed how he had their names or had tracked them down. At the time, that had just made him seem even more terrifyingly omniscient. 'You told him our names?'

'You think that was the worst thing I did? You can't begin to imagine. Pat agreed to help me – he treated the whole thing like a joke – but he made it very clear that

302

there was a price to pay. Part of that price was giving him your names. He said that was his insurance in case we tried to double-cross him later. You can guess what the other part of the price was.'

'I'm so sorry.' There was nothing else Margaret could say.

'I did what I had to.' She shook her head, slowly. 'That wasn't the worst thing. I just persuaded myself it was a sacrifice I had to make. Not just for me, but for all of us. The worst thing was what happened to Jayne Arnold.'

Margaret didn't want to hear this, didn't want to know. She turned away, trying to avoid the woman's eyes.

'They carried her into the house. Pat told me she was unconscious but not dead. I didn't know what to do, but Pat said I should just leave her with them. After that, he took me upstairs and – well, I don't need to tell you. I can barely even remember it myself after all these years. I've just blanked it out. I don't know how long I was up there. It felt like hours. When I came down, there were two of them waiting downstairs with Jayne. The son and the man who owned the house. I thought Pat might want – but, well, he just sent me on my way, telling me to keep my mouth shut. I don't know what happened to Jayne.'

Margaret stared at her in horror, thinking about those moments. Thinking about the fate they'd condemned Jayne Arnold to. Thinking about Pat and Ryan Challis, and the other man, and about what they must have done. About her own complicity in everything that had happened.

'I don't know how I made it back to the school,' the woman went on. 'I went to the sickbay, but I could barely speak or stand up. I don't even know what happened after that, until my parents came to pick me up the next day. All I know is that I didn't say anything, and I let it happen.'

She stood for a few moments, saying nothing. 'I've paid the price ever since. I don't know about the rest of you. I've watched Alice and Lavinia, and I know it's eaten away at them.'

'Ryan Challis has extracted his share too,' Margaret said. 'From me and from Lavinia. Years of blackmail. Years of twisting the knife.'

The woman nodded. 'And yet, in the end, for what? Years of torture. Years of guilt. Years of fruitless penance. The bones still wouldn't lay buried. Time and teenage curiosity were enough to drag it all to the surface. What was it all *for*?' The expression in the woman's eyes had changed. 'In the end, we all came back, and now it's time to finish it.'

'Where's Alice? You said she was resting.'

The woman pushed open the door of the living room, turning on the light as she did so. 'She's in here. I've put her to rest.'

Alice Cartwright was curled up on the floor, her motionless body frozen in a defensive posture. Her face was a gruesome mass of blood and bruising, her dead eyes staring upward in horror.

The woman turned back to Margaret. 'And now you can rest too.'

Chapter Forty

The main school gates were closed for the night, and Annie had been told to drive round to the side entrance. She'd called ahead and spoken to Andrea Bennett, the head's secretary. There was still no sign of Diane Astor, and still no response on either her school or personal mobile phones.

Andrea Bennett was waiting for them under the archway before the main entrance, and she raised a hand as Annie drew into one of the visitor parking spaces. Bennett hurried over as Annie and Zoe climbed out of the car. 'Still nothing. It's not like Diane at all. I shouldn't say it, but Lavinia was the one for going AWOL. Diane's normally utterly reliable.'

The rain had finally ceased, although a strong wind was still blowing in off the hills behind the school. The sky was clearing, and occasionally a sickle moon was visible between the clouds scudding across the sky. The school buildings loomed above them, now in darkness except for the lights showing from the main entrance.

'When did you last see her?'

'Early afternoon. I didn't really register the time, but it can't have been much after two. She'd seemed distracted all morning, as if her mind was on something else. But she's had a lot on her plate, so I wasn't surprised.' Bennett looked around, as if worried that someone might be listening. 'I'd heard Mr Challis gave her a tough time at the governors' meeting.' She shook her head disapprovingly. 'I don't like to speak ill of anyone, but I don't like that man. He doesn't seem to me to be the kind of person we should have representing the school. From what I hear, he was flexing his muscles, showing who was boss before Diane had got her feet properly under the table. I could tell she wasn't happy about it.'

Annie was keen to stem Bennett's flow of anxious verbiage. 'She didn't give you any indication of where she might be going?'

'She didn't say she was going anywhere. She just said she needed to pop out for a while. I thought she meant just for a few minutes. Then she didn't come back, and I thought she must have been waylaid by someone. That's the nature of the job, and Diane can be a bit of a soft touch sometimes. She always wants to be able to sort out other people's problems.' She stopped, clearly conscious that she was talking too much. 'Anyway, she didn't come back. I wasn't too concerned. I just assumed she'd got caught up in something and went back to my own work. It was only when her husband called that I really registered how long she'd been gone.'

'She wasn't teaching this afternoon?'

'We've juggled the timetable to free her from teaching duties while she's covering the head's job. She didn't have any other meetings scheduled.'

'Do you know if anyone else saw her this afternoon?' Zoe asked.

'I've asked around the staff. No one seems to have seen her.'

'What about her car?'

Bennett blinked. 'That's really stupid of me. I hadn't thought to look. She normally parks in the staff places at the back of the school.'

'Let's go and see.'

Bennett led them into the main entrance, then through the lobby into a corridor leading to the rear of the school. The rear door was a fire exit, accessible from the inside. Bennett pushed it open and peered out. The staff parking area was empty of vehicles, except for a couple of cars parked close to the school.

'That's Diane's.' Bennett pointed to a small Fiat. 'That suggests she's still around the school somewhere.'

Annie made her way out to the car. She placed a hand on the bonnet. 'Feels slightly warm. I think the car's been driven recently.'

Bennett had been propping the door open behind them. 'You mean she's been somewhere and come back? So where is she?'

Annie looked around, as if Diane Astor might suddenly appear from out of the surrounding bushes. 'If she'd gone back into the school she'd surely have headed back to her office.'

Bennett nodded. 'Everything else is locked up for the night now.'

Zoe pointed to the far edge of the car park, to where lights were visible among the trees. 'What are those buildings?'

'That's part of the teachers' accommodation for those who live on site,' Bennett said.

'Is it possible she might have gone to see someone there?'

'It's possible. Especially if someone caught her with a problem as she was heading back to the school.' Bennett was looking mildly embarrassed. 'I suppose that's an obvious explanation. I should have thought of something like that.'

'It still wouldn't explain why she disappeared without telling anyone,' Annie pointed out. 'But let's go and check it out.'

She began to walk towards the cluster of cottages, Zoe and Bennett following close behind. Then she stopped and turned back to look at Zoe, her face baffled. She gestured to a spot at the edge of the car park, hidden in the shadow of the trees. There was a car parked there, almost invisible in the darkness.

'That car,' Annie said.

Zoe caught up with her. 'What about it?'

'It's my mother's.'

'Your mother's? Are you sure?'

'I'd know it anywhere. That silly personalised number-plate, for a start. What the hell's she doing here?'

Annie could feel her unease growing. Part of it, she told herself, was just that her mother's presence anywhere rarely heralded good news. A bigger part was simply that something felt very wrong.

Andrea Bennett pointed out the entrance to the resid-ential cottages, and Annie made her way into the court-yard. There were lights showing in most of the cottages now, and no immediate clue as to where they should try first.

Annie stood for a moment, looking round and listening for any sound audible above the buffeting wind. Then she heard it – a sharp cry, as if of pain or surprise. She took another few steps forward and saw that the front door of one of the cottages was standing open. 'Who lives there?'

Bennett frowned. 'Number three? That's Alice Cartwright's.'

Annie gestured to Zoe and walked cautiously towards the open doorway. She could hear something from inside. A crash. The sound of something being knocked over. Another bang.

Then, before Annie could react, there was another cry. Louder, this time, and more agonised. A cry of pain, gradually mutating into a scream. Then Annie was running into the house, wondering what the hell she was going to find.

Chapter Forty-One

It took Annie several seconds to take in what she was seeing. She had already registered, in her peripheral vision, a figure lying curled on the floor of the small living room to her right. Ahead, in the kitchen, there was an even more bizarre tableau. A body coiled defensively on the ground, being savagely and repeatedly kicked by someone seemingly lost in a frenzied fury.

Annie grabbed the attacker by the shoulder, dragging them away from the figure on the floor. A fist slammed towards Annie's face, but she was able to grab the wrist and steer the assailant back against the kitchen wall. It was only then that Annie recognised the person she was wrestling with.

Behind her, as if in confirmation, she heard Andrea Bennett say, 'Diane?'

Astor was almost unrecognisable, her face contorted with rage. She pushed Annie back and then, reaching into the pocket of her coat, she withdrew what looked like a kitchen knife. Annie took a step back, as the blade narrowly sliced past her face.

'Diane—'

'Let me finish.' Astor almost spat out the words. 'Let me do this.'

Annie looked down at the figure on the floor, already knowing what she was going to see. It was Margaret curled up in the corner, her arms wrapped round her face. 'Mum. It's Annie. Come over here behind me.'

The sounds Astor was making seemed more animal than human. Margaret was still lying, as if paralysed, on the floor. Annie shifted her position so that she was between Astor and her mother. 'Whatever this is about, Diane, let's stop it now. Before it's too late.'

Astor's mirthless laugh was unexpected. 'It's forty-six years too late.' She was still waving the knife, and Annie was contemplating the odds of her being able to grab Astor's arm before she could make a lunge. Astor was relatively elderly, not heavily built. Annie should have no difficulty in overcoming her in any ensuing struggle.

It was the spark of madness in Astor's eyes that gave Annie pause. Whatever the reasons, this was not a rational woman. She was less concerned with her own fate than with achieving whatever obsessive goal she'd set herself. And part of that goal, for whatever bizarre reason, clearly involved Annie's own mother.

Annie had placed herself fully in front of Margaret, and was tensed for any movement from Astor. She tried hard to keep her demeanour and voice as calm and emotionless as possible. 'Just give me the knife, Diane. I don't know what this is all about, but there's a better way of dealing with it.'

Astor's eyes were dark fathomless holes. 'There's nothing to deal with. This has been all about deals. Too many deals. Too many sordid deals. We just need to end it. Whatever it takes.'

Her lunge towards Margaret was sudden, but didn't quite take Annie by surprise. As Astor thrust herself forward, Annie threw her arms around the other woman, trying to prevent her using the knife, struggling to force her back away from Margaret. Zoe was trying to seize her from behind, while Andrea Bennett stood back in the hallway, her face aghast.

Astor was stronger than Annie had expected, and she dragged herself free of Annie's grip. Then she stopped and laughed as if she'd unexpectedly thought of a joke she'd once been told. She pointed the knife out towards Annie and said, 'You, girl!'

It was the voice of a schoolteacher, but it didn't sound like Diane Astor's natural voice. It sounded more as if she was impersonating some much older teacher from her own schooldays. 'You, girl! I say, stop!'

'I said stop.' Astor was laughing now, as if at some private joke. 'Are you being wilfully disobedient, girl? Are you listening? Or have you gone stone deaf?' Astor had adopted a different accent, a mocking representation of someone from deep in her past. 'Wilfully disobedient!'

Astor had taken another step forward, the blade of the knife now inches from Annie's face. Annie was raising her hands to defend herself when Astor tumbled sideways, falling against the doorway.

It took Annie a moment to work out what had happened. Margaret had thrown herself forward from the corner of the kitchen, wrapping her arms round Astor's legs, dragging her off balance. Astor fell, and for a second Annie thought that she was going to plunge the knife into Margaret's face. At the last moment, Margaret parried the blow with her arm, driving Astor's hand back.

Later, Annie was unable to describe what had happened after that. It had all occurred too quickly for her to see clearly the interaction between Margaret's flailing and Astor's falling body. Whether it had been an accident or something else, she could never say, but somehow, in

312

those seconds, the knife blade had ended up embedded firmly in Diane Astor's neck.

Chapter Forty-Two

'Food's nearly ready.' Sheena was standing in the doorway of the living room brandishing a wine bottle. 'Do you want a top-up?'

Annie looked at the empty glass in her hand. 'If by top-up, you mean a refill, I won't say no.'

'Going to be one of those evenings, is it? Can't say I blame you after the last few days.'

Annie held out her glass. She was stretched almost horizontal on the sofa. 'It's not all bad. At least young Andy Metcalfe has enhanced his reputation. Even Stuart Jennings is singing his praises.'

'He'd better watch his back then.' Sheena lowered herself onto the sofa beside Annie and took a sip of her own wine.

'Stuart's not so bad. He's been pretty supportive.'

'What's the latest? If you feel ready to talk about it now.'

Annie rarely talked shop with Sheena, given the sensitivity of their respective work. But Sheena had been there when Melanie Donnelly had died, and she probably deserved to know where it was likely to end. In any case, Annie needed to talk about this. 'The good news is my mother is saying she wants to make it easy for everyone.'

'First time for everything, I suppose. How do you mean?'

'She's coughed up the whole story. Or at least she's told us a lot, and it mostly hangs together.'

Annie had visited her mother earlier that afternoon. For the moment, while the investigation continued, no charges had been brought against Margaret, although she had been interviewed at length under caution. Annie had been withdrawn from the case to avoid any conflict of interest. She hadn't been sure whether it was wise even to speak to Margaret, but Jennings had raised no objections.

As it turned out, the visit had been shorter than Annie had expected. She'd thought that her mother would have been changed by what had happened, and perhaps somewhere inside she had been. On the surface, though, she remained as difficult and abrasive as ever.

'I suppose you've come to gloat?'

'*Gloat?*' Annie had looked round Margaret's flat, thinking for the first time that it looked a little shabby, a little neglected. 'I came to see how you are.'

'Well, you've seen that I'm fine.'

For all the superficial bravado, Margaret hadn't really looked fine. She looked diminished, fearful. Her face still showed signs of bruising and her left wrist was bandaged. Annie noticed that when her mother made them both coffees, there had been a slight tremor in her hands.

'So what's going to happen to me now?' Margaret had asked, once they were seated back in the living room. It was still raining, the drizzle falling ceaselessly on the skylights above their heads. The sky was a dark metallic grey.

'I'm no longer on the case, Mum. And even if I was, I couldn't talk about it.'

'Not even to me?'

'Especially not to you. You know that.'

Margaret had swallowed a mouthful of her coffee. Her hand had trembled again as the mug reached her lips, though Annie could see her mother had been trying to conceal it. She'd carefully replaced the mug on the table and said, 'We didn't kill her, you know. That wasn't us. I want you to know that.'

Annie had sighed, unable to stop herself responding. 'I don't know if you killed her. I do know that, even by your own account, you bullied her. You attacked her. You left her for dead. And you left her for something worse than death.'

'And I've paid for it every day since. What do you think it was like for me? Carrying this secret, this guilt?'

'Christ, Mum, this isn't all about you. What do you think it was like for Jayne's parents? Decades of not knowing what had happened to their daughter, just because you did this sordid deal to save your own skin. Didn't you ever consider their feelings? Not even when you had a daughter of your own?'

Margaret had offered no immediate response. She'd sat in silence, her eyes closed, her face expressionless. Finally, in a much quieter voice, she'd said, 'You just can't imagine it. I know what we did. I know what the consequences were. I've never been able to forget that. But I had to go on. I've had years of not allowing myself to think, to feel. Years of cutting myself off from any real emotion. Years of trying just to keep it all buried.'

'Like Jayne Arnold's body?' Annie had regretted the words as soon as she'd spoken them.

'If you like.'

It made sense, Annie had thought afterwards. It perhaps explained the woman Margaret had become, the kind of mother she'd been. The way she'd interacted with Annie and with everyone else. Unable to acknowledge what had happened, what she'd done, she'd had no option but to close in on herself, gradually hardening like a fossil under all those years of pressure.

Annie had left Margaret's flat shortly after that. She'd wanted to stay, wishing she could find a way offer some comfort or support. But in the end she'd simply had no answers. She'd felt there was nothing more she could say, nowhere else to go. Her mother had remained where she was, staring into space, seemingly almost unable even to recognise her daughter's presence. When Annie had returned home, she'd fallen into Sheena's arms and cried, for minutes on end, as if releasing years of emotion. Sheena, sensitive as ever, hadn't pressed her on the reasons, and it was only now, an hour or so later, that Annie felt able to talk about it.

'What a bloody mess. God, I'm sorry, Annie.' Sheena stretched her arm around Annie's shoulder and held her as she had earlier. 'She's still adamant they didn't kill Jayne Arnold?'

Annie shrugged. 'But then she would say that, wouldn't she? Whatever really happened.' She looked up and read Sheena's expression. 'Oh, don't look so surprised, Shee. I'm sick of defending her, sick of all the crap she's been responsible for. Sick of the mess she made of her own life and the mess she's tried to make of mine. Yes, she's my mother. But I'm not doing it any more.'

Sheena nodded. 'Fair enough. I can't imagine what it's like in your shoes.'

'I'm just beginning to find out myself. Anyway, if they didn't kill Jayne Arnold directly, they left her to die, and that's almost worse. They left Diane Astor – or Eleanor Mason, as she was in those days – to sort the mess out.

317

And she did that nightmare deal with Pat Challis. Astor sacrificed herself for that, but she must have known she was condemning Jayne to an even worse fate.' Annie shuddered, her body tensing even at the thought of what must have happened after that bleak transaction. What must have happened to Jayne Arnold before her body had finally been consigned to that concealed grave.

Sheena put down her wine and took Annie fully in her arms. 'Jesus.'

'It looks as if Challis kept his side of that bargain, but he more than extracted his pound of flesh over the years. He and Ryan spent years blackmailing my mother and Lavinia Ellsworth. It was almost a joke to Ryan — another bit of lubrication in his dodgy business empire. Meanwhile, Diane Astor seems to have spent her life trying, in her own bizarre way, to atone for what she'd done. She couldn't drag herself away from Meresham.'

'You said she bought Jayne Arnold's former house?'

'As if she wanted to forge some sort of link with Jayne, find some way of paying her respects. I suppose the stranger thing is that Ellsworth and Cartwright couldn't tear themselves away either. You'd have thought they'd have wanted to get as far away from there as possible, but somehow they all ended up gravitating back. Maybe it was to keep an eye on each other, or on the scene, but I think it was really just that they couldn't let it go. Even Ryan Challis, in his own unique way, though again maybe that was just his idea of a black joke.'

'Where did Melanie Donnelly fit into all this?'

'That seems to be what triggered Astor's breakdown, alongside the discovery of Arnold's remains. She was afraid of what Melanie might reveal, and where that might lead.

It looks as if she was being fed inside info on Challis's business by his own daughter.'

'Why would his daughter do that?'

'She hated her dad. Don't know why. Maybe just teenage angst. Or maybe Ryan had the same proclivities as his father—'

'Oh, Christ.'

'We're trying to talk to her, but I don't know how much we'll get out of her now. Anyway, for whatever reason, she'd handed Donnelly some pretty explosive material.'

'And Melanie saw that as the route to her big journalistic break? Poor kid.'

'Something like that. Though I don't really know how interested the media would have been. Dirt on a relatively small-time provincial businessman. Maybe not worth getting yourself killed for.'

'You think Astor did that?'

'Seems most likely, though I guess we can't rule out the possibility that it was Ellsworth or even Alice Cartwright. If so, that might have been what triggered Astor. What I'm not sure about is whether all this was self-protection on Astor's part – taking out those who might expose her – or whether she saw herself as enacting some sort of belated revenge for Jayne Arnold. The savagery of the killings certainly suggests she saw herself as an avenging angel. But it was something of both, maybe. Either way, it was always likely to end with her taking her own life.'

'You reckon that's what happened?'

Annie hesitated. 'I was there, but I couldn't confidently say either way. It all happened so quickly. I'm not saying that to protect my mother. I'm long past that. If I'm feeling cynical, it might well be convenient for her that there are no surviving witnesses to what really happened all those years ago. She's not tried to deny her part in it, but she's also claiming it was Ellsworth who was the ringleader.' She paused. 'We've only her word for that, and I'm not sure I believe it.'

'So what's going to happen to her?'

'That's up to the CPS. There's no hard evidence to tie her directly to Jayne Arnold's death other than her own confession to participating in the attack on her. She's adamant they didn't kill Jayne, so there's the question of what she'd be charged with. We'll see.' Annie was silent for a moment. 'I've a feeling this might get buried again, just like before. Too many reputations at risk. So in the end the only person whose reputation gets trashed is me, just for being my mother's daughter.'

'It won't be like that. No one's going to hold you responsible for your mother.'

'You reckon? It's not stopped them before.'

Sheena smiled. 'They'll have me to answer to if they try.'

'The ferocious backbencher?' Annie finally returned the smile. 'That might work, I guess.'

'Of course it would.' Still gripping Annie's hand, Sheena reached out for her wine. 'By the way, how's Zoe now?'

'You're just changing the subject, aren't you?'

'Obviously. But I also want to know. I like Zoe. She's still off?'

'Signed off for at least a month. She's been having these dizzy spells and attacks, whatever they are, for a while. Gary and her GP have finally persuaded her to get it properly checked out. It may be something psychosomatic, but the docs reckon they can't rule out a physical cause. They're doing brain scans and a round of tests.'

'What do you reckon?'

'I had a long chat with Gary. He's afraid there's some physical cause, but he also reckons there's still something Zoe's not wanted or been able to talk about, even to him. She was telling me how much she hated her own schooldays, so maybe this case just brought all that a bit too close to home.'

'Christ, we really do screw over our children, don't we?' Sheena said. 'Parents, teachers, the lot of us. We get screwed over, and then we screw over the next generation in our turn. Like that Philip Larkin poem. That stuff about man handing on misery to man.'

Annie raised an eyebrow at the allusion. 'Or, in my case, woman. Tell me about it, Shee. Tell me about it.'

Acknowledgements

Writing tends to be a solitary business, and, as a result of the Covid pandemic, the last year or so has been more solitary than ever. I've had to carry out most of my research online or by telephone, sitting in my little writing room overlooking the Cromarty Firth, with only a brief visit to my former stamping grounds around the Peak District when the regulations allowed.

Even so, there are countless people to thank for their contributions to the book, most of them necessarily remaining anonymous (but you know who you are). This includes all those who answered my sometimes idiotic questions about boarding schools, television production and the precise duration of the long hot summer of 1976. The answers were invariably invaluable and thought-provoking, even if my versions are heavily fictionalised. Any remaining mistakes, as ever, are entirely mine.

More specifically, I should thank my wife, Helen, who's continued to tolerate me and my writing even though we've barely been able to leave the house for the last year. Helen's always my first reader, fiercest critic and biggest supporter, and the perfect person to sort out any plot tangles.

Finally, thanks as ever to everyone at Canelo, especially the ever-excellent Louise Cullen – full of smart ideas and incisive insights, and always a joy to work with. And to my agent, Peter Buckman, for his unswerving support over however many years it is now.

Do you love crime fiction and are always on the lookout
for brilliant authors?

Canelo Crime is home to some of the most exciting
novels around. Thousands of readers are already enjoying
our compulsive stories. Are you ready to find your new
favourite writer?

Find out more and sign up to our newsletter at
canelocrime.com